Praise for the Boo

"The Cook-Off Mystery series by Devon Delaney … of a series. Readers will be glued to their seats wrestling with continuing reading the story or getting up to get a tasty treat to eat . . . I highly recommend getting something to eat before you sit down to indulge yourself in the story . . ."

—*Cozy Mystery book Reviews*

"This is a very fun and rollicking mystery that stays light-hearted even as the case gets more complicated, building toward a get-all-of-the-suspects-together-in-a-room conclusion. Cooking, holiday celebrations, and moving family drama all make for the perfect end-of-the-year escape."

—*Kings River Life*

"I've read several in the series and enjoyed them all. It was interesting to see Sherry acting as a judge rather than a competitor. The book kept my interest from the beginning but any book that combines cookies and murder has to be interesting. The characters are varied and seem like a lot of fun. I look forward to more in this series."

—Alicia F.

Books by Devon Delaney

Cook-Off Mysteries

Expiration Date
Final Roasting Place
Guilty as Charred
Eat, Drink and Be Wary
Double Chocolate Cookie Murder
A Half-Baked Alibi
Murder for Good Measure
Serving Up Spite

Serving Up Spite

A Cook-Off Mystery

Devon Delaney

BEYOND THE PAGE
PUBLISHING

Serving Up Spite
Devon Delaney

Cover design and illustration by Dar Albert, Wicked Smart Designs

Beyond the Page Books
are published by
Beyond the Page Publishing
www.beyondthepagepub.com

ISBN: 978-1-960511-42-3

Chapter 1

Sherry glanced at the wall clock. Six minutes of class time remaining. "I almost forgot the most important question of all. Raise your hand if you or your family have a vegetable garden." Sherry scanned the fifth-grade class and counted eight hands raised. "Amazing. That's wonderful. Now the rest of you, even if you don't think you have the outdoor space, the time, or even the interest, I'm here to tell you otherwise."

"Miss Sherry?" a prepubescent male voice called out. Sherry squinted at the hand-drawn nameplate taped to the corner of his desk. He was one of the students that hadn't raised his hand.

"Yes, Magnus."

"Me and my mom moved here during the summer. My dad's been here for, like, around a year. Was kinda late to start growing anything for this year, I think. We never had a garden before, but one would be awesome."

"Welcome, first of all," Sherry said. "You'll love it here in Connecticut. I'm from Augustin, the next town over. You have the Long Island Sound to the south, lovely hills to the north and farms all over the east and west for gardening inspiration. This week I hope I can teach you all how to start and maintain a productive garden for the coming warm season. Before you know it, spring will be here. February is the perfect time to plan. I hope you and your family start a garden."

A hand darted skyward. Before Sherry could read the name in large upside-down block letters, the girl in pigtails spoke. "My mom says you're a sick cook and that you crush the competition at cook-offs. She said the name Sherry Oliveri is synom, synom, oh, what's the word?"

"Synonymous?"

"Yeah, she said the name Sherry Oliveri is synonymous with cook-off champions."

Mrs. Turpin, the homeroom teacher, who was positioned off to the side of the classroom, cleared her throat. "Sherry, sick is slang for wonderful."

"Mom wanted to come sit in on the class in case you taught us any cooking. I would have died of embarrassment if she showed up. I told her to stay in her lane. And how come you didn't come yesterday?"

Sherry laughed and swatted a stray lock of mousy brown hair from her forehead. "I work at my family's store, the Ruggery, Mondays. I'll be visiting your class every day this week thru Friday. A short week but we'll work hard. Your mom sounds very nice. Yes, one of my hobbies, besides gardening and working at the Augustin Community Garden, is entering cooking competitions. You'll have to tell your mom I can't teach cooking. I have to stay in my lane, too."

"Why can't you teach us cooking?" the girl in pigtails asked.

"As much as I'd love to teach cooking to kids and adults, I can't be paid for any food-related job or I'll lose my amateur status. That means I wouldn't be able to compete in the cook-offs or recipe contests I love so much."

"That seems like a bogus rule," the young girl said.

"Not to me," Sherry said. "I don't want to compete against professional chefs. They're on a whole different level of trained expertise. I'm a self-taught home cook and I like it that way." The girl shrugged as she took in the information, seeming unconvinced by Sherry's logic. "Thank your mom for calling me sick. I'm not, but I've won my fair share of contests."

"I'm sure her mother used a more endearing term rather than sick," Mrs. Turpin said. "Either way, we appreciate her kind words. I think it's so exciting Miss Sherry is here for some class time for four days. This year's fifth-grade garden will be the best in school history. Today's time is almost up. Anything else you want to say, Miss Sherry?"

Sherry opened her mouth to bid the class farewell for the day, when Magnus's waving hand rose over his head.

"Yes, Magnus," Mrs. Turpin said.

"My dad said he'd like to print an article about Miss Sherry after our week with her is over," Magnus said. He wriggled in his seat.

"Magnus's dad works for the *Coastal County Beacon*," Mrs. Turpin explained to Sherry. "He gave the kids a talk on career day. Interesting man with interesting ideas." She turned back to Magnus. "Miss Sherry has a wonderful story about how she got into cook-offs and such."

The girl with pigtails called out, "Can you tell us?"

Mrs. Turpin glanced at the wall clock. "We have two minutes. Would you mind?"

"Of course not," Sherry said. "The quick version is I entered a recipe contest on a whim when I found an ad in a magazine. The theme was to create a recipe that showcases bread. I got lucky and won with my Orange Dusted French Toast Fingers with Maple Dipping Sauce. After that I was hooked on the creativity of reimagining and inventing recipes. I've been competing for longer than I care to admit."

"That sounds so cool," Magnus said. "My dad needs to hear all that stuff."

Mrs. Turpin said to Sherry, "I wasn't the one who suggested Magnus's dad write about you in his paper. I wouldn't do that to you. I certainly wouldn't want to be associated with that rag."

Sherry's eyebrows arched. "Oh, okay. Any publicity is good publicity."

Sherry's follow-up chuckle died a quick death when Mrs. Turpin raised her enthusiasm level once again. "That was so much fun to hear. The kids are so interested. They look forward to tomorrow's class. Right?"

The class cheered, putting a smile on Sherry's face. "You're so nice," Sherry said. "I've had the best time today teaching you all seed-saving techniques. Tomorrow we'll cover prepping the garden for planting. Thanks, everyone." Sherry gathered her material and her winter outerwear. She left the classroom with a warm heart.

She found her ride home waiting in the parking lot. She climbed into Don's pickup truck and gave him an enthusiastic kiss on his day-old scruff before he could turn his head and move in for the kiss.

"Beautiful smile. You're one happy lady. How'd it go?"

"As you know, I was nervous about whether I could keep a bunch of twelve-year-olds' attention for forty minutes, but I think I smashed day one. I would even go so far as to call myself sick."

"Sick, eh? I would never doubt you're shaping the minds of the next generation with your sick garden wisdom," Don said. "Not only are you one of the most successful cook-off champions, your work at the Augustin Community Garden benefits so many families and kids who might never learn gardening. That's how you were recommended to teach these kids for a week, isn't it?"

"Sure is. The middle school has worked with the community garden in the past and someone spoke to someone who recommended me." She watched her boyfriend reach around the driver's seat and lay the newspaper he had on his lap down on the backseat. "What'cha reading? That doesn't look like the *Nutmeg News*."

"A new paper covering our Hillsboro County. I'd never heard of it until today. The guys at the boat storage unit were making all kinds of intriguing remarks about the content. Pro and con. Discussion even got heated at one point. I asked if I could have a copy when they were done. I felt left out."

Sherry glanced over at Don, who was fastening his seat belt. She never tired of stealing a glance at the man who captured her heart. "Is that how you spent your time while I was in class? Debating a newspaper's viewpoints?"

"Not on purpose. I went to visit my boat, not enter a jousting match, but that's what it felt like. The guys were going at it. After reading some of the articles, I can see both sides of the debate have merit."

"As long as you left the feistiness at the boathouse. How's your baby?" Sherry asked. "I miss her."

"She's lonely. Won't be long before she and Captain Don resume ferrying the commuter crowd to Long Island and back. She's happily in dry storage during the depths of winter, safe and sound."

"Does helping Dad manage the Ruggery's books fill the void left in your captaining heart?"

"For the winter, yes. Then it's back to anchors aweigh for me."

"My siblings and I appreciate the help so much."

"Three years and no one has taken a look at the numbers except him? Shame on you and Pep and Marla." Don wagged his finger at Sherry. She snatched the accusatory finger out of the air and kissed it. "Your brother and sister shouldn't put this all on Erno."

"That's not exactly the case. Amber's been helping keep the books, too. Reluctantly. She feels like her role as the store's assistant manager shouldn't include learning the family business's financial secrets."

Sherry pictured her friend working alongside her father in his artisan hooked rug store. Amber Sherwin had become a most valuable employee but, admittedly, wasn't keen on number crunching. Her strength was customer relations and the overall running of the front end of the store.

"Under Dad's tutelage, Amber's doing an okay job with the books. Not really her thing, though," Sherry added.

"She was a family and marriage therapist before she moved to Augustin, isn't that right?" Don asked.

"Sure was. And she still writes an online advice column. When I met her at a cook-off she needed a career change. And Dad needed an assistant manager. Perfect fit."

"I'm happy to help Erno," Don said. "I have a strong numbers nerd background."

"Keeps you busy in the off-season. Perfect fit since you're the smartest guy in the world."

"Thanks, cutie pie." Don shifted the truck into reverse. "I'm happy to work for your dad doing financials. I was curious to see if I remembered how to add two numbers together. I pay someone else to keep my books. It's always better to have an outside set of eyes on the numbers, in my opinion."

"If you're too rusty and give up, you can always help me prepare for my next cook-off. It's only a week away. It can be my birthday present to you."

Don laughed. "I'll help you whether I'm rusty in accounting or not. I'm the world's best sous chef, as you know. If I hadn't been sous chef for my sister at the New England Fall Food Fest, you and I may never have met."

"I owe a lot to cook-offs," Sherry said.

"My future was bleak before that day. And I don't need any presents for my birthday. I'm lucky it falls on Valentine's Day. You're my present."

"Awww," Sherry said. "You're so sweet."

"By the way. There's an ad for the cook-off in that paper. Maybe they're a sponsor?"

"Let me think. There are a few food product sponsors, a cutlery sponsor and, yes, you're right. The *Coastal County Beacon* Media Group. I didn't make the connection. There was a boy in my class today who said his father worked for the *Coastal County Beacon*."

"Then his father's got a fight on his hands when Augustin digests the tone of the writers," Don said. He adjusted his knit cap and swiped the bangs that peeked out the front. "I won't spoil the ending for you, but the paper has a lot to say about what's wrong with Augustin."

Sherry reached out toward Don and tamed an errant curl of his hair, finishing the grooming he began. She kept her gaze on his face. From working outside on his boat all spring and summer and up until the end of December, his complexion had grown ruddy. A January spent mostly indoors moderated his wind-blown appearance. Don Johnstone would have made a fine partner for any woman looking for stability. She had won the lottery when they started dating. Fast-forward to the adventurous, entrepreneurial Captain Don. A move to Connecticut to be near Sherry, plus the purchase of a new boat, and his commuter business was launched. No one was more surprised than Sherry and the changes suited her to a T.

"Are you staring at me again?" Don asked.

"Can't help myself. You're so handsome, I was picturing Summer Don versus Winter Don. Love both versions."

"You're the one who's sweet," Don said.

"The classroom teacher, Mrs. Turpin, wasn't a fan of the paper the boy's father worked for. Her inflammatory opinion was shocking. I think people sometimes think teachers thrive on neutrality, but she told me through gritted teeth the paper was a rag. A rag! What exactly is the paper's viewpoint?" Sherry asked.

"The majority of the articles are about Augustin and the other towns in Hillsboro County needing to get with the times and modernize. Stop the focus on preserving the past and act now to make the future happen. There was loads of criticism of current policies the towns have in place that stonewall growth and progress. It's a stark contrast to the *Nutmeg News*, which honors tradition, the past, and who got us where we are today."

"New England's quaintness should never be snuffed out," Sherry said. "My dad's business thrives on an heirloom artistry."

"The letters to the *Beacon* editor are very interesting, to say the least. Not a lot of gray area. In a nutshell, the *Beacon* dictates the towns' need to cater to business, tourism and technology. They claim the towns will shrivel up and die if honoring the past remains the focus. Augustin especially."

Sherry was left speechless. She knew what side she was on.

Chapter 2

"Thanks for the ride," Sherry said as she leaned her head into Don's driver's-side window. She kissed him goodbye. "Call me when you're done at the Ruggery."

"Will do, gorgeous," Don said as he pulled out of her driveway.

"Sherry. Sherry. Over here," a familiar voice called out. The same voice that summoned her almost every time she arrived home or went out her front door.

"Hi, Eileen." She waved to her neighbor across the street.

Bundled in a heavy sweater and a brightly colored knit hat, Eileen returned the wave.

"I see Elvis Purrsley has earned himself some freedom outside," Sherry said. The tabby cat was trekking up a pile of snow as if he were intending to plant a flag on the summit of Mt. Catnip. His leash was trailing on the ground behind him. From her driveway, Sherry could hear her Jack Russell, Chutney, barking with insistence for a similar freedom. She could see his little snout pressed up against the sidelight of her front door.

"I know in this cold, Elvis won't go too far. Something must have left a yellow marking on the snow pile. Elvis is all about ID-ing every critter that dares to come onto our property," Eileen said with pride in her voice. "He wants to protect his human."

"He's a good watch cat," Sherry said.

Eileen took a few steps down her driveway, the packed snow crunching under her boots' treads. "Dear, as your friend who only wants the best for you, when are you going to marry that fine fellow?" She pointed to Don's truck far down the road.

Sherry was used to Eileen's well-intentioned remarks, as pointed as they often were, but the spontaneity of this question stunned her momentarily. Sherry made an instantaneous decision to take the upper hand.

"Well, with Valentine's Day and Don's birthday right around the corner, maybe the time has come. Who knows?" Sherry tipped her head as she admired her own candor. She seldom shared what was lingering in the back of her mind, whether Don would ever take the next step. Maybe if she put the idea out in the universe things would move along in that direction. A twinge in her stomach unsettled her. "If not, we're still very happy and very much together."

"Okay, dear. That's what I want for Chutney's mother." Eileen clutched the broom she was using to sweep snow drifts off her driveway. As soon as she began, Elvis attacked the offending bristles. "Speaking of happy, I'm very worried about the collective mindset of our town. Have you seen that newspaper, the *Beacon* something or other? Spouting all sorts of chatter about bringing Augustin into the twenty-second century. Skipping the twenty-first completely. Whatever happened to living for the moment?"

Sherry threw up her hands, which Elvis took to mean *release the broom*. He scampered back up Mt. Catnip.

"I agree with you. Let's enjoy what we have instead of rushing time forward. And let's remind ourselves how much there is to learn from the past, both good and bad. Augustin is a wonderful place as is." Her rumbling stomach told her to keep her opinion concise and get inside for lunch.

"One of the letters to the *Beacon* editor said Augustin was as unwelcoming to newcomers settling among its age-old residents as ranchers around Yellowstone were to the reintroduction of wolves. I take offense at that nonsense. My cribbage group is divided. Helen says new ideas usually mean growth. She should work on her card skills rather than stir the pot. She lost every game last month."

"Looks like I'm late to this party. I better do some reading and catch up on current events," Sherry said as she watched Elvis do an Olympics-worthy roll across the snow. "You've got a snow cat on your hands."

Eileen laughed. "Let's talk after you've had a chance to get up to speed." Eileen began her trek back up her driveway. After a few steps she stopped in her tracks. "I'm glad your sister, Marla, is here for a visit. She's such a lovely gal. So strong. She looks like she could wrestle one of her misbehaving calves single-handedly and put it in its place." Eileen flexed her arm under the bulk of her sweater.

"Running a ranch in Oklahoma will do that to a body," Sherry said. "I'm glad she's here, too. See you soon." Sherry knew that wasn't a meaningless statement. She saw Eileen at least twice a day on average.

Once inside, Sherry peeled off her outerwear and headed to the kitchen to find her sister. Finding no one, she began preparing lunch.

"Sherry? I hope that's you and not an intruder," Marla called from the second floor. A moment later, Marla appeared in the kitchen holding a book. "I thought you were heading straight from school to be interviewed for Patti Mellit's podcast."

"Don dropped me home so I could get a quick bite. I'll take my car if you don't need it. How was your morning?" Sherry lifted her knife from the mound of kale she was trimming. Her gaze landed on Marla's book. "*Finding Yourself a Better You*. That sounds interesting."

"Finished it. The search for a better me is underway."

"I love the you you are," Sherry said.

"It's a book recommended by our marriage counselor," Sherry's younger sister said.

"I'm happy you and Grant are doing so much better. We were all very worried about you two."

"I appreciate that. We're working hard to get back to where we were and grow even stronger."

"Different ending than my marriage to Charlie," Sherry said. She lowered her head a touch.

"For sure. You guys decided to split up. You came out okay on the other side. You and Charlie are still good friends. Heck, to have a lawyer as an ex has its perks, if you're on good terms. Grant and I wanted to weather the storm. It's a process," Marla said with a nod. "Enough about me. Tell me what Patti's podcast is about. Food-related, obviously, since Patti is a food journalist."

"I'm sure she was inspired by next week's cook-off. Problem is, she contacted me only yesterday to see if I'd speak about my favorite kitchen tool. I can only choose one. You know me, I've been stewing over my choice for the last twenty-four hours." Sherry poked around her salad fixings while Marla rummaged through the refrigerator. "Wanna guess what tool I chose? Let's see how well you know me."

"This is a loaded question." Marla tossed backed her auburn hair. She puffed out her cheeks and surveyed the kitchen. "The wooden spoon?"

"Yes! You got it." Sherry lifted the knife. A ribbon of kale flew off her cutting board and landed on the floor. Chutney was on the green in no time.

"I have a visual of you, wooden spoon in hand, etched in my mind's eye. Remember when you chased me and Pep with the weapon a few times as kids when we pestered you?"

"Hah, yes, I do. You were pests, always in my business."

"We're your siblings. That's our job. There you go. That's how well I know you," Marla said as she dusted her palms together. "I can't wait to hear the podcast. Is it being prerecorded?"

"That's right. I'll ask her when it's airing. I think there'll be other guests on the show before or after me. Why don't you come? We don't have to stick around when I finish."

"I thought you'd never ask. I can be ready in two minutes, as usual. It doesn't take much to achieve the ranch look." Marla straightened the collar of her red and green flannel shirt. "There, I'm ready."

Sherry let out a burst of laughter, the hearty variety only her sister's off-the-cuff comments could prompt. "No rush. I need to eat first. I wouldn't mind stopping by the Ruggery after the interview. Don's putting in some hours there."

• • •

Half an hour later, when they reached the MediaPie Center City Studios, Sherry, Marla and Chutney checked in with the security guard, whose gold nameplate read *Clem*. Clem shared the bad news that the elevator was out of commission. He explained the problem was some sort of "cable malfunction mumbo-jumbo." That was all Sherry had to hear to know the stairs were the only safe option. By the time they climbed the four flights to Patti's office, both women were huffing and puffing.

"I thought I was in decent cardio shape," Sherry said as she reached for the stairs' door handle. "That was a killer."

"I know I need more cardio," Marla said. "But I'm as strong as a bull." She gently pushed Sherry's hand aside after two failed attempts to open the door. With a mighty yank Marla forced the heavy stairwell door open.

"Good afternoon, ladies," Patti said as she appeared in the hallway outside her office door. "I got a call from downstairs you two were on your way up. Sorry about the elevator." She lifted the leg of her pants to reveal a blackish purple bruise across her knee. "I had a devil of a time climbing four flights of stairs with my bum knee. I fell on the ice yesterday. Doc says it's a bone bruise."

"I shouldn't have complained. My misery is due to my own spotty commitment to exercise," Sherry said.

"Follow the limping show host. Right this way." Patti led the sisters through her office door to the podcast waiting room. She was dressed in a navy blue pants suit with a winter white cable-knit scarf around her neck. She had a cornucopia pin attached to her lapel, reinforcing her reputation as a foodie. The small laptop secured under her arm gave away her journalist side. "Sherry, you're on in eight minutes. The others aren't here yet. They follow you after your thirty minutes is up. Thank you for not revealing your kitchen tool of choice ahead of time. I want to be surprised."

Sherry peered down at her tote containing the wooden spoon.

"Make yourselves comfortable," Patti said, pointing out the love seat and chairs. "Hammy, my intern, will come get you in about four minutes. Does Chutney need any water?"

"He's fine, thanks for asking," Sherry said as she handed the leash to Marla.

Patti went into the adjoining room and shut the door behind her. The *standby* sign over the doorframe lit up.

"Wow, we cut that close," Sherry said.

"Better not sit around thinking too hard about what you're going to say," Marla said in her characteristic casual tone. "Just let it flow."

The office door opened and in walked four men and a woman. At the same time, a young man with round glasses and a quilted vest poked his head out of Patti's studio.

"Welcome. Have a seat, we'll be right with you. I'm Hammy."

He gestured toward the metal seats before ducking back in the studio and shutting the door. Each man was dressed in corduroy pants and cradling a winter coat in his arms. The woman was sporting a puffy commuter coat that went down to her knees. Her fashion sense didn't stop there. She wore shearling-trimmed suede boots that pulled the entire outfit together. On her head she donned a knit hat boasting silver threads woven throughout and a shimmering pom-pom at the crown. Sherry envied her toasty outfit, which had form and function, something Sherry knew was usually lacking in her wardrobe choices. Function ruled with her busy schedule.

Before Sherry could offer her name and a greeting she was summoned into Patti's studio by Hammy.

"Good luck," Marla called after her sister before the door shut. Chutney yanked at his leash to follow Sherry, but his efforts were rebuffed.

Chapter 3

The thirty-minute interview sped by. Sherry had tons of facts about the origin and uses of the wooden spoon. The many ways she used the tool gave Patti lots of fodder for an engaging chat, as if they were comfortably seated in Sherry's kitchen sipping tea. After the interview she thanked Patti and returned to Marla in the waiting room. A group brushed past her with a mumbled word as they entered the studio. Two men remained seated across from Marla, their eyes fixed on their cell phones. Neither showed interest in a hello.

Sherry was running on adrenaline when she picked her coat up off the chair next to Marla and then plopped down in it. She couldn't help but notice one man's gaze lifted from his phone and settled on her. His blonde hair and square jaw were reminiscent of a famous Swedish tennis player she watched win a tournament on TV. If he donned a horned helmet and unsheathed a sword he could pass for a Viking with ease.

"Was the wooden spoon a good choice?" Marla asked. "What did you say makes it your favorite, besides how well it frightens your brother and sister during a chase."

Sherry's body flowed with unspent nervous energy. She straightened up and cleared her worn throat. "So many reasons. The material never gets hot to the touch because wood doesn't conduct heat. They don't scratch any of my pans. They season themselves naturally. They're a breeze to clean. They don't have any weird reactions to acids. All natural. Strong as all get out. You couldn't snap my spoon in half if you tried. Well, maybe you could. Heck, you could use it as a weapon if need be. I only pretended to when we were kids. Oh, and they are the prettiest tool in my kitchen drawer. Are you convinced?"

"I am," the Viking said. "All great reasons. Like you, I love my wooden spoon. One of the other guys was choosing the wooden spoon, too. I think he switched choices at the last minute. Not because of you, because of me. I'm not even being interviewed. Thomas, you still have my spoon?"

The man two seats down from the Viking, most likely related judging by their strong resemblance, peered up from his phone. "Yes, and I'm holding on to it until the others come out. You've riled them up too much." His phone buzzed and his attention returned to the device.

"You've convinced me I need a wooden spoon," Marla said. "My favorite kitchen utensil is the ice cream maker. Do you know how hot Oklahoma can get? Ice cream's a great source of cold refreshment."

Sherry saw her opportunity for a connection when the man ended his call. "Excuse me," Sherry said.

The man raised his sights from his phone.

"Are you being interviewed by Patti for her podcast? About your favorite kitchen tool?"

"Not on her podcast, no. Neither one of us."

"I brought my favorite kitchen tool to impress her," the first man said. "Turns out I'm not the only one who loves wooden spoons. You stole my thunder."

"Sorry about that." Sherry couldn't read the man's tone, sarcastic or unhappy. "What's that smell?" Sherry asked. "Reminds me of Halloween for some reason."

Marla scrunched up her nose. "I don't like it."

Sherry gave the men a moment to chime in but there were no takers. "Doesn't seem like I'm having any luck making a friend," she whispered. "Time to go?"

"Let's do it," Marla said. She wriggled her arms into her coat sleeves.

Sherry stood and did the same. "Have a good day," Sherry said. Both men gave the women a smile and a nod.

Sherry and Marla labored down the steps until they reached the ground floor. Even with tiny legs Chutney hopped down each step with ease. They found Clem at his station by the exit.

"Do you need us to sign out?" Sherry asked.

"I can mark you down," Clem said. "Have a good day." He held the door open for the sisters and Chutney.

"Glad that went well," Marla said as they strolled down the sidewalk. They took their time with each footstep. Black ice was everywhere. "You handle cooking interviews so well."

"There's always a moment of panic before we start that I'll be as dull as dishwater, but thanks. The subject is my comfort zone."

"Wonder if the others will be as knowledgeable as you on their favorite tools," Marla said.

"Patti wouldn't have invited them if they weren't. Did you get a sense of who they were? I didn't have any chance to ask Patti. I was escorted in and out without any small talk."

"I did get a few tasty tidbits of info. The three who went in after you were judges at the upcoming cook-off. Of the other two, the one who brought the wooden spoon was Patti's boyfriend and that was his brother attached to his phone," Marla said with a nonchalance Sherry couldn't fathom.

Sherry's mouth hung open until she gathered her thoughts. "What? More of a smorgasbord than a tasty tidbit. I don't know which is bigger news. The fact those were the cook-off judges or that Patti has a boyfriend. I haven't seen her since before the holidays. I have no idea what she's been up to."

"I didn't speak more than a hello to him."

"How did you connect the dots he was her boyfriend?" Sherry asked.

"From a remark that sounded like he was as mad as a wet hen. One said, 'If I weren't your brother, I'd walk away,' to which the other replied, 'Go right ahead. Patti treats me like the good boyfriend I am.'"

"They were arguing?"

"While you were out of the room, he and his brother were busy having words in an aggressive whisper for the first ten minutes. I couldn't hear some of what was said but the mood was somber. Two bulls in the height of rutting season would be more compatible than those two."

"That's too bad. Brothers fight, I'm sure they'll make up."

"Always the optimist," Marla said.

"What did you learn about the judges? Where are they from? The cook-off contestants weren't provided any details as to who the judges are. Maybe they weren't even decided on until very recently. I'm so curious."

Marla's reply was as slow and deliberate as their footsteps on the icy sidewalk. "I bet you are. Let's see. I hope I'm getting this right. After the edge was off the brotherly feud the conversation became civil. I learned the woman was a cookbook author who specializes in international cuisines, quick and easy. Those are her words. Sienna Warren is her name. I browsed her copy of her latest cookbook, which she brought along. Signed for Patti. I was drooling at the photos when I flipped through it."

"I haven't heard of her," Sherry said. "I like the theme of her book."

"Another was an expert in food and ingredient trends, Gunnar V.," Marla said. "He said his last name, but man, it was nearly unpronounceable, so he uses his last initial, V. when he introduces himself. And one was the home and food section editor for the *Coastal County Beacon* newspaper, Carl Carlson. All good choices to judge your cook-off. Isn't the theme international recipes?"

"More specifically, the cook-off is titled Round the World's Pantry—Cuisine and Culture Cook-off. Entrants had to submit a main course or dessert recipe of their own design, using at least one of seven listed sponsor ingredients." Sherry lifted her sights skyward as she recalled the eligible products. "Black beans, coconut milk, balsamic vinegar, peanut butter, goat cheese, gooseberry preserves." Sherry silently counted how many ingredients she had named. Only six. "Oh, and the seventh was chocolate-hazelnut spread."

"Those are quite diverse flavors. Easy to be overwhelmed by too much choice," Marla said.

"Absolutely. You know how these contests work. The judges want a recipe that the general public hasn't seen, isn't put off by, and can make at home."

"If it were me, I'd use all seven products in one recipe hoping to lure in one judge," Marla said.

"I know you know better than that. Cramming in too many of the sponsor ingredients isn't a good idea and doesn't impress the judges. And it's transparent that you're trying to cast a wide net," Sherry said, shaking her head.

"If there's one lesson I've learned from you it's that less is more in most recipe contests. Choose the star ingredient, maybe two, then shape your recipe around those ingredients," Marla said.

"Don't forget to stick to your theme. You'd be surprised how many people let that simple rule slip away in the heat of battle."

As they passed Augustin Dry Goods, Sherry admired the Valentine's Day–themed window displays. In the left front window was a chainsaw decorated with a red ribbon that was in the process of carving a heart into a piece of wood. In the right side window was a romantic picnic setting with all the amenities needed to woo a loved one. Both displays conveyed the holiday perfectly. Sherry imagined her ex, Charlie, was more likely to find inspiration in the picnic scene, with its orderly and refined aura. Don would just as likely present Sherry with a chainsaw-carved token of his affection, reflective of his new outdoorsy profession. Both windows represented the store's diverse inventory any small-town country store would be proud to carry.

"Do the Nagles still run the dry goods store?" Marla asked. "Tony and Penny?"

"Absolutely," Sherry said. "Want to hear something interesting about them?"

"Sure," Marla said.

"Recently Augustin's planning committee asked the Nagles if they wouldn't mind changing the name of their store."

"Why would they do that? Dry goods is what they sell."

"Mayor Jenkins sent his chief of staff over to meet with the couple in hopes they'd modernize the name. Something short, flashy, and trendy, to attract a younger clientele. With deep pockets."

"Not a bad idea," Marla said. "I see by the store's familiar sign they haven't changed the name. These things take time, I imagine."

"Not going to happen," Sherry said. "The Nagles say Augustin Dry Goods represents the town's history, which is anything but flashy and trendy. Remember, Augustin started as an onion farm. The town was established by simple folk who liked their day-to-day supplies found in a one-stop shop. The dry goods store was born from that desire."

"Two sides to every argument," Marla said.

"No argument it's a fun window," Sherry said. "The Ruggery needs to step it up. Who knew Valentine's Day would take so much effort. Too bad I won't have much time to devote to my valentine this year. I still have work to do on my cook-off entry for the finals. Is there such a thing as a Valentine's Day rain check?"

"No way. You need to put in some effort to make Don feel special. You know he'll be doing something special for you. What recipe did you enter in the cook-off?" Marla asked.

"The sponsor products I used were peanut butter and coconut milk. I made my version of Snappy African Groundnut Stew."

"Groundnuts are peanuts, right?" Marla asked.

"Right. The stew's so good, if I do say so myself. Chicken, chutney, creamy peanut butter–coconut milk sauce, sweet potato chunks." Sherry licked her lips for emphasis. "Rich, well-seasoned, and the leftovers are to die for. When a meal tastes better the second day, it's a winner."

"Yum. But that was only round one in the contest?" Marla asked.

"That's right. I passed the first test. Next week the finalists are asked to cook a new recipe from a different country. It must incorporate a pancake or tortilla or a similar thin, circular unleavened flatbread, along with a story that explains the inspiration behind the choice. It's a little more work than usual but I'm excited for the challenge."

Sherry stopped as they neared the Ruggery. As if she were seeing the store for the first time, she took in the beauty of the building that housed her family's business. The bones of the structure were over a hundred years old and boasted the architectural accents New England was famous for. Her favorite was the paneled wood door and the dental molding that framed the entryway. Flattened columns were inlaid on the sides of the door and the detail invited customers in with a visual welcome. The combination of features beckoned all to experience her father's latest hand-designed hooked rugs.

"You're admiring the building again, aren't you?" Marla asked.

"Guilty. The family's so lucky to work at this address where old Augustin meets new Augustin and they coexist perfectly.

"For sure," Marla said.

Chapter 4

The walk to the Ruggery had been a chilly one. Sherry didn't wear her hat to the podcast, fearing a case of hat-hair. The icy February wind left her scalp numb to the touch as she rearranged her tussled hair before entering the store. As they opened the door the sisters greeted their father, Erno. He was busy locating a customer card in the Rolodex, Erno's version of a computerized system. When he selected the card, he raised his eyes.

"Look who's here. My favorite daughters," Erno said. "And my favorite terrier." Chutney wagged his stubby tail when Erno knelt to pat his head.

"Hi, Dad," Sherry said. "We came to see if Don is free for dinner tonight. And you, too. Where are you hiding that young man?"

"Don worked on the books for a few hours and took a fresh batch home with him. He said he was heading somewhere to check out the latest in nautical radar systems. I think he's trying to figure out how next year he can miss less time on the water in the winter," Erno said. "He must really like his job. It's dang cold out there."

"Maybe working on the Ruggery books is giving him haunting flashbacks of his previous career," Marla said.

"Working at the Ruggery is a privilege, not a nightmare, young lady," Erno said with a wag of his finger.

"Doesn't sound like he'll make it back by dinner. He can spend hours being entertained by the latest and greatest in the boating industry," Sherry said. "If I weren't so secure in our relationship, I'd be jealous of his passion."

"How about you, Dad?" Marla asked. "Want to join your daughters for some slow-cooker beef and barley soup with garlic toasts? Sherry set it in motion early this morning."

"Sounds like an invite I can't turn down," Erno said. "Except this time. I can't miss a dinner with my valentine, Ruth."

"Looks like it's you and me tonight, Marla," Sherry said. "I'm making dinner Friday night for Pep, Charlotte and little Mimi. The recipe for next week's cook-off. Dad, you'll come to dinner Friday, right?"

"That's a solid yes," Erno said. He was applying tape to the frayed edge of the card he was holding. "Pep's free that night?"

"Pep doesn't work Friday," Sherry said. "His food truck is having some maintenance done. You'll have all your kids gathered around you like baby chicks to the rooster."

"Cock-a-doodle-doo. How was your podcast?" Erno asked. "Can one of you show me how to listen to the interview? Setting those things up is the devil for me. My interest in technology only goes so far. Speaking of tech, Don wants me to computerize everything, including the Rolodex." The seventy-something man pointed to the device crammed with well-loved cards. "How in tarnation will I ever be able to do that? I have every piece of vital customer information on each card." His voice was gathering momentum.

"That's what computers do best, Dad," Marla said. "Chewing up data and spitting it back out in a way you can make sense of."

"The problem is," Sherry said, "only you can interpret those cards with your shorthand and your Erno Oliveri secret symbols. Even our dear Amber Sherwin, who knows the business in and out, has trouble discerning your notes. She likens them to a doctor's hand-written prescription."

"Don't be silly. God made hands so we could put pen to paper, not type on a computer," Erno said.

"Hard to argue with that," Marla said with the subtlest of eye rolls.

"I'm not even going to try," Sherry said. "I'll plant the bug in Don's ear to keep next winter open to computerize the store, just in case you come around to the modern age, Dad."

"You and Marla are coming into the store tomorrow to help me with inventory tracking for a few hours, I hope. It's been lonely here without Amber."

"She'll be back soon. She was overdue for a vacation. I bet she's having a great time."

"Guess what? I put Don to work for an hour manning the register."

"Does Don even know how to work that old-fashioned bean-counter?" Marla pointed to the register, which was celebrating its fortieth birthday this year.

"He's tech-savvy. I'm sure he had no trouble," Sherry said.

"Not sure there's any tech in that old thing," Marla added.

"Do you need one of us to stay on this afternoon?" Sherry asked.

"No, no. All is well. You two be on your merry way," Erno said. "I'll get some work out of you tomorrow."

"In that case, we're homeward bound," Sherry said as she edged toward the door. "I need to do some prep work for tomorrow's gardening class. I go every day for the rest of the week for thirty or forty minutes to teach the kids how to have a successful garden in the spring."

"The youth of Augustin is in your hands. Speaking of Augustin, you girls hear any scuttlebutt about that new newspaper in town?" Erno asked.

"Seems an awful lot like someone's trying to teach the town's next generation to forget the past and stomp all over tradition."

"I seem to be the last to know," Sherry said. "I haven't had a chance to read what everyone is talking about."

"Don left the paper here. I've read enough. Here, take it." Erno gathered the open paper from the side of the sales desk. "Business is tough enough without writers bending people's ears on how Augustin is living in a fog of antiquity." He forced the crumpled sheets into Sherry's hand.

Sherry spent a moment ironing out the paper folds until she could neatly tuck it under her arm. "Mandatory reading. See you tomorrow."

"Bye, girls. Enjoy your afternoon," Erno said.

"See you tomorrow, Dad. Give Ruth our love," Marla said.

• • •

Back at Sherry's house, the sisters went their separate ways until dinner prep time. Sherry worked on Wednesday's class notes. Garden planning was the topic. Or should garden planning be Thursday's topic? Wednesday could be waking the garden after winter's wrath. No matter, she would prepare for both days and shuffle content as she saw fit. If Mother Nature could be fickle, she could too.

Marla had retired to her bedroom to call her husband, Grant. Judging by the snores Sherry heard as she passed the guest bedroom, a nap followed. Sherry's dinner prep was a solo act. The simplicity of the soup earlier in the day—basically an ingredient dump into the ceramic crock—gave Sherry time to ponder what she might prepare for the upcoming cook-off.

Curiosity got the better of her and she rounded up the newspaper she brought home from the Ruggery. She flipped to the Home and Food section and scoured the content. One article in today's paper suggested topped toasts were a trend to be taken seriously.

Sherry decided she'd save the article for Pep. She knew he'd appreciate having reinforcement that he chose a trending theme for his food truck. Maybe he could even get mentioned in the next article. A wave of pride for the success of her brother's young business swept over her. Then she wondered if there were any new trends in the paper she might be able to work with.

She thumbed through the next two pages, learning she had made a correct call with her Snappy African Groundnut Stew because island flavors were "in" this year and her recipe contained many. She also learned fish in a tin can was a current trend. Odd. Who knew sardines, mussels, and anchovies would be making such a comeback? She'd take that recommendation with a grain of salt. She flipped to the page back and found the name she was looking for—Carl Carlson. He was the author of many of the articles and he was the section's editor. From what Marla said, he was a judge at the cook-off.

The temptation to adopt one of his trends for the recipe she would be creating was enticing. More enticing was the challenge to show the judge and journalist she had her own ideas of a good trend to put on the cook-off menu. She knew she was up to the task. A little more thought and inspiration was all that was needed.

• • •

When she and her sister finally sat down to dinner hours later, the slow cooker soup was a hit. Marla was the family beef eater. Sherry reserved her red meat consumption primarily for the times her fully carnivorous sister visited. She admitted to herself it was an indulgence she shouldn't make a habit of, as flavorful as the meaty broth was. Chutney, too, was mesmerized by the aromatic broth from the moment Sherry lifted the slow cooker lid. He sat expectantly at the base of the kitchen counter while Sherry ladled out two bowls. Six hours of low and slow cooking produced fall-off-the-bone meat shreds that melted in Sherry's mouth. It was too good not to reward his admiration of her cooking skills with a taste, so she pinched off a shred and fed it to her patient Jack Russell. She could have sworn his eyes rolled back in his head with delight.

After dinner and cleanup Marla settled in to watch her favorite reality television series while Sherry sat at the dining room table and continued her schoolwork. Waking up the garden in the spring was a favorite topic. Sherry began her list.

Raised garden beds thaw faster than in-ground beds.

Resist the urge to turn over the earth until planting time. The action disrupts the earthworm family dynamic and spreads weed seeds.

Don't weed with vigor. Often those sprouts are unrecognized regrows from the previous season, saving you seeding efforts.

Jotting down the words was enough to drive Sherry's enthusiasm for the upcoming spring's warm weather. Sherry would be back volunteering at the community garden, Don would be back on the water where he prospered, Marla would be raising baby calves on her ranch, and Pep would be serving up tasty toasts for the outdoor lunch crowd from his food truck. Amazing how one entity had a connection to another and another with no other apparent thread than a goodbye to the cold.

Chapter 5

The next morning Sherry slept through one cycle of her alarm before succumbing to the annoying squeal. "Sherry, your alarm," Marla called out. "And the coffee's ready."

"I hear it," Sherry called back. Phone in hand, she came down the stairs, bedhead unbrushed. "You're up early." Her phone buzzed in her hand. "Someone else is up early, too." She double-checked the name on the screen. Unusual. Patti seldom called, choosing to text instead when she reached out. And either method of communication was rare to nil so early in the day.

"Hi, Patti."

Patti sucked in a deep breath. "My friend, Sig, is missing. They think he might be dead. His brother, Thomas, called me. It looks like he fell through the ice on Harmony Lake."

The raspy voice on the other end of the phone chilled Sherry to the bone. Patti's usually robust, clear tone was her trademark. All Sherry could hear through the phone was sheer terror. "Patti? What did you say?"

Sherry squeezed her eyes shut while she processed what Patti was telling her. The shocking news before she had even taken her first sip of morning coffee was extra difficult to digest. Figuring out the words to console her friend was equally difficult.

"I didn't know who else to talk to. You saw him yesterday. At the studio. I'm not sure if I introduced you two. I meant to but time was getting away from me."

"If he was one of the two men seated in the waiting room while the other three went inside your studio, then yes, I saw him. I didn't formally meet him," Sherry said. "Marla may have. I exchanged only a few words with those two. They were busy on their phones."

"Don't you think this sounds very suspicious?" Patti asked breathlessly.

"Suspicious?" Sherry said. She was confused. Had she missed something? "I'm sure he'll turn up. Or was there a tragic accident? When exactly did this happen?"

"Yesterday. After dark. I got a call from Thomas around ten last night. Maybe earlier, I don't even know."

"Thomas?" Another unexplained detail. Sherry did her best to remain lucid. A sip of coffee was the remedy. She collected a mug while trying to keep her attention on Patti. Marla came to the rescue and prepared her coffee the way she liked it, with oat milk creamer and a spoon of sugar. The creamy caffeine went down easily. Sherry put the phone on speaker mode so Marla could listen in.

"Thomas is Sigmund's brother. He was also at my office yesterday." Patti was practicing breathing techniques between bursts of information. "Thomas was there because one of the men I interviewed works with him. He wasn't in the actual podcast."

"Sigmund is your friend?" Sherry asked. She held off on using the "boyfriend" label in hopes Patti would get provide a full picture of who she was concerned about and why.

"New friend. We've been on a number of dates. I liked Sigmund a lot. He was different. Had a lot of layers I hadn't had enough time to peel back."

"His brother called you saying he was missing? Or in an accident? What exactly did Thomas say?" Sherry asked. If she could get Patti to stay on track she might be able to sort out the story. As it was, she was lost as to what had actually happened. Sherry took another sip from her mug.

"The details are sketchy. Thomas was in a rush. He delivered the stunning news as if he were only telling me Sig has come down with a cold. He was strangely calm but left me no chance for questions. He told me Sig was missing and it looked like he drowned in the lake after falling through the ice. He said he knew Sig thought of me as a wonderful friend." Patti went quiet. Sherry let her take her time. When she collected herself, Patti said, "The last word Thomas spoke was *sorry*."

"I'm sorry, too, Patti. I didn't know him, or that you two were, whatever you two were. But if he meant something to you, I'm sorry you have to go through this."

"Thank you. But something's not right. Something smells bad. Sig's an Icelander, for heaven's sake. They know ice. They don't fall through the ice. He was murdered, Sherry. I'm sure of it."

Patti's words tumbled out with such emotion Sherry was left dumbstruck. Her arms sprouted goose bumps. She didn't know what to ask next to make her friend feel heard. Marla's reappearance shored up Sherry's courage.

Icelander. Sherry let the word rattle around in her head while she pictured the country's landscape. "I thought the men had accents I couldn't pinpoint. How long have you known Sig?" Sherry grimaced as she realized the question may not drum up any pertinent information. It just felt like a natural progression to get to the heart of the matter. Whatever the matter was.

"He's been in the area for less than a year. We hit it off one day when I was reading the back label of a mustard jar at the grocery store. He came up behind me and said, 'Ah, a label reader. My kind of consumer.' Wasn't that cute?"

Sherry was still lost, as if she had entered a movie theater halfway through the film and was expected to follow the plot. "Is he in the food industry?"

"He was a food importer."

"Less than a year. You and Sigmund were in your early days. Would you say the relationship was going well?" This conversation was in uncharted waters and Sherry was having trouble with choosing what to say. Of course, the relationship wasn't flawless if Patti thought her boyfriend had an enemy capable of murder.

"As much as I had in common with Sig, we had as many differences. One being his temper. I'm pretty even-keeled. He got rattled easily."

"I saw that side of him," Marla whispered over Sherry's shoulder.

"He was buttoned up about some family issues. He didn't like to talk about his upbringing in Iceland. How could I not be interested in hearing all about a country I've never visited? He shut me down every time I broached the subject. Even discussing his brother, Thomas, was treading on thin ice. Oh, I shouldn't have said thin ice." Patti whimpered.

"Why are you jumping to the conclusion he was murdered?" Sherry asked.

"A gnawing feeling. To make matters worse, I'm not so sure Thomas wasn't suspicious of me," Patti said. Her voice cracked when she said the word *suspicious*. "When I argued Sig couldn't have drowned, that he would turn up, he agreed Sig was adept at recognizing unsafe ice. But he said there were signs of trouble at the lake, and he went so far as to ask me if we had a fight that day. The frustrating part was he gave me no chance to respond."

"He doesn't know you, obviously. That's ridiculous," Sherry said. "Your emotions are getting the best of you."

"You're right. Thomas doesn't know me, and I don't know him well at all." Patti's voice trailed off. After a short silence, she added, "How would he have known we had a spat. Maybe more than a spat." Her voice was trembling. "Yes, Sig and I did have a major disagreement. I told him I didn't want to see him again. I didn't mean it. The others saw it. That's not going to get out, is it?"

"I couldn't tell you." Although Sherry could tell her she assumed it would, but she didn't want her more upset. "But murder? You're really going to the extreme here. That doesn't add up if his brother said he fell through the ice."

Patti sucked in an aggravated breath. "Thomas said Sig's phone was found submerged near the shore of the frozen lake. Emergency services were notified and found a disturbing scene at the lakeshore. There were footprints in the snow on the fishing dock."

Sherry visualized the scene of chaos when Sigmund may have slipped on the dock, the phone flying from his hand as he catapulted into the frozen lake. Assuming the death was murder was a whole other level of concern. "The police will give this the thorough investigation the case deserves. In the meantime, Patti, don't give up hope. You don't know that he's dead."

"Thank you, Sherry," Patti said. Her voice sounded more like herself. "I know you're busy with your class and preparing for the upcoming cook-off, not to mention your sister is in town. You're the first person I thought of when the word *murder* popped into my head."

Sherry whispered a half-hearted "thank you." *Thank you* wasn't the right phrase. Uttering *murder* and thinking of Sherry wasn't an association she was interested in being a part of.

"I mean you're very good at solving murders." Patti sighed. "I'm frazzled. I better go before I say more stupid stuff," Patti said. She clicked off and the line went silent.

Sherry and Marla exchanged glances.

"Relax your forehead, she's right," Marla said. "You *are* good at solving murder mysteries."

Chapter 6

"At her studio, did you learn anything about Patti's boyfriend? This is all catching me by surprise," Sherry said as she reached out to open the cabinet containing her school supplies.

"Only what I caught snippets of, which wasn't much," Marla said. "Who knew I should have been a better eavesdropper, like you." She held Sherry's canvas tote bag while Sherry loaded in seed packets, soil samples and a shiny new trowel. "It makes sense you're such a good sleuth. As a kid you knew all the secrets."

"I was in the right place at the right time," Sherry said as she double-checked her inventory. "What snippets can you remember?"

"Let me think. He seemed like a decent dude after his salty mood simmered down," Marla said. "When he said they'd be having lunch together the twinkle in his eye was cute. Another indication something was going on between the two. He was taking her out after the podcast was over. Would you say you know Patti well?"

"At first, she and I had a working relationship. She wrote some articles about my cooking wins, and I was very grateful. Time went on and we continued to hit it off. She's serious about her food knowledge. More than that, she's become a dependable friend and super helpful during some of the more trying times, especially when I've been involved in murder investigations."

"That's a quality not everyone can boast having," Marla said. "Comes in handy."

"I can't deal with this right now," Sherry said with a wave of her hand. "I'm going to be late for school." She ran up the stairs and finished her look with a swipe of the blush brush and a wipe of the mascara wand. It was more makeup than she'd worn since her last dinner out with Don. One peek out the window and she had no trouble choosing her footwear. Another day of waterproof boots.

The light coating of snow that fell overnight would be cleared from the middle school's walkways long before Sherry arrived for her class. She was fully aware Connecticut had a higher tolerance for snow and rarely canceled school days for it, unlike the states south of New England. Still, she briefly wished on this day school authorities would have reevaluated by the time she pressed her alarm's off button a few hours ago. She was still rattled by Patti's phone call.

"See you soon, boy," Sherry said as she waved the small bundle of elderly canine energy forward. "Marla will be your company this morning. See you both soon."

Sherry gathered her class materials and drove to the middle school. Facing a sea of eager faces, she listened as Mrs. Turpin introduced the class topic to the students. Sherry launched into her program on how to wake up a garden space after a frigid New England winter. It wasn't long before hands were raised.

"Yes, Magnus. How are you today?"

"Not so good, Ms. Sherry. I wanted to tell you my uncle disappeared last night, they think he might have died. He was a big fan of yours, like my dad is."

A chill crawled up Sherry's spine. "I'm so sorry, Magnus. I wonder if I ever met him?" Again, Sherry turned to Mrs. Turpin for an idea how far to take the questioning.

"I think you met him yesterday. My dad said you saw him and Uncle Sigmund in Augustin when you were doing an interview. After you left this class. Don't you remember them?" Magnus's expression implored Sherry to revisit the previous day and picture the men in Patti's waiting room.

"Your dad works for a newspaper, you said? The *Coastal County Beacon*?" Sherry asked, trying to put the pieces together. The men Marla described as bickering bulls.

"That's right," Mrs. Turpin explained. "Magnus's father, Thomas Helguvson, is the editor in chief of the *Coastal County Beacon*. Thomas was the first in the family to relocate from Iceland last year. The rest of the family soon followed. The family has had to make many adjustments this year. It's been hard on Magnus." She lowered her voice to a whisper. "The paper's lean isn't making them popular with the old guard in our Hillsboro County, either."

Surprised by the sudden mood swing in the room, Sherry only nodded so as not to misspeak.

Mrs. Turpin flipped on her teacher switch and addressed Magnus in a warm empathetic tone. "As I said earlier this morning, we are so sorry, and that includes Miss Sherry. But we must continue with the lesson. Her time is running out."

The air was thick with awkward silence as Sherry tried to construct a sensible segue back to gardening. "Okay then. Who has an idea why we shouldn't turn over the soil that is thawing out from the winter freeze?"

"We don't want to squish the worms with shovels, or chop them in half," a boy called out.

"Please raise your hand, Louie," Mrs. Turpin said. "Was he right?"

"Absolutely," Sherry said. "And the topsoil that's been developing naturally all winter long needs to cook a bit longer as the sun warms the soil. Nature makes layers of soil for a reason. When you disrupt the organized layers and toss everything together, the weeds and their seeds are spread around, the worms struggle to find their home and the nutritious microbes in the soil get disturbed. Only till just before seeding, not too much. Just enough to punch in a hole for the seed or baby plant. Leave the surrounding soil alone to do its thing."

"Till?" the girl with the pigtails asked. "What's that?"

"Great question. Tilling is breaking up the soil and turning it over and over."

"That'll squish the worms," Louie called out.

"Raise your hand, Louie," Mrs. Turpin repeated.

"And we don't want to do that," Sherry said. "There's a whole community down under the soil we don't want to disturb. Let worms live in peace. Speaking of worms, Friday we'll get into composting. Worms play an irreplaceable part in composting."

"Okay, everyone. Time's up," Mrs. Turpin said after the bell announced the next period. "See you tomorrow, Miss Sherry."

"Thanks. See you all tomorrow." Sherry gathered her tote bag from under the teacher's desk. She hustled down the row of student desks before stopping by Magnus. He was in the midst of stacking textbooks in his arms.

"So sorry about your uncle. I hope this is all a mistake and he shows up. I do remember seeing him yesterday. Your uncle and father were at the studio, but I didn't have a chance to introduce myself. I certainly would have if I'd known he was your dad. My sister told me later who your uncle was and I'm making the connection now. She didn't know who your father was exactly except for the fact he was your Uncle Sigmund's brother. It's so interesting he runs a newspaper in the county."

"Dad's very busy." Magnus lowered his voice. "He probably didn't go out of his way to introduce himself. Some people don't like my dad because of what he prints in his paper. He says he's just trying to bring Augustin into the modern age. Maybe folks here don't like us because we're from Iceland. Dad was frustrated with living there. It's different there than here, but also kind of the same. If Iceland was a garden, we'd be the worms. No one has tilled the soil there in so long the worms never had a chance to see the world up above. Do you know what I mean?"

"I think I do. Iceland. Wow. Did you like it there?" Sherry asked.

Magnus reached into his desk and pulled out a pencil. He checked the wall clock. "The land is beautiful. The food is kinda gross. People believe in weird stuff." He shrugged. "I don't know. I gotta go."

The students flowed out of the classroom, leaving Sherry and Mrs. Turpin behind.

"He's a nice boy in tough circumstances," the teacher said. "He'll find his way. Your gardening class is cheering him up. He'll be one of the first to plant one this year."

• • •

Before Sherry drove out of the school's parking lot, she read two texts on her phone. One was from Don saying he had some Ruggery issues to discuss, no rush. The other was from the last person she wanted to hear from under the circumstances, Detective Ray Bease. He had led the murder investigations she had been involved with in the past. She enjoyed seeing his name on her screen most of the time. It usually meant he was following through on his promise to learn to cook. He had become a generous friend and usually whatever he wanted to talk about was welcomed. But the timing of this call suggested it wasn't a social call. The second she connected with him her fear was confirmed.

"Hello, Sherry," Ray began. His greeting wasn't so formal on a recipe-related call. "I have a few questions about your friend Patti Mellit. Is she involved with a man named Sigmund Helguvson?"

"Hi, Ray. Yes, Patti was dating him. A new relationship. A couple months. That's about as long as it's been since I've seen or talked to her. Maybe they're not even dating. Maybe spending friendly time together," Sherry said. She knew that when Ray was on duty his questions were time-sensitive and Sherry's wordy speculations tested the limits of his patience. She didn't mind if he was fussy. It was part of his charm.

"You've given me a multiple-choice answer to a simple question," Ray said. "Moving on. Have you seen them together? Do they seem like a romantic couple or friendly time-spenders, as you put it?"

"I only recently found out they were somewhat of an item. Yesterday, in fact. I can only hope they're happy. Patti is my wonderful friend and my go-to source for all things food. I've even forwarded some of your recipe questions on to her. Even after not seeing each other for months we pick right up where we left off. Usually something about food. In that way Patti is to me what I am to you. But what is this about?"

"I spoke with her about twenty minutes ago," Ray said. "She told me that she informed you Mr. Helguvson is missing, and there are signs of foul play. She said you were with the Mr. Helguvson at the MediaPie Studios yesterday. Is that correct?"

"Yes, no," Sherry said. "Not exactly *with* him." Her circuitous reply prompted Ray's mild groan. "We were never even introduced. I only found out who he was when my sister, Marla, who was waiting for me, told me, after the fact, who the two men and one woman were. I passed by them as they went in for the interview. Well, Patti's friend didn't go in for an interview. I'm not exactly sure why he was there except maybe to take her to lunch. Marla and I left the studio soon after I was done."

"Interesting," Ray said. "I would like to speak to Marla. Maybe she overheard something. Is now a good time? Is she with you?"

Sherry gave his question some thought. "I should be home in about fifteen minutes. Can I call you back then? Let's arrange a meeting."

"Twenty minutes. We'll speak soon. As for a meeting, my time is limited, so unless . . ."

"Ray. I've known you a few years now. Have I ever wasted your valuable time?"

"Nope. Never. Remember, the first twenty-four hours of an investigation are also the most valuable in terms of hot, fresh evidence."

Mrs. Turpin's feelings about Thomas rang in Sherry's ears. Sigmund may have been murdered, she thought, but it was Thomas who has a county full of enemies. The thought dissolved as quickly as the falling snow melted on the windshield.

Chapter 7

During the drive home Sherry passed a billboard on the side of the county road advertising the cook-off she would soon be participating in, Round the World's Pantry—Cuisine and Culture. It was just six days until the cook-off. The African-style groundnut stew she entered in the first round of the contest was good enough to get her into the finals, along with twenty-four other amateur cooks. The next step was to come up with an international recipe from scratch, along with a related story. Her family would be her taste-testers Friday and she'd take their opinions to heart.

First things first. She should check in with Patti. After she arrived home, she walked up the front path. She needed to shovel the path of its new layer of snow before the night's freeze turned the light fluff to perma-drifts.

"I'm home." No reply. "Marla? Chutney?" Nothing. "Where is everyone?" Sherry hung up her coat and began a search for her sister. Finding the house empty, she organized the newspaper she had only read the food section of. She took a seat on the couch. The *Coastal County Beacon* was a good name for a local newspaper. Beacon was a ray of light. Maybe a clue to the name choice. Shining a new light on a town stuck in the dark ages. What was she thinking? Sherry loved her stuck town. She hadn't even leafed past the front page when she heard Marla and Chutney enter through the front door.

"Hey, sis. I've walked Chutney and his bladder is now empty," Marla said. She joined Sherry in the living room, basking in the elusive winter sun shining through the picture window.

"Hi. Thanks. You're the best. Did you find his snow booties? I let them dry on top of the heating grate and forgot to mention that. The ice is rough on the pads of his paws."

"Found 'em. I couldn't locate his little hat and scarf though."

The visual alone caused much-needed laughter. Sherry set aside the newspaper.

"What do you think of the *Beacon*?"

"I haven't gotten past the food section, so I'm keeping an open mind," Sherry said.

"Once you get past all the articles about improving Augustin and Hillsboro, read the letters to the editor. They're downright volatile. Pro and con modernizing the county in a fast-track plan."

"Will do," Sherry said.

"How was your class?"

"Amazing. The kids are sponges, soaking it all in." Sherry paused. "Coincidentally, one of the kids in the class is a boy from Iceland. Just moved to Bridgeton, the town north of Augustin."

"Iceland. I've never met anyone from Iceland. That kid's probably never met anyone from Oklahoma. I know I hadn't until Grant lassoed me. My sweet cowboy. Why is the boy from Iceland a coincidence?"

"His father is the editor of this paper. That's not all." Sherry rattled the sheets of newsprint. "His father's name is Thomas Helguvson."

Marla opened her mouth to speak but was beaten to the punch.

"And, Thomas Helguvson's brother, Sigmund, was Patti's friend who's missing and presumably fell through the ice. Both of whom you saw yesterday at the studio."

"Wow. Bonanza of news. Poor kid's family is dealing with tragedy. That's a kick in the pants," Marla said as she took a seat next to Sherry.

"Not only that," Sherry said, "Magnus, that's the boy's name, was disturbed his father had ruffled so many feathers in town with his paper's content. When that kind of news trickles down to the youngsters in the family, it can do serious damage. His dad might be his hero and now he's under attack."

"Lucky for us, we have the world's greatest dad, who'd never cause us worry like that," Marla said.

"I agree. The rest of the class time was fantastic. More of the same tomorrow."

"I'm glad class is going well. Sorry for the Helguvson family. And Patti."

"I'm worried about her. I'm going to call to make sure she's okay."

Sherry was reminded returning Don's call was on the agenda too. She was procrastinating because she knew she'd see him at dinnertime and always preferred to hold their conversations in person. She'd promised Ray she'd call him back, too.

First up, Patti. She seemed calmer than before, and they scheduled a walk down the river boardwalk. Patti's sore knee was healing, and she insisted she needed fresh air. Sherry's next call was to Ray. With a little creative persuasion Sherry was able to include Ray in the mix at the boardwalk. Killing two birds with one stone, or one walk, seemed like a good idea. She just hoped Detective Bease didn't upset Patti.

"Are you sure Patti's up for a walk?" Marla asked as she climbed into Sherry's car.

"Best thing for her is to stay engaged," Sherry said. "She's frustrated, hurting, and doesn't even know if Sigmund is alive or dead. Worst of all, Sigmund's brother stopped just short of accusing her of murder. That's too much to deal with alone."

"I'm confused. Why would Patti murder her new boyfriend?" Marla asked.

"You're not the only one who's confused."

"Now I understand. That's what the walk's about."

Sherry shrugged at the ease with which her sister unraveled her motive.

Sherry and Marla met Patti by the Augustin Library steps. They proceeded shoulder to shoulder down the boardwalk parallel to the Silty Pretzel River, being careful to sidestep icy areas. Snow flurries came and went, leaving a layer of snowflakes on everyone's hats. As they neared the river, the Canadian geese who neglected to migrate farther north honked in a panic and scrambled awkwardly on webbed feet across the ice chunks floating with the current. After the gaggle took flight quiet returned to the gray scenery.

With small talk about the weather out of the way, Sherry jumped right into the difficult subject. "I talked to Detective Bease. He called me because you told him I was at MediaPie the day Sig disappeared. Why do they think he drowned?"

Patti took some time to answer. A lone gull cried overhead. When the black and white bird flew out of sight Patti stopped walking and turned to Sherry. "They haven't recovered the body, but there were signs of a struggle. The detective said they were looking at all possibilities."

Sherry tipped her head from one side to the other, weighing how much to share. "Let me explain something to you. When I first met Detective Bease I made plenty of mistakes that set the tone for our relationship. I had a lot to learn about the etiquette for dealing with an on-duty detective. First, never expect him to offer more information than you've asked for. Even then, there's a good chance he won't be willing to give you an answer when dealing with work issues. It definitely wasn't give-and-take until I made peace with his style. Since the first murder investigation I was involved in, he and I have come a long way. I was the prime suspect, which had everything to do with our collision course meeting. Since then, we've become friends. I've lent him a friendly hand when he lost his mother, suffered one or two loves lost, and needed recipe advice. The line is drawn, though, when it comes to him performing his detective duties. Work first, friends second."

"How do they confirm Sigmund's dead with no body? Why not assume he might still show up?" Marla asked.

"He might," Sherry said. "But if not, my first thought is he dropped his phone and made a move to intercept it before it hit the water and somehow fell in. Who hasn't tried catching their falling phone with their foot before it hits the floor?"

"There was evidence of a scuffle on the dock," Patti said. "A trail of blood leading to the edge of the dock. Thomas told me the ice was disturbed a few feet off the dock, as if he were pushed or tossed in after possibly being knocked out." She grimaced. "A torn jacket was hanging on a piling. And a broken wooden spoon was found under the jacket. With his blood on the splintered end."

"How awful," Sherry said.

"The police sent their dive and water rescue unit but the conditions in the snow squall last night made the search treacherous. The lake is the deepest there with a severe drop-off." Patti's voice weakened. "They had to abandon the search."

"They'll keep trying," Sherry said. "When they get a break in the weather."

"A wooden spoon with his blood on it?" Marla directed her attention toward Sherry. "Remember when we were in Patti's office and Sigmund mentioned a wooden spoon?"

"That's right. Sigmund brought a wooden spoon with him to your studio. He mentioned it. His brother had it at the time so I never saw it," Sherry said. Staying put too long was chilling her. She balled her fingers up for warmth as much as she was able while wearing her restrictive gloves.

"He brought the spoon to the podcast, hoping to show me his favorite utensil. He wanted to tell me about the value of the spoon to Icelandic culture."

"Sounds like a popular choice."

"There were enough facts about the wooden spoon's importance in cooking for everyone to have shared. Did you know spoons were found in burial sights from the year two hundred and fifty years BC?" Patti said.

"That's old," Marla said. "And amazing."

"If Sigmund wasn't on the podcast, why was he there, if you don't mind me asking?" Sherry asked.

"He was so inspired by the topic that he stopped by during his busy day to see how it was going. That was his first visit to the studio, which, as you know, is owned by MediaPie Corp, who also owns the *Nutmeg News*. Sig's brother's newspaper, the *Coastal County Beacon*, is their direct competitor."

"The Van Ardans from Augustin own the MediaPie group of television, radio and newspaper outlets locally, as I recall?" Marla asked.

"That's right," Patti said. "Their newspaper, the *Nutmeg News*, loves Augustin just the way it is."

Sherry nodded. "Good thing. Change comes slowly in Augustin. If there are any changes to be made in Augustin, the citizens vote, rally, petition and, even then, usually change still moves at a snail's pace. Everyone seems to be fine with consistency or they move away."

"Not necessarily a recipe for keeping up with the times," Patti said.

"How do they feel about Sigmund's brother Thomas coming into town and throwing a wrench in the works?" Marla asked Patti. "Trying to ignite a movement toward modernization at warp speed. Taking the *Nutmeg News* complacency head-on."

"The Van Ardans are my employers, but I don't have to support their view. In fact, I haven't made up my mind which way the wind is blowing," Patti said. "Unfortunately, the town's getting fractured."

"Yup," Marla said. "Might help newspaper subscriptions if the banter continues."

"Or agitate so many, the town's reputation for keeping calm and carrying on goes down the tubes," Patti said with a frown.

"Yesterday's *Beacon* had an article about how Augustin would benefit from digital parking meters. Income is lost daily until the town acts, the reporter wrote. The money collected could pay for a face-lift for the town's marina. More boats equal an uptick in business revenue. But more boats require dredging and cause the destruction of wetlands. More infrastructure will be needed to support an increase in volume to the downtown. On and on. The domino effect. Some say it's a win-win all the way around," Marla said. "No need for the meter maid. She scares away tourists with her gruff demeanor, he wrote."

The corners of Sherry's mouth turned up slightly, as if she herself may agree. "Our job-for-life meter maid, Layla? She can't help how serious she looks. She loves her job."

"Get rid of the Augustin Community Garden, another article suggested. It's an eyesore that squats on commercially valuable land that, if developed, could bring a boom to a sagging local economy," Marla said. "I didn't have the heart to tell you, Sher."

"What?" Sherry's jaw dropped. "That's not going to happen under my watch. My hours of volunteer time at the garden spent teaching underserved kids have been my happiest times. The *Beacon* is going too far."

A couple crossing their path stopped steps in front of Sherry.

"The *Beacon*, ugh." The woman was bundled as tight as a burrito in a fluffy faux fur. "Those so-called journalists would love it if us forever Augustonians dried up to dust and blew away. Reface our beautiful Town Hall in a cubist modernist architectural style just to attract a younger population to settle here? No way. Horrible idea. And Wi-Fi in our treasured donut and coffee shop, Sweets and Sip, so people can stare longer at their computers rather than chat face-to-face? Horrendous idea." She swatted her male companion on the arm with her gloved hand. "Right, Oscar?"

"You're being a tad dramatic, honey. Some of the ideas aren't half bad," Oscar said, risking another battering. "I did like the idea of benches and planters in front of stores so us husbands have a meeting spot while you gals shop. And storefront awnings. Augustin always fought that plan because it might encourage loitering rather than shopping. Times have changed and maybe Augustin should, too." Oscar side-eyed the woman Sherry assumed was his wife.

"Oscar. After all these years I can safely say I don't know you as well as I thought. I'm sorry but we need to agree to disagree. You're for the *Beacon* and I'm for the *Nutmeg News*. You're for time to speed up and I'm for savoring what was and is." She threw up her hands. "I hope Augustin can weather this storm." She hooked her arm in Oscar's and led him away.

Chapter 8

"That woman was right," Patti said. "Augustin is becoming divided, all thanks to Thomas Helguvson and the power of the printed word. Since the damage has been done, I suggest the Van Ardans ramp up their paper's viewpoint to ensure the town's heritage isn't buried and dead. Might as well fight on equal terms."

"You're for an escalation of the town's division?" Sherry was incredulous her friend would take the stance she did.

"You have to fight the battles before you win the war," Patti said. She resumed the walk.

Sherry scanned the surroundings in hopes of catching sight of Ray. She was more than curious whether there were any new developments.

"The town's problems aside, I think it's best if you pull out of the Round the World's Pantry cook-off," Patti said.

"What? No. Why would I do that?"

"Sig may have been murdered and there's a good chance his brother's affiliation with the newspaper was the reason why. The *Beacon* is a sponsor of the cook-off. You're my friend. I was Sig's special friend. It's too dangerous for you if whoever is behind Sig's disappearance feels the need to kill again." Patti paced a few steps back and forth as she explained her reasoning.

"Patti, I don't want to contradict you, but you have to admit, there's still a chance Sig will show up. And if not, his death could have been an accident," Sherry said.

Patti stopped pacing and faced her friend. "That's okay. You're just trying to be nice. I'd like to believe he had no enemies, but I know better."

"Excuse me, ladies. Sherry mentioned I might have a chat with Marla here this afternoon. Am I interrupting something?" Detective Bease asked as he slid in alongside Sherry.

Patti blew out an extended breath. "This can't be a coincidence. Sherry? Meeting the detective here has your signature all over it. What did you hope to gain from this?"

"Patti, Ray wanted to speak with Marla. I thought he could take some of the worry off your shoulders at the same time."

"I didn't say that," Ray said. "I'm not known for taking worry off of anyone's shoulders."

"I've already talked to Ray," Patti said. "He knows everything I know."

"There are a few new details that complicate this case," Ray said.

"Especially concerning Marla."

"Me?" Marla asked.

"Thank goodness it's not me," Patti said. "I've said all I have to say."

"Ray, before you talk to Marla, I have a question," Sherry said, hoping to smooth over the sudden waiver in Patti's calm demeaner. "Why are you investigating Sigmund's disappearance as a murder if no body was found? He might not even be dead."

Typically, Ray would state he was the investigator. The person whose job it is to ask questions. Much to Sherry's surprise he elaborated on his answer rather than changing the subject.

"Police photos from the scene are consistent with a struggle. The break in the water's surface was a distance from the dock, suggesting something big and heavy broke through the ice at that point. It's very unfortunate we have not recovered a body. As you know, weather conditions dictated a stoppage in the search. The investigative unit's job would be straightforward if we had found a body. Mr. Thomas Helguvson reported his brother, Sigmund, missing, presumed dead, and we are acting on that report."

"Do you have any other evidence he's in the lake?" Marla asked. "Besides an ice hole and a messed-up jacket on the dock?"

Sherry silently thanked her sister for asking the tough question.

"I have a contact at Augustin United Bank. She examined Sigmund's accounts for me and there has been no activity of any kind for days. No telltale withdrawal or deposit. Which is all consistent with a sudden death. It led the unit to approach the case as a murder rather than a missing person search."

"Maybe Trooper, from the town's K-9 unit, would be helpful," Marla said. "He is such a ridiculously talented police dog. Sherry couldn't stop bragging about him and how he cracked the last murder investigation she was involved in."

"She's right. Trooper's going down to the lake when the weather lightens up," Ray said with a tinge of pride. "The good news is the frigid weather, followed by the predicted thaw, will preserve the scent. If there's a scent track to be followed, made by Sigmund Helguvson, Trooper will find it."

Patti stayed quiet. Her eyes were glazed over as the discussion of her boyfriend's search was detailed.

"Did you have questions for Marla?" Sherry said, in order to draw closer to the end of the topic. She could see Patti was losing interest in pursuing the group conversation since Ray showed up.

"Ask me anything you want, Ray," Marla said. She winked in Ray's direction. "Taking a page from your detective manual, I may not answer."

"Another sassy Oliveri. My prayers have been answered," Ray said, returning the wink. "Do you mind if we take a seat at that picnic table?" His gaze was directed toward a row of snow-blanketed tables lining the edge of the river.

Ray followed the three ladies to the water's edge. They dusted off the thin layer of snow on the benches.

"Are you limping?" Ray asked Patti.

"I fell on the ice. A hazard of winter we all need to be careful of. It's getting sore again. I'm happy to sit." Patti moaned when she bent her knee to squeeze her legs under the picnic table.

"Marla, you met Thomas Helguvson in the MediaPie podcast waiting room. Correct?" Ray asked.

Marla nodded and pushed around some snow on the table in front of her. "Thomas arrived with the group to be interviewed after Sherry was done. We did some fast greetings around the room."

"And Sigmund?" Ray asked.

"Yes, he came in with them," Marla said.

"Why did Thomas come if he wasn't on the interview schedule?" Ray asked with a glance in Patti's direction.

"To accompany Carl Carlson, his employee. Maybe since Carl was entering enemy territory, he wanted to assure his safety," Patti said.

"Marla, did Thomas have words with Sigmund at that time? And if he did, what did you hear them discussing?" Ray asked.

"I heard Sigmund tell Thomas he couldn't believe he would show up at MediaPie when his goal as editor of the *Beacon* was to usurp their newspaper's dominance on the newsstands. Sigmund called Thomas a few choice words, describing the bold move without caring about the consequences." She pursed her lips in silence for a moment. "Thomas blamed Patti for corrupting Sigmund's perspective."

"Corrupting? He said 'corrupting'? What a . . ." Patti stopped short of designating her boyfriend's brother as something other than Mr. Nice Guy.

"Don't worry. Sigmund came to your defense," Marla said. "He said he would choose Patti over Thomas to spend time with in a heartbeat."

"Any reply?" Ray asked.

Sherry could see Marla had the answer on the tip of her tongue, when Patti clapped her gloves together. "Brothers banter. It's what they do. It doesn't mean a thing. I invited the *Beacon*'s food editor, Carl, to participate in the podcast because the *Beacon*'s a sponsor of the upcoming cook-off. Carl will also be a judge at the cook-off. As Marla said, Thomas is the editor in chief of the paper. It made sense Thomas would tag along, no doubt taking the opportunity to scout out his paper's competition. He was a welcome visitor. How was I to know there'd be a row?"

"Maybe you did have some inkling the two brothers weren't on the best of terms?" Ray asked. "Sigmund may have dropped a hint during a conversation?"

"We talked about his family maybe three times in all the time I've known him. He shut me down each time, saying he and his brother were working through some issues and when the relationship became more cordial, we would all sit down to a meal together. He made it sound like it was worth the wait. I took him at his word," Patti said.

Sherry glanced over at Ray. She wondered if he was thinking the same thing she was. That Patti constructed the plan of bringing two battling brothers together under the guise of sharing a common interest, food, and rebuilding a brotherly bond. All for the sake of peace and tranquility. Look how that turned out.

"Let me get two details straight," Ray said. "Patti, did you specifically invite both Thomas and Sigmund to the podcast interview session?"

"Okay, yes, I did," Patti said. "They both came. I was happy about that."

"They had to have known the other was coming," Sherry said. "It's a good sign they both showed up."

"Maybe," Ray said.

"I imagine Thomas was interested in his food writer putting the paper's best foot forward in the podcast. Sig was very excited about the podcast content," Patti said. "I'm sure he knew Thomas might show up. I assume another reason Sig wanted to be in the studio was because he felt somewhat protective of me, in case the mood went sour. That's silly, I don't need protection."

"Why would you predict the mood would go sour?" Ray asked.

Sherry noted Patti was responding well to his gentle tone of voice until he challenged her.

"I didn't mean that," Patti said. "Like I said, Sig mentioned he and Thomas had hit a bumpy patch. I took that with a grain of salt and something that could be remedied with some outside intervention."

Sherry weighed the options of asking her next question and decided she'd proceed even if Patti took offense. The answer might help her friend out in the long run.

"You didn't think having the editor in chief of a rival newspaper in the MediaPie building would cause friction? Maybe putting more pressure on the Helguvson family?" Sherry asked.

"Ridiculous. I'm given the freedom to invite whoever best fits my podcast themes. Carl Carlson fit. I'm the food editor of the *Nutmeg News*, so our paper was well represented." Patti's lips pursed as she appeared to mull over her next words. "Maybe I was hoping to ignite some talk about the hot topic in town. If the conversation about the two newspapers' divergent opinions bloomed organically, I had the beginnings of my next podcast."

"Patti's got the journalistic nose for stories," Sherry said. "She can smell the importance of digging up dirt."

"That's a real compliment, Sherry. Thank you."

"That's why your podcast is number one in Connecticut," Sherry said. "Will the kitchen utensil podcast still be airing? After all that's gone on?"

"Of course. And there definitely will be spin-offs from the topic. I don't want to give away any podcast content, you'll have to subscribe. Spoiler alert, Gunnar, whose job it is to spot trends in the food-o-sphere, thinks the wooden spoon will be among this year's top utensil trend list," Patti said. "That's one reason he was going to choose the wooden spoon."

"What's old is new again sometimes, they say. Whoever *they* are," Marla said. "Maybe you should bring your wooden spoon to the cook-off. For good luck."

Ray lifted his wool cap and itched his scalp with his gloved hand. "It always seems to come down to cook-offs, doesn't it?"

"Interesting suggestion." Sherry stored Marla's comment in the 'tips for cook-off success' compartment of her brain.

"Did you bring your spoon to Patti's studio?" Ray asked.

"Of course," Sherry said. "And it's back home safely in a drawer. Unbroken."

"You mentioned Sigmund brought a wooden spoon to the podcast," Ray said.

"He did," Patti said. "He called me and asked if he could bring his favorite wooden spoon to the studio along with his knowledge of the utensil handed down by many generations of his family cooks back in Iceland. I didn't get a chance to hear his stories until all my guests were interviewed. I only heard a few words from him before he excused himself, saying his intentions were stomped on. He's always been a bit emotional. Homesickness is my diagnosis. He was so close to sharing that aspect of his life with me."

"Marla, how did the conversation between Thomas and Sigmund de-escalate?" Ray asked. "Or didn't it? Can you recall?"

"Sure. After grumbling like wild cats they relaxed and sat down in their chairs. Gunnar stepped between the two brothers and began a quieter back-and-forth. Gunnar was blocking their faces at that point, so I didn't hear much. Their hissing whispers were effective at masking the words." Marla paused. "The tension died down when the guys ran out of steam."

Ray, not one for wasting precious seconds on dead air, asked, "Anything else?"

"I was remembering something," Marla said. "I did hear one of the men say something about the whole situation with the Bankless Brothers being window weather.'"

"Window weather?" Ray asked. "Explain."

"I had no idea what window weather was, so I googled it, right then and there," Marla said. "Window weather is an Icelandic term meaning what you see isn't always what you get. The weather changes so often in Iceland people resort to looking out the window to predict it. But seeing isn't believing. It may look spring-like through the windowpane, but the temperature might be forty degrees colder than the tranquil scene portrays."

"And Bankless Brothers? Any idea what that refers to?" Ray asked.

"No idea," Marla said.

"Bad timing for a squabble to be witnessed," Sherry said. "Hours before one of the squabblers vanished."

"Back in Oklahoma we settle arguments between sparring bulls by playing symphony music in the field. Patti, you should try that next time your guests become unruly."

"That's a unique solution. It must be awful for Thomas to have his last encounter with Sig be so quarrelsome," Patti said.

Ray cleared his throat, a sign he was interested in keeping the questioning on track. "Did Sigmund do anything special with the spoon he brought while Sherry was being interviewed?" he asked.

"He handed the spoon around the room," Marla said. "The mood had lightened, and he was like a kid at show and tell."

A light snow began to fall again. The vapor of Marla's breath was heavily visible as she spoke. If Ray's questioning didn't end soon Sherry was going to have to stand and start jogging in place to keep warm, as the temperature was dipping.

"Everyone including me touched it," Marla said. "The last I saw the spoon it was in Thomas's hands," Marla said.

"You never left the room at any time?" Ray asked Marla.

"No one did. Not until Sherry finished her interview," Marla said. "There was too much entertainment going on."

Sherry wasn't at all surprised when Ray abruptly ended the meeting.

"That's all for now, ladies," Ray said as he slid his rear end down the picnic bench to release his trapped legs. He turned back to face a seated Sherry. "Sherry, you know how to reach me if you have any follow-up."

"Thanks, Ray. I'm busy prepping for next Tuesday's cook-off but I'll keep my ear to the ground."

Ray lifted his snow-dusted cap and itched his scalp with his gloved hand again. "Keep me posted on that front, too, please."

Sherry grinned. "Will do."

"Good day, ladies," Ray said. He disappeared down the boardwalk.

It was Patti's turn to face Sherry head-on. "Tell me, Sherry. Is the detective going to make finding Sig's killer a priority?"

"If Sig's dead, he will. He's the one for the job."

"That's high praise coming from you," Patti said. "You've built quite a reputation for yourself when it comes to being an amateur sleuth who gets the job done."

"You're giving her a big head, Patti," Marla said.

"Deservedly so."

"What's next on the agenda?" Marla asked. "Our mission is to cheer you up. Anyone up for a hot chocolate and donut from Sweets and Sips?"

Sherry glanced at her phone. "We'll have to take them to go. We told Dad we'd help with inventory this afternoon."

"Don't worry about me. I need to go as well. Getting back to work is the best medicine." Patti wedged her legs out from beneath the picnic table and slid across to the edge of the bench. "Thanks for the distraction, girls. I fully appreciate the time away from my cluttered headspace."

Chapter 9

Thursday was no warmer or less cloudy than the day before. It was, though, a day closer to Don's birthday, Valentine's Day, and the cook-off. So much to plan for in the next few days. Who is born on Valentine's Day anyway?

Checking her phone's weather app and seeing the same dull forecast repeated for the next three days, Sherry was inspired to brighten up her class's topic with the promise of warmer weather to come. Sharing her knowledge of the importance of earthworms, ladybugs and winged pollinators in the garden was just what the doctor ordered. Who wouldn't have warm and wonderful feelings after hearing how hard the little creatures work to make gardens more fruitful. Projecting some photos stored on her computer to the whiteboard at the head of the classroom would bring the outside in and give life to her words. The creepier and weirder the insects, the more engaged the children. If her years working alongside the juvenile members of the Augustin Community Garden taught her nothing else, she learned slimy and wriggly equals attention grabber.

Marla was asleep when Sherry left the house. If it weren't for her anticipation of the kids' excitement about the day's topic, Sherry, too, would have considered sleeping in. The momentary thought was dismissed when she drove into the school's driveway. There was a thrill about teaching young receptive minds the successful harvest methods used for centuries. Productive gardening was a testimony to hard work rather than modern shortcuts. Her goal throughout the week was to get that point across to the crop of kids raised on googling rather than discovering answers through seasonal trial and error, the truest gardening method. She entered the classroom to a round of "Yay, Miss Sherry's here." She couldn't have started off on a more positive note.

Three-quarters of the way through her presentation, Sherry had the kids mesmerized. Their hands continually jutted skyward as they volleyed questions as fast as the slides were advanced. When the lights were turned up Sherry had a question of her own for the class.

"I wanted to spend the last minutes asking a question you all might think is a little out of left field." She gazed around at the faces awaiting the question. Assured she had everyone's attention, she continued. "Next week I have a cook-off I'd like to win. It's a hobby I'm passionate about for many reasons. The creativity, the competition, the cooking, of course, and the camaraderie of the other cooks who share my passion for inventing new recipes. The question is, I would like to know if any of you have a favorite kitchen tool you or the cook in your family can't live without? The answer might help me channel the right method of putting my recipe together."

The kids chattered among themselves. When the talk settled down, hands went up.

"Yes," Sherry said as she pointed to a girl with untamed hair and tortoiseshell glasses.

"My mother says her stick blender is the bomb. You'd think she discovered the thing cures Dad's snoring how much she loves it." The class giggled, as did Sherry and Mrs. Turpin.

"What's a stick blender?" a boy in the back row called out.

"It's a handheld mini appliance with a motor on one end and a spin blade on the other," Sherry said. "Plunging the blade into softened, chopped veggies makes a smooth soup. I love mine."

"We have soup twice a week and that's her magic wand to make it creamy," the girl said. "Cream of tomato is my favorite."

"That's wonderful," Sherry said with a broad smile. She was in another of her happy places talking food stories. She bypassed a few raised hands to get to the one she was seeking. "Yes, Magnus. I'm interested in what your Icelandic family loves to cook with."

"Wooden spoon," Magnus said. "My dad loves to cook. He says our family's food history is on that spoon."

"Gross," a boy, seated one desk over, groaned. "Doesn't he ever clean it?"

"Chill, Josh. Obviously, he does," Magnus said.

"Magnus used a hyperbole to make his point. He intentionally exaggerated to get his point across, and he did," Mrs. Turpin said.

Magnus ran his fingers through his blonde mop of hair. "My dad's a journalist. He says he likes to paint a picture with his words."

"Exactly, Magnus," Mrs. Turpin said.

"Dude, that's awesome," Magnus's seat neighbor said.

"What's cool is the story of the Spoon-Licker Yule Lad," Magnus said. "Kids in Iceland believe in trolls that come down from the mountains in December to find good and naughty children before the holidays. Spoon-Licker licks your wooden spoon to taste all the holiday goodies baked in your home. It's best to leave him a used spoon so you don't get a potato in your shoe rather than a gift. Or worse, he may kidnap you."

"Bleh. I'd rather get a potato than lick a yucky spoon." The boy stuck out his tongue. This boy wasn't one to speak up often in Sherry's class. She enjoyed his participation even if it involved him pretending to choke on the idea of licking a soiled spoon.

"Probably tastes great, *fiflingur*," Magnus said.

Mrs. Turpin instantly cleared her throat in a not-so-subtle directive for civility. "I know what *fiflingur* means, Magnus, and it's not nice to say."

Magnus made a half-hearted apology for calling the boy a dimwit in his native land's tongue.

A girl behind Magnus spoke up. "He means if my mom, for example, stirred her yummy turkey stuffing with cranberries, sausage and pecans with the wooden spoon she would skip the rinse and leave the spoon where the Spoon-Licker could sneak a taste. I'd get a gift, not a shoe potato."

"Or my dad's cheesy mashed potatoes," a student said.

"My mom makes the best green bean casserole with crispy shallots over the holidays. Spoon-Licker would love those," added another student.

"Okay, folks, we get the idea. Let Magnus finish his story," Mrs. Turpin said.

"Iceland sounds magical," the girl with the wild hair said.

The corners of Magnus's mouth lifted and his eyes brightened. "Could be."

"Do you have any more to add, Magnus? About the wooden spoon?" Mrs. Turpin asked.

"Just that wooden spoons are simple to look at but important. That's it."

"Great story, Magnus. Thanks for sharing," Sherry said. "Sorry I didn't get to hear from more of you, but I'll be back tomorrow. Thank you all again and have a good rest of your day."

The class clapped and Sherry's heart was warmed.

Mrs. Turpin closed in on Sherry. "Magnus's father is waiting for you by the principal's office."

"Magnus's father? Hmmm. Okay," Sherry said as she gathered her supplies. Her thoughts raced with curiosity. The man was going out of his way to meet her at the end of class. For what reason? If he wanted to interview her for his paper she wasn't really prepared and would ask for a reschedule. If he wanted to talk about Magnus's garden class experience, she only had glowing comments to make about his son's enthusiasm.

After Sherry left the classroom, she stopped by the administrative office to sign out and locate Magnus's father.

"Sherry Oliveri?" a man's voice accented with a foreign lilt called to her.

Next to the man was a tall blonde woman wearing a long down coat with a furry collar. Sherry hoped it was fake fur because the coverage was the size of a full-grown fox. She hated to think the animal gave its life to adorn the woman's neck when it would be more useful to the animal.

"Yes, hello. Are you Thomas Helguvson?" she asked. She held out her hand to shake.

"Yes," he said.

"So nice to meet you. We were two ships that passed in the night at Patti's office. You were very busy on your phone. I didn't want to interrupt you," Sherry said.

"I don't get much of a break. I was trailing my employee while trying to negotiate another's contract and follow a breaking news report. So sorry if I was rude," he said.

After what seemed like a long wait Thomas shook Sherry's hand. "I've enjoyed working with your son this week. I'll be sad when my week of teaching gardening skills is over."

"Thank you," Thomas said. "Magnus raves about the class. He can't wait until the spring thaw. We're going to have to trade emails so we can pepper you with questions."

"Absolutely," Sherry said. "I'm giving all the students my email on the last class day. All questions are welcome."

Sherry's gaze drifted to the woman at Thomas's side. The awkward pause in introductions gave Sherry reason to question her assumption that she was with him.

"And this is Lilya." No last name offered.

Sherry shook Lilya's hand. She had on the softest leather gloves. "Nice to meet you." She returned her sights to Thomas. "Did you have something you'd like to talk about?"

"Let's go in this room. They said we could use it for a few minutes." Thomas tilted his head toward the school secretaries sitting at their desks behind a counter. Two young women holding folders were in a conversation huddle, not too subtly discussing Lilya's fashion choices, or possibly her association with the father of one of their students. Whatever the topic, Lilya was clearly the focus of their glances.

"This way." Lilya followed behind Thomas, as did Sherry. He shut the door and each took a seat at a conference table. Lilya and Thomas opened their coats as the room was overheated and the air was stuffy.

"Sherry, Lilya is a private investigator from my hometown in Iceland. Just outside of Reykjavík, if you've heard of the city."

"The capital. Yes," Sherry said.

As Lilya was peeling off her gloves her watch rang. Her eye-catching manicure was fresh. Brilliant red, matching the color of her lipstick. She pushed up her sleeve and read the tiny screen.

"Secret agent watch?" Sherry asked with a smile.

Lilya raised her eyes to meet Sherry's. "Sort of is. Yes."

"Lilya's come looking for my brother Sigmund," Thomas said

Sherry ping-ponged her gaze from Thomas to Lilya and back again.

"This is about the investigation of your brother's disappearance?"

"That's right," Lilya said. "We're afraid progress has stalled."

"It's only been a few days. And Detective Bease said the body hadn't been recovered, unfortunately. That's got to slow everything down," Sherry said.

Lilya and Thomas exchanged glances.

"If you're thinking I can add any information to the investigation, I can't. I've only been in a room with Sigmund once and can't even say we had a conversation. I know Thomas's son better than I know you or your brother."

"Interesting," Lilya said.

"I need to go soon. My dad owns a hooked rug store in Augustin and I work part-time there. This is a Ruggery workday for me. Sorry to not be of help. Hope you didn't go out of your way to seek me out here. Good luck with the investigation. We'll probably hear the body's been recovered in no time. That'll speed up the process." *Jump in any time,* Sherry silently urged. Her comfort level was on par with having a root canal. She rose halfway out of her seat as Lilya began to speak.

"The body won't be recovered because he's not dead," Lilya said.

Sherry's breath caught in her throat. She sat back down. She was uncomfortable continuing this conversation at a middle school with the father of one of her students. "If he's not dead, I'd say that's good news and the search for his body can be called off. I doubt Trooper was keen on mucking around in the mud sniffing for signs of the man in the middle of February."

"Trooper?" Thomas asked.

"The sole member of Augustin's K-9 unit. He was about to be put on search duty at Harmony Lake, I heard," Sherry said. "From what you're saying, Detective Bease has one less murder investigation in his caseload."

"It's not good news that Sig's not dead. He faked his death. He's a selfish and manipulative human being," Lilya said. "I am very sure he staged it to look as if he was murdered at Harmony Lake. I'm in town to gather evidence to prove what he's up to."

"Wow," Sherry said, unable to come up with another word to verbalize her reaction to what she was hearing. "Are you working for Thomas?"

"No, ma'am," Lilya said. "I've been hired by Sigmund Helguvson's wife, Nora, to find him. He's been gone without contact for longer than she's comfortable with. Living alone in Iceland can't be easy for her. He promised to send for her when he had his new business affairs in order. He's gone radio silent on her. It's admittedly not the first time, but it's the longest time."

"Business affairs," Sherry repeated. She lowered her voice. "That's not the only affair his wife should be brought up to speed on." The question in the forefront of Sherry's mind was whether Patti was aware of Sigmund's marital status.

"I thought my brother had changed," Thomas said, shaking his head. "Nora doesn't deserve this."

"Thomas, let me be the angry one," Lilya said. "You don't need more aggravation. Maybe there is a legitimate explanation as to why he's taken such a drastic measure."

"I'm sorry for what's going on with your family, whatever that may be. I'm especially sorry for my friend, who was grieving Sigmund's disappearance and likely death and now has a whole new situation to adjust to. That being said, what do you want from me? I didn't know where his body was when he was supposedly dead. I certainly have no idea where he is if he's alive and on the run." Sherry raised her hand to her temple to massage away a developing dull ache.

"Ms. Oliveri," Lilya began.

"Sherry, please," Sherry corrected.

"Sherry. I have reason to believe your friend Patti Mellit aided in Sigmund's so-called drowning death. They staged a physical altercation on the dock at Harmony Lake to make it look like a crime scene. Fast-forward to no sign of him since. Now he's presumed dead and can start a new life with a new identity. The woman has a new chance to be with a man who's living an unfettered life."

"That sounds very far-fetched," Sherry said. "I'm glad Detective Bease isn't here to witness this fabrication. He would have walked out halfway through your theory. What evidence do you have any of this is true?"

"What evidence is there that it's not?" Lilya challenged.

"Detective Bease is sorting through clues as we speak," Sherry said. "I have it on good authority there has been no activity with Sigmund's finances in the recent past. At least at the Augustin United Bank. To me that speaks volumes."

Thomas scoffed. "Iceland had a horrific banking collapse in the early two thousands. It was bad timing for me and my circle of industrious, hardworking friends, including my brother, who were well on our way to financial independence. We got some bad advice to put our money in one of the country's big three banks, which were run by, let's see, what's a good word to describe their abilities—*morons*!"

"That's rough," Sherry said.

"We thought we were invincible being fresh-faced go-getters. We took our big losses and licked our wounds. Some took it better than others. To get over the crisis we banded together. We called ourselves the Band of Bankless Brothers, pulled out what remained of our devalued kronas, and stuffed our mattresses. Sigmund was the first to find the next place to rebuild our so-called wealth." Thomas paused. "Actually, he wasn't the first. We were going to go into tourism, but Sig convinced us otherwise. Hindsight is twenty-twenty, as I keep reminding the other boys. Tourism in Iceland is now huge. We missed that boat. Anyway, the point is, tracing all Sigmund's finances might be like finding a needle in a haystack. Some money may be here, some money may be there."

"Well," Sherry said with diminished conviction, "I have no doubt his body will be found and Nora will have to reset her thinking. And what's the chance she has something to do with his disappearance and/or murder? Pretty good if you ask me."

"Sigmund's wife hired me to find him because she has unfinished business with her husband and would like closure. As for your friend, a scorned woman knows no bounds. Even murder. But that's not my concern. I need your help to extract Sigmund's whereabouts from Patti." Lilya was clinical in her delivery, to such a degree Sherry grew concerned for Patti's well-being.

"Enough. Stop right there," Sherry said. Her scalp bristled and the heightened volume of her voice betrayed her attempt to stay cool in the school setting. "Patti had nothing to do with Sigmund's death, his disappearance, or anything else he's done in the past." Thomas was studying her with such intensity she upped her defense. "Don't waste your time going down your fabricated path. Patti is the most decent, wonderful person. She wouldn't harm a fly. Even if she was terribly wronged."

Lilya opened her well-appointed lips to speak. Sherry put up a hand to stop her.

"Love is blind," Lilya said. "Especially forbidden love."

"I highly doubt Patti knew about Nora. Patti's an upstanding member of the Augustin community and wouldn't knowingly entangle herself with another woman's husband. I'm certain of that."

Lilya's silence spoke volumes.

"Thomas, I adore your son, but I don't know you from a hole in the wall. From what's been said here *you* have plenty of reasons to be frustrated with your brother. I'm trying to keep my cool but for you two to waltz in and try to tarnish my friend's character with your accusations, well, that just boils my biscuits."

"I understand why you're prickly, Sherry," Thomas said. "If you would cooperate with Lilya, we can put this whole episode behind us and move on. Sig will pay the price for his bad behavior and I'm sure Ms. Mellit will get off with just a slap on the wrist for acting out of passion." He paused. Raising his eyes to meet Sherry's, he continued. "I'm keeping my brother's disappearance out of the paper. For now. When I feel the time is right to publish an article, I'm obligated to include Patti Mellit's name unless it's been proved she's in no way associated. I'm doing you and her a favor for the time being."

Sherry subscribed to the motto of getting to know someone before drawing a conclusion on their character, but these two were testing her resolve. They came in hot with their accusations against Patti and Sherry's hackles were up.

"The answer is no. If you were hired to do a job, then do it. Detective Bease will be working on the murder investigation and when he discovers who killed your brother, your theory will blow up in your face." Sherry surprised herself at how forcefully the words spilled out. She gathered her belongings and stood. "I have to go."

"Sherry, on another note, good luck in the cook-off," Thomas said. "My paper is a sponsor and I have a reporter covering the event. I'm excited to see you home cooks at work."

"Thank you," Sherry said, amazed at how seamlessly Thomas could change topics. She left the middle school with a cluster of questions swirling in her brain. Foremost was whether or not she sacrificed her chances at the cook-off by vehemently defending Patti.

Chapter 10

"Marla, I'm home. We need to get over to the Ruggery soon. Any chance you made extra lunch?" Sherry called out.

"Tuna salad, raring to go. Just giddy up over to the kitchen table and I'll lasso you up some tuna salad," Marla said with an inflated Midwest accent.

"Did I mention I'm glad you're here," Sherry said as she sat at the table.

Marla delivered two plates, with Chutney tagging along two steps behind her. "How was your morning class with the young gardeners?"

"Great. Tomorrow, I think we'll design the school vegetable garden, in a way that makes sense. That's an art." Sherry swallowed the savory tuna combined with mayonnaise, a touch of Dijon, diced celery, capers, and shallots, the way she taught Marla to make it. "Have you ever heard of someone faking their own death?"

Marla didn't bother swallowing her bite before speaking. "That's a question I didn't see coming. Let me think. Yes, once. On *Dateline*, or was it *20/20*? Maybe *NCIS*. The guy faked a boating accident and started a new life on one of the islands south of Florida. He was in deep embezzlement trouble. He couldn't figure any other way out. He was eventually tripped up and caught. Why do you ask?"

"Thomas Helguvson met me at school today after class, along with a private detective who hails all the way from Iceland. Both are convinced Sigmund faked his death."

"For what reason?" Marla asked, returning from a search in the refrigerator for Ranch dressing. She poured a pool on her plate and coated the tuna wrap in the creamy dip.

"To start a new life after making a mess of his current life. Surprise! He has a wife. She is the one who hired the PI."

Marla concentrated on the final bite of her wrap. Sherry could always count on her sister's enjoyment of most any food. She missed having her around more often as one of her chosen taste-testers when she created a new recipe.

"Poor Patti. Do you think she knew about wifey? And if she did, how long did she know?"

"I've only known about Sigmund's existence for a few days. I certainly wouldn't have suspected he was married. Why would I, unless he was sporting a band on his left ring finger and waving his marriage license around

Patti's studio the day we crossed paths?"

"Have you spoken to Ray about this?"

"Should I? I'm sure he knows. If he hasn't come up with this nugget in his research of Sigmund Helguvson, he's slipping. Besides, why didn't he tell me, knowing how much my friend Patti has been affected? Maybe he thinks I'm getting too involved," Sherry said.

"Ray appreciates your input," Marla said. "He sometimes has a funny way of expressing his appreciation, that's all." Marla dabbed her mouth with a napkin. "I'm sure he was about to fill you in on the cad's status as a husband."

Sherry groaned. "I don't know who to believe. I was so flustered when Thomas and Lilya, she's the PI from Iceland, asked me to get the truth from Patti, since she's my friend. That's Lilya's job. Not happening."

"It's not like you to not want to dig a little to get at the truth. What's up with that? I can smell something else brewing," Marla said.

"Bingo. Lilya strongly suggested Patti is a willing cohort in Sigmund's plan. If she is, I'm the world's worst judge of character. I was so nauseated by that woman I couldn't get out of the meeting fast enough. The nerve of her. No way. Not happening." Sherry stood and took her plate to the sink.

"You don't have to tell me twice," Marla said.

"I'll do these dishes later. Let's get down to the store. I need to see what Don called me about." Her words tumbled out with a hint of aggression.

"Putting off the dishes until later?" Marla said with a wry smile. "That's not like you either. That woman must have really gotten under your skin. Hold up, I'm right with you."

• • •

"Ladies, it's inventory time," Erno announced to his daughters before they even unzipped their coats. "I'm assigning each of you sections of the store. The yarn and dyes are the most difficult. I need product codes and exact color descriptions. Double-check as you count that they are in the correct locations. I'm so appreciative of your help. I'll be up front here if there's any questions."

"Hey, pretty sisters," Don said as he emerged from the small kitchen in the back of the showroom. He planted a lingering kiss on Sherry's lips.

"Hi, Don," Marla said. "How are the books treating you?"

"Not as fun as a full-throttle boat ride, but happy to have Erno's company while I sort through the past adventures of the Ruggery's sales," Don said and laughed. "Sher, I'll keep you company for a few minutes, if you don't mind."

Sherry and Don crossed the room and stopped at the wall of yarn bins. The daunting task of hand-counting the lamb's wool skeins had to begin somewhere. Sherry took the opportunity to procrastinate a moment.

"Sorry I haven't called you back about the Ruggery issue. I'd rather speak in person. I hope there's not a problem." Sherry's voice was soft.

"I haven't traced back far enough in the store's history yet to see what the issue is, but what I've discovered is Erno isn't taking his full salary recently. Do you know why that might be?" Don asked.

She had no idea why her father had made a change in the salary he draws from the store. Sherry glanced over at her father, who was lovingly folding a canvas he had designed and drawn by hand. The lucky customer for whom the canvas was designed would either hook the rug using a selection of the hand-dyed wool yarns Sherry was about to take stock of, or have the rug completed by one of the artisans Erno worked with.

"Dad came into some money recently, as you know. He inherited a parcel of land, and he made a tidy profit selling the land. He did have to do a pricey renovation of the store's bones and mechanics, but I'm certain the inheritance easily covered that. Did you ask him?" Sherry said.

"My job is to balance the books and look for any red flags. So far, that's the only red flag that's stood out. But no, I don't feel comfortable asking until I've finished all my analysis. I thought you could provide some of your powerful insight."

"Sorry. First I've heard of this. But keep me posted. That's why we hired you to unravel any mysteries in the numbers." Sherry pointed to the waiting bins of wool. "I better get a move on here, lots to do. You're coming to dinner tonight I hope."

"Wouldn't miss sitting with my two favorite Oliveri gals," Don said. "Are Marla and I being treated to your cook-off practice recipe?"

"Not tonight. I need one more day to get my act together. Tomorrow everyone's coming over and I'll have made my choice of recipes." Sherry lifted the inventory clipboard and clutched it to her chest. "Now, get back to work."

"Yes, ma'am. And may I say I love a woman boss."

Hours later, inventory was complete with the exception of the returns and damaged products. Erno needed to put his expert eye on those and come up with a plan for their future. The customer wasn't always right when something was returned, for reasons of damage or otherwise. Erno kept very close tabs on his patrons' actions if only for his own satisfaction. Sherry loved the detail-oriented side of her father and knew that was a gene she had inherited from him.

• • •

On their drive home Marla volunteered to make a wild rice salad with hummus crostini for dinner, forgoing any meat for the evening. With the night's menu set, Sherry was thrilled to have some extra time to plan for her last day of class and narrow down her options for the cook-off. All that went out the window when she found Patti on her front porch.

"Hi, ladies. It's me again. Sherry, you probably know why I'm here. Can we have a chat?"

"Hi, Patti. You must be freezing. I hope you haven't been waiting long. You should have called first, we would have hustled home," Sherry said as she let Marla and Patti inside. "If you don't mind, I have to walk Chutney while we talk. We've been out since lunchtime. Marla's going to be busy putting dinner together." She scanned Patti's light down coat. "Will you be warm enough? And how about your knee? Is it up for a short walk?"

"Absolutely. I'm happy for a moment of your time no matter what the form," Patti said. "I wrapped my bruised knee in case you took me on one of your outdoor excursions."

With Chutney leashed, Sherry and Patti made a quick turnaround and left.

"You talked to Thomas and that woman private eye," Patti began. "Who does she think she is? I understand Sig's wife would want him alive, not dead, but he's gone. Forever. I just know it. And I certainly had nothing to do with his disappearance, dead or alive. Help me prove that, Sherry."

Sherry glanced over at her friend, who was wiping away a tear, not a simple task with a bulky glove on. "How did you know I talked to them? Did one of them contact you directly?"

"Thomas called me. I got a glimmer of hope when I saw his name on my caller ID. By the end of the phone call all my hopes were not only dashed but my whole spirit was dashed. Why is he after me?"

"I lit into him about suspecting you of all people of staging Sigmund's disappearance," Sherry said as she watched Chutney sniff a full circle around the neighbor's boxwood. "He went after you anyway. I wish I could help clear your name, but I don't know the Helguvsons at all. There was something else—how long before this story is made public? Thomas said he was squashing the details of the story for the present, in respect to his brother, I imagine."

"He's probably also interested in keeping the Helguvson name somewhat clear of an adultery scandal," Patti said. "Imagine my side of the story. I had no clue the man was married until a few days ago."

Sherry stopped and dusted off one of Chutney's paws. "You knew? You didn't tell me. It might be hard to defend someone who involved herself with a married man. It probably provides a good look to have Thomas go after you rather than place the blame on his brother."

"Ugh. So many angles to this story. If the court of public opinion gets their hands on the scuttlebutt I'm the one who suffers," Patti said.

"Would the *Nutmeg News* print a story involving a beloved employee without knowing all the facts?" Sherry asked. Not giving Patti any time to wallow in self-pity, she answered her own question. "Highly doubtful. We have time."

"For now, the Van Ardans are keeping the story under wraps, as a sensitive subject concerning an employee and a competitor's family. Nothing will go out in the *Nutmeg News*. They sent me a note saying as much. They are the fairest of fair. They won't sell papers with sensational content just to up their sales if something isn't right. But that sentiment can't last forever once the story breaks through other outlets. I'll probably lose my job."

Sherry stopped again when Chutney veered off the cleared sidewalk. She hadn't dressed him in his booties and feared he'd come up lame if he stepped in the deep snow. Balls of snow and ice tended to build up between his tiny toe pads, causing discomfort when he walked. She was relieved when he did his business and returned to the cement walkway with no limp. Patti, though, was hobbling noticeably. Sherry reversed course and headed home.

"I was thinking. What about the cook-off judges? They might know something. Marla said there was a ruckus during my podcast interview." Sherry paused. "Or maybe you can hear the dialogue from the podcast recording you made?"

Patti groaned. "What a good idea. If only."

"If only?"

"Yesterday I stayed late at work and was able to filter out the background voices on the recording. The tech has gotten so sophisticated. It's like photo editing software, you can remove all interference when you learn how to use the tool correctly. Unfortunately, now I'm not sure I didn't blot out useful evidence. I take that back. I'm sure I did."

"Then we need to speak to the judges. They may be sitting on crucial information. Thomas is on Lilya's side. He believes Sigmund's alive. At the same time, being newish in the area while running a growing newspaper, it's in Thomas's best interest to keep his family's collective nose clean or risk damage that can't be repaired. He has a lot at stake. Between his brother's possible disappearance or his murder, I would imagine deflecting the blame to someone else would accomplish a better outcome for him and his business. He and Lilya are going to work hard to find Sigmund, even if they're in Ray's way. Rather than helping their cause like they asked, I need to come at them with surefire evidence someone killed Sigmund. For your sake. Even if the someone turns out to be Thomas."

"With no body?" Patti asked. "I don't even want there to be a body. That would end the notion he may be alive. I don't hate him. I don't wish anyone harm. Maybe a tiny bit of misery." She measured the size of her wish in the space between two insulated fingers.

Sherry closed her eyes as she was reminded of the missing link. The body. She opened them with a renewed sense of purpose. "Minor roadblock. We have to forge ahead as if he were murdered. For your sake, we have to."

"And if you uncover the fact Sig is alive and faked his own death?" Patti asked.

"Then we need to prove you weren't in on it," Sherry said. She studied her friend. "You weren't, were you? I'm sorry, I must ask."

"Sig and I were getting close. He was reserved when it came to sharing his personal history, and I was fine giving him the space he seemed to require. In my heart I don't think I saw our relationship as long term. I love my life as is and not sure I'm looking for a long-term partner. Certainly not him, anymore." Patti let out a weak chuckle. "Was that your stomach rumbling?" She reached into her coat pocket. "Here, have a candy." She presented a tin. She lifted the lid and Sherry made a choice from the two remaining pieces.

"It's so embarrassing. My tummy is so loud. Thank you. Are you sure? You only have one left."

"I don't even like them. I tried to like licorice but the flavor's too strong for me. Sig lived on these things. Please, take both."

Before she could refuse, Patti slipped the small tin into Sherry's coat pocket.

"Thanks," Sherry said. Hurting her friend's feelings by not accepting the gift wasn't an option.

"To answer your question, no, I didn't have any knowledge of him faking his own death. I wouldn't have helped him if he presented that silly plan to me. Definite relationship deal breaker."

Sherry admired Patti's honesty. She was a modern woman comfortable in her own skin.

"His wife isn't a suspect if he was murdered?" Patti asked.

"You'd think so. Especially if she knew about you."

"Ugh," Patti moaned. She put her gloved hands up to her face.

"I didn't mean that. You had no bearing on what his wife might be capable of."

"What a nightmare," Patti said. She dropped her hands. "I have no idea if she knew I existed before the private investigator told her."

"I wonder if Thomas had contact with her since moving to the States. It didn't seem as if they were all that close. That would be rough news to hear from your brother-in-law."

"I'm trying to put the pieces together. Sig had become increasingly irritable lately. Emotional. Defensive. It was not fun to spend long amounts of time with him because his moods swung like a pendulum. An indication the truth was eating him alive?"

After a pause, Patti continued. "I was thinking about when Thomas told me on the phone about Sig's disappearance. At the time Thomas truly believed Sig was dead, whether by accident or at the hands of a murderer. Now he's convinced his brother faked his death. We need to find out what makes him so sure, or if he's covering something up, for either himself or someone else, like his sister-in-law."

"Mind if we head home? Don's coming over and Marla's treating us to a vegetarian feast."

"I thought you'd never ask," Patti said.

Sherry walked Patti to her car where it was parked along the curb beyond her driveway. Patti's gait was lumbering. The bruised knee accounted for some drag. The other reason was probably the weight of the dark cloud of uncertainty swallowing her. Sherry frowned in the face of her friend's predicament.

"Sherry, I can't thank you enough," Patti said as she reached for her car door handle. "I feel like the vultures are circling above me and about to pick my bones. I need your help. I didn't mean to do anything wrong."

Chapter 11

Don arrived at Sherry's house with a craft beer six-pack and a bottle of wine, which paired perfectly with Marla's salad. Wild rice, goat cheese, pecans, toasted pepitas, dried cranberries, and honey Dijon vinaigrette were some of the tasty, colorful ingredients tossed on a bed of arugula leaves. Marla broiled garlic Parmesan toast slices to accompany the main course salad and the menu was complete.

Sherry eagerly sat down to fill her belly. "What a treat. You've upped your dinner game."

"That's right," Marla said. "Who knows, one day I might be on the cooking competition circuit with you."

"Speaking of competitions," Don said as he scooped up a forkful of rice. "Have you made a decision on what you'll cook next week?"

"You mean for your birthday, Valentine's Day, or the cook-off? They're all on the same day," Sherry said. "When it rains it pours."

"Can't we combine them all?" Don said.

"You deserve your own dedicated tribute," Sherry said with a grin. "For putting up with me. I'll make you something special, or we can go out." She crunched on the remaining toasted pecan bathed in tangy dressing left on her nearly empty plate. "For the cook-off I have a recipe that might fit the bill. A French crepe recipe. The crepe will be the 'round' item for the theme, and I'll come up with a nice story behind the popularity of crepes in France. Will that wow the judges?"

"Sounds good to me," Don said.

Sherry looked to Marla for approval and only saw a blank stare. "No good?"

"Not bad. Kinda boring," Marla said. She directed a bite of rice to her mouth. After savoring it, she swallowed. "Where's the wow factor, the twist, the 'I've never seen that before, why didn't I think of that' factor the judges will be expecting from you. Remember, one of the judges is an international food trend expert. He's seen it all and then some."

"Now I'm nervous," Sherry said. "Back to the drawing board."

The conversation stayed light, ranging from the weather to the time frame for Don's commuter boat to be returned to the water. The elephants in the room—the murder investigation and the town's growing division—stayed off to the side for the time being.

"I'll tackle the dirty dishes while you two brainstorm Sherry's recipe,"

Don said. "Marla, you've made tomorrow night's family dinner a challenge. I can't wait." Don stood and took his plate to the kitchen. A moment later he called out, "Any ice cream in the freezer? I need a reward for good behavior."

"Vanilla, chocolate chip and chocolate. Scoop out some of each in three bowls and we'll come grab them," Sherry said. "Be right back, my phone's ringing." She collected her phone from her purse on the front hall table. "Ray. You were on my list to call."

"I'll go first," he said with no preliminary greeting. His tone was business serious. "Patti Mellit had a reason to kill Sigmund Helguvson. The man was married. She was scorned. Do you know where Patti was the night of Sigmund's disappearance?"

Scattered thoughts buzzed around Sherry's brain. She had to separate what Patti may have explained of her whereabouts the evening of Sigmund's disappearance from any speculation of unaccounted-for periods of time. Why hadn't she asked Patti the details of that night? And how did Ray flip the script, going from being the one who didn't tell Sherry about Sigmund's marriage to her being in trouble for not knowing Patti's whereabouts?

"Patti told me she stayed at work after the interviews with myself and three cook-off judges about our favorite kitchen utensils. She had to edit the recording." Sherry's response stalled. She wasn't sure she should share the reason for the surgical edit that had to be done. She should leave revealing that detail up to Patti.

"Her whereabouts from afternoon to late evening need to be verified. Before I approach her, do you have any insight?"

"I don't know beyond her time at work," Sherry said.

"Because you're afraid of what the answer implies?" Ray asked.

"Not at all." Sherry heard a rustle of paper through the phone.

"Another question. There were two men from Iceland, actually one relocated to Iceland, where the Helguvsons hail from, at Patti Mellit's studio the day you were there. What was their kitchen tools for the podcast?"

"I didn't personally speak to them beyond two words. Marla may have. Hold on." She clicked the phone's speaker button and entered the dining room. "Mar, do you recall the kitchen tools the judges chose to talk about? Did they mention their choices?" Sherry returned to her seat at the table.

Marla thought for a minute. "I know all three judges' tools. Gunnar Vilhjálmsson, good pronunciation, right? He had kitchen shears. Sienna Warren had a cast iron skillet and Carl Carlson had tongs. They all said they had trouble making a final decision on their choice."

"Did you hear that?" Sherry asked.

"I did," Ray said.

"Shears and a heavy skillet could kill someone, but not the tongs, unless they're used quite creatively," Sherry said.

"I'd like a word with the three from the studio," Ray said. "In your opinion, or Marla's, were any of the three aggressive or quarrelsome with Sigmund?"

"I wasn't with the judges for more than a few seconds," Sherry said. "Marla? Did you hear Ray's question?"

"Yup. There was a quarrel, for sure. But you're barking up the wrong tree. The judges weren't the instigators of the heated argument that went on. Thomas and Sigmund were. Thomas was aggressive with his brother. They were like two bulls banging horns, and from what I picked up, making more noise than sense."

Sherry muffled a giggle at her sister's analogy. She hoped Ray appreciated the visual.

"And the others?" Ray asked. "Any of the other three bang horns, as you say, with Sigmund?"

"Sienna kept to herself for the most part. Except when she and I were discussing her cookbook. Carl was disturbed by the brothers going at it. So was Gunnar V. At one point when the chatter exploded into anger, Carl reminded the boys they should get along. That they were once a tight group called . . ." She paused as her gaze swept skyward. "The Band of Bankless Brothers. The name doesn't exactly roll off the tongue. Carl tried to talk them both off the ledge with a lecture in brotherhood. Finally, everyone settled down. If that argument continued after we left, I'm sure that was the ruckus Patti had to filter out from the podcast."

Sherry and Marla exchanged glances. Marla put her hands up to her head. That cat was out of the bag.

"Did Patti mention that to you, Ray?" Sherry asked. "That she had noise interference in the background of her podcast recording?"

"She didn't. I've made a note of it for follow-up," Ray said. "And Carl Carlson? Where's he from?"

"Carl Carlson is Norwegian. Did you know Norwegians are known as the peaceful people?" Marla asked.

"I did not. Thank you for all your tidbits of info, Marla," Ray said. "You Oliveris are a knowledgeable clan."

"Happy to help, Ray. Carl mentioned his country's description, as if he thought the words would transfer peace to the room," Marla said. "It kind of worked."

"With no body to examine, how can you move forward? It must feel like the blind leading the blind," Sherry said.

"I would never concede the success of the investigation so early in the process," Ray said. "Circling back to the wooden spoon. Do you have any idea what Sigmund's reaction was when he found out you also chose the wooden spoon to talk to Patti about? Did Patti mention anything about that?"

"I'd hope he thought great minds think alike," Sherry said with a chuckle. "Why do you ask?"

"Could be if he were in a mood already, he might not have taken kindly to you stepping on his toes."

"Not much I could do about that," Sherry said. "Funny. Now that you mention it, I wish I had as good a story as the Icelanders' story of the wooden spoon. Thomas Helguvson's son told me a fascinating story about the importance of the wooden spoon in Iceland. Around the winter holidays there's a Yule Lad that comes around from the mountains to lick wooden spoons and taste what families have been preparing. People leave their spoons on the counter overnight to appease the little guy's needs. He also finds naughty children and either steals them away or leaves them with a booby prize rather than a present."

"What cultures pass down through generations is amazing," Ray said.

"Cooking methods and recipes are the glue that keep cultures alive and thriving," Sherry said.

"Is a wooden spoon something I should add to my kitchen drawer?" Ray said.

"One hundred percent yes. I have one for you, too. I've won so many I could build a fence with them," Sherry said with a laugh.

"Thank you. I'll take you up on that offer," Ray said. "One wooden spoon, not a whole fence."

"Consider this. Learning about the Icelandic food culture might be of help in this case. Possibly the broken wooden spoon has more meaning than just having Sigmund's blood on it at the scene of his disappearance," Sherry said.

"I've taken note."

"Am I getting my point across that Patti shouldn't be on your radar? She didn't do anything criminal, especially commit murder. Certainly not aiding and abetting a faked death."

"You've heard from that private detective from Iceland? Faking a death is her theory, not my department's."

"I spoke with her, yes," Sherry said.

"I figured, since you didn't seem surprised at the revelation Sigmund was married."

"She and Thomas Helguvson found me after I taught a class at the school Thomas's son attends. His son is in my class. They went out of their way to meet with me when I was leaving school. Surprised the heck out of me."

"You're helicoptering the case, Sherry. Aren't you?" Ray said.

He wasn't scolding her, but she suspected a caution was about to be suggested. She'd heard it before.

"Let us do our job. This is getting complicated. It's unclear who is after who in this case. What is clear is someone has likely been murdered. We don't know the motive and we don't know the killer's identity. Those are the ingredients for someone else to get hurt. You and I both know you'll do most anything to help a friend out of hot water. Please be careful."

"I hear you. Patti's my friend," Sherry said. Her sincerity seeped through the phone and Ray sighed. "I want to help her if I can. She's lost someone she shouldn't have trusted. She's embarrassed. Worse, she's a suspect. That detective from Iceland isn't making her life any easier. Lilya has some nerve. Shouldn't she focus on the enemies Sigmund has, rather than the person who liked him?"

"I understand your judgment of her. She reached out to my department. They patched her through to me. She doesn't bother with the pleasantries when she makes initial contact, dives right into the nitty-gritty."

"Must be like looking in a mirror," Sherry said to lighten the mood. She was certain Ray could see the broad grin on her face. The comfortable banter reminded her their friendship evolved after a rocky start. It was a relationship growing with trust and mutual respect of each other's strengths and weaknesses.

"Maybe," Ray said. "Any details of the meeting with Lilya you'd care to share?"

"According to Lilya, Sigmund faked his own death in order to restart his life. A do-over. Ha. There are plenty of times I'd have liked a do-over." Sherry waited for a confirmation from Ray that was slow to come.

"No need for you, my dear. You are perfect the way you are. Quirky, but acceptable."

"Thanks, Ray. At the meeting I was asked by Lilya and Thomas to prod information out of Patti Mellit as she most certainly was in on the scheme. I refused."

"You did the right thing. I don't work for Lilya or Thomas or anyone other than my department head. You certainly don't work for Lilya or Thomas. My mission in this case is to find Sigmund Helguvson, or find his murderer. If in the process another scenario is uncovered, I'll steer the ship in that direction. Until then, my job is far from done."

"I was thinking," Sherry said. "Patti said Thomas told her first responders were summoned to his location at the lake. When they arrived, they found the phone in shallow water. No sign of Sigmund. Let's say he didn't plan his demise and was really in trouble. Would he have had enough time to dial 911, before or after being attacked, then pushed in the water before dropping his phone?"

"Are you edging over to Lilya's side?" Ray asked.

"It's a sound question," Sherry said with confidence. "Staging your murder properly so as not to make the scene appear sterile takes planning and timing. A murder goes bing bang boom. If the moment's right, the deed gets done in an instant.

"Speculation," Ray warned.

"Of course it is. I must present a scenario out loud to see if you give it credence," Sherry said. Ray could be so frustrating at times.

"One of your facts is incorrect. He didn't dial 911. He had the latest version of smartphone. A sensor calls for help if the phone has been battered in a jarring accident. That's another reason I'd back the bing-bang-boom theory of murder. If he wanted the phone to alert his staged demise and the phone wasn't jarred enough to sense a fall, he'd have to go through a second phone drop, and the phone would already be wet and may not work at all." Ray was proud of his clear analysis of the scenario. His triumphant tone betrayed any attempt at humility.

"The phone drop did alert the authorities. Okay. I'm confident Lilya has no evidence Patti aided Sigmund in faking his death," Sherry said. "If she did, she didn't tip her hand to me when we met."

"Maybe they haven't dug deep enough," Ray said.

"What do you mean?" Sherry asked.

"In my conversation with Patti I made an interesting discovery. Sigmund leases an electric luxury vehicle."

"Not that shocking," Sherry said. "Good for him to save the planet."

"His phone has a car app. That's how you start the car and initiate all sorts of personalized services, like preferred seat position, interior temperature settings, bells and whistles galore."

"That's what you pay lots of money for," Sherry said.

"And there's a capability for a second driver profile on the app. In case a second person uses the car frequently. Thomas knew the password and the forensic lab discovered the second profile is Patti Mellit."

Sherry stayed silent for a moment, taking in the implications. "It means Sigmund trusted Patti. You'd trust her, too, if you got to know her."

"He may have trusted her, yes. But she can also use the app to track where the car is at all times. The primary driver can't sneeze without the second driver saying a remote 'gesundheit.' During the time you say Patti was editing the podcast she also had the tools to track Sigmund and know exactly when he had reached Harmony Lake. If the faked death scenario were in play, she could have snuck out of the MediaPie building undetected, helped his plan come to fruition by sending out a distress signal from his phone by whacking it hard on something before it was submerged, and driving him in her car, not his, to an undisclosed location to begin a new life while his car remained parked at the lake."

"Speculation. More proof is needed." Sherry said. "Patti needs to account for her entire evening."

"Right answer," Ray said.

The corners of Sherry's mouth lifted. "MediaPie has a capable and duty-bound security guard on duty, day and night. He has his pulse on all the comings and goings in the building. Patti couldn't have gone out without logging out."

"Work to be done," Ray continued. "Trooper will be at the lake the moment the weather breaks from this snowy pattern. Tomorrow, we're hoping. Officer Sedgeman, his handler, has been on vacation. Trooper's been staying with another officer who's not fully qualified to conduct a K-9 search. If I'm not mistaken, your friend Amber Sherwin is on vacation with him?"

"That's right. Their first trip together," Sherry said. "They're back tonight."

"Right," Ray said with a lightness in his tone.

"Will Lilya be at the lake for the search, or would that be an admission she may be barking up the wrong investigation tree? Can private investigators even be involved in murder cases? Seems like that's police territory," Sherry said.

"Private investigators don't typically investigate murders. That's what my homicide department does. PIs are hired by citizens to track a cheating spouse, get dirt for a divorce proceeding, locate a missing person, uncover missing finances, any of which can apply to Sigmund Helguvson. As I understand it, Nora, his wife, hired Lilya to prove Sigmund was alive and well and living under a new identity. He left Iceland with the promised intention of finding an opportunity for his import-export business and then sending for her. That dream never materialized. She wants closure. In addition, she suspects he's hiding assets here in the U.S., some of which she's most likely entitled to, although I'm not up on Icelandic marriage rights."

"I got the same story," Sherry said.

"We continue to monitor his financial activities since his disappearance. As of now, nothing. If he faked his death he committed to it," Ray said. "And circling back to your story of the wooden spoon licking Yule Lads, interesting stuff. I'll take your advice and do some research on Icelanders." He inhaled a crisp breath and spoke the words that warmed Sherry's heart. "Thank you. There you go, a pleasantry. I have plenty more to share if need be."

"Thanks, Ray."

"By the way, what the heck do Icelanders eat, I wonder?" Ray asked.

"I'm sure lots of fish. It's an island, after all."

"Makes sense."

Sherry couldn't let the phone call end without introducing one more opinion. "Ray, one more word. Lilya and Thomas are so far off. When the body's been found, all this nonsense about a faked death will be squashed." Sherry reconsidered what she'd said. "Not that I'm rooting for murder, or any death at all. Ugh, you know what I mean."

"I've gotten pretty good at interpreting your Sherry-speak. If you're determined to do some snooping, I'd like to know what Sigmund was doing at the lake that evening," Ray said. "Snow was in the forecast. There are flags all over the lake property warning the frozen lake's not safe to walk on, even though it may appear so. If he did plan his demise he chose a good night for it, weather-wise. With snow falling, any arriving or departing car tracks were blurred and unidentifiable. We'll talk soon." He clicked off.

Sherry talked into the phone, knowing no one was on the receiving end. "He's gone. He always gets me with his lack of a formal goodbye. One minute he's there, the next second he's out. One day I'll get the last word in."

• • •

Don entered the dining room balancing three bowls of ice cream like a well-trained server. “That was quite a phone call, full of information I couldn’t help overhearing. Now I don’t need to be filled in on any of the latest developments,” Don said. He set the bowls down in front of each diner.

“Sure was,” Sherry said. “There’s one takeaway from this crazy event.”

“What could that be?” Marla asked.

“I’ve made an African groundnut stew for the preliminary round of the cook-off and that was a hit with the judges. What do you guys think about an Icelandic recipe for the final round?”

“I couldn’t name one if you waved a hundred-dollar bill in my face,” Marla said.

“Can’t say I’ve sought out an Icelandic recipe to fill a craving,” Don said.

“That might be a gamble,” Marla said. “What do you know about the cuisine up in those parts?”

“That’s the point of the cook-off. To introduce something reimagined to the judges and the audience based on a traditional dish from a certain country.”

“You thrive on culinary risk. I say go for it. Maybe something positive will come out of all the shenanigans,” Marla said.

“Except, didn’t you say one of the judges is from Iceland? Won’t it be difficult to impress him with his own cuisine?” Don asked. “While you’re pondering my question, let’s dig in before the ice cream melts anymore.”

Sherry savored a spoonful of chocolate chip. “Gunnar V., yes. He’s from Iceland. And Thomas Helguvson is.”

“Don, you may want to rethink your words,” Marla said. “Sherry loves a cooking challenge. It always elevates her game.”

“I take it back. What was I thinking?” Don chuckled as he scooped the cold, creamy goodness into his mouth.

“I guess after tonight’s research I can answer Ray’s question of what the heck people in Iceland eat. And I have to make their recipe my own by adding my Sherry twist to a tried-and-true recipe. It won’t be easy. I’ve got some work ahead of me.”

Don, true to his word, washed every dish when the ice cream bowls were empty. While he cleaned up Sherry and Marla took the opportunity to research Icelandic cuisine. An online search failed to inspire her, as did browsing through many of Sherry’s cookbooks.

“Moving on to plan B. My last hope is in class tomorrow. I’m going to ask Magnus what his favorite meal from his home country is,” Sherry said.

"You don't think he'll go home and tell his father you've asked for a recipe for the cook-off?" Marla asked.

"I won't be doing that. I'm asking the whole class for their favorite family meal for the purpose of garden planning," Sherry said. "No sense planting a garden full of veggies no one would cook and eat."

Chapter 12

Friday began with an uncharacteristically early awakening by Marla. Sherry would never have been the wiser had her sister not unloaded the dishwasher with enough clattering to wake Sherry and draw her downstairs.

"What a nice surprise," Sherry said. "You're hired."

"Hah," Marla chuckled. "Couldn't sleep. Needed something to do. Too excited for what we're cooking for dinner tonight."

"Really? I thought I was the only one to lose sleep over food prep," Sherry said and laughed. "I'll be back from school before lunch. Then we'll plan dinner." She poured a mug of coffee. "It's my last day teaching. I'm sad. I've really had a nice time with the kids. Kudos to them for their enthusiasm about a project months away that can only be visualized in the depths of winter. That takes some commitment to future success on their part. Most kids I know thrive on instant gratification."

"And kudos to the teacher," Marla said. She gave Sherry a golf clap. "You should take the scenic route to school and skip driving through town this morning."

"Why's that?" Sherry asked. She doused her coffee in almond milk creamer.

"I saw on MediaPie's local news site a call for an impromptu protest around Town Hall," Marla said. She dried her hands on her pajama bottoms. "All done."

Sherry grimaced. "I have a towel you could use." She pointed out the kitchen towel rack by the oven.

Marla shrugged. "This works for me."

"Are you sure there's a protest? I edited the mayor's newsletter a few days ago. On the mayor's calendar I specifically recall there is a meeting this morning with local media groups about improving connectivity in commercial space, cell phone towers, and laying new cables. To be followed by a proposal for redesigning the Augustin Marina for day-docking large vessels. That way personal watercraft can bring shoppers and diners to town."

"Yup. The call-to-action plan is a simple one. Protest. One group backed by the *Beacon* newspaper is calling for sign holders to represent progressive advancements. A second group is being solicited to hold signs for preservation of the town's core values. No new unsightly cell phone towers. No new anything."

"Sounds like you've chosen your side," Sherry said.

"Augustin shouldn't cut off its nose to spite its face," Marla said. "Wow, I never thought I'd be old enough to use that phrase, let alone know what it means."

"Discussion to be continued. Thanks for the heads-up on the protest route. I need to get a move on." Sherry carried her coffee mug upstairs and got dressed for her final day of fifth-grade gardening class.

On her way to school Sherry disregarded Marla's warning to stay clear of Augustin's town center. On the contrary, her curiosity got the better of her and she steered the car toward Town Hall. From a distance she could see the mayor's reserved parking spot was occupied by his sports car. The surrounding Town Hall property appeared tranquil. She passed the historic brick building, home to one of her part-time jobs. Sherry never tired of entering the ornate marbled-floored space to chat with the mayor or his secretary about the submissions for the newsletter.

The feeling of contentment she experienced was washed away when her car was stopped in its tracks by a crowd of people pouring out from behind the building. Carrying signs mounted on posts, two distinct groups were chanting back and forth. *Preserve and Protect, Hands Off the Past, Augustin Strong, The Future Is Now, Our Town Needs Life Support, Everyone's Leaving Because No One's Believing* were some of the sentiments hand-drawn on staked posterboard. When Sherry picked up her dropped jaw, she shifted the car into reverse and followed Marla's suggested scenic route.

"The town is splitting. This is terrible," Sherry said aloud as she glanced at the scene in her rearview mirror. She couldn't get to the school fast enough.

Shaking off the upsetting start to the day, Sherry's spirit lifted as she entered Mrs. Turpin's classroom. More hand-drawn signs on posterboard adorned the room, only these contained uplifting words of thanks for Sherry's time with the kids. She received a round of applause when she settled in front of the class.

"Before we start today's last class, I'd like to tell you we had a few students and their parents make you a meal of their favorite things to eat. I emphasized healthy as a guideline, so I'll leave it at that," Mrs. Turpin said. She swept her hand across her desk. In front of Sherry were four lidded containers decorated with cards and ribbons. "Makena, would you like to describe what you made for Ms. Sherry?"

A girl, who seemed to have been ill-fitted with an undersized school desk, smiled. Her legs spilled out from under the desk across the aisle into the next row of student desks. "My mom and I made you tomato chicken stew. My grandma came here from Africa and this is our Sunday night dinner every week. We just made some a few days early for you. Mom says since you're teaching me how to grow tomatoes, we'll use those in the stew next summer. I only brought you enough for one. I didn't know if you were married or any stuff like that."

"Thank you so much, Makena. Please tell your mom I'm so thrilled to eat this," Sherry said. She patted the top of the container.

Sherry also was gifted tofu lettuce wraps, with the promise of hand-picked garden lettuce next year rather than store-bought, along with a tub of homemade pumpkin seed pesto. The final container came from Magnus, saving Sherry the task of prying his favorite meal choice out of him.

"Dad and I made you dessert. Do you like chocolate hazelnut spread?" Magnus asked.

Sherry nodded with enthusiasm.

"It's the bomb in Iceland. Everyone loves it. It's practically the national dish. You spread the chocolatey goo on, like, pancakes after you warm them up and plop some cream on top. We didn't make the spread, but we did make the pancakes."

"Look at your classmates' faces, Magnus. I think you'll have to bring enough for the whole class next time," Sherry said.

"We're drooling, brother," a boy said from the desk at the end of the row.

"Thank you so much, everyone," Sherry said. "An embarrassment of riches today."

"Back to work, kids," Mrs. Turpin said. "Sherry, what gardening wisdom have you got for us on your last day?"

"The class designed some great food and we're going to design the contents of your school's spring garden," Sherry said. "I couldn't have asked for a better segue. Let's get this garden party started." Forty-five minutes later, what seemed to Sherry like the blink of an eye, her week of garden classes came to an end.

• • •

On the trip home Sherry bypassed the town center to avoid any residual protesting. She was also interested in preserving the uplifting satisfaction of her classroom success. At home she unloaded her armful of class materials and food containers. She set the mountain of items on the front hall table, hung up her coat and removed her sunglasses. She found Marla at the kitchen table munching on a piece of buttered toast.

"You were right, Marla. The center of Augustin was jammed. I had to turn around at Town Hall. I hope Dad and Amber got to the Ruggery without trouble."

"The town's fired up," Marla said. "Lucky for them, the protesters were gifted some sunny skies. Chutney and I took advantage of the warmer temps and walked around the neighborhood."

"Thanks for that," Sherry said.

"My pleasure. How about the cook-off recipe?" Marla said. "Did you get any ideas from the kids at school? Have you decided on your choice? That's why I got up so early this morning. The suspense is killing me."

Sherry was amused at her sister's increasing interest in the cook-off. "I've come up with a recipe."

"You're still choosing an Icelandic recipe, aren't you?" Marla said.

"The choice is written in the stars. Not only did I bring home tasty treats from the kids at school, but Magnus gave me a great idea. Hold on. I left all the food in the hallway." Sherry dashed out of the room and collected the containers off the front hall table. She returned to an impressed Marla. She set down what the kids gave her, side by side, on the kitchen counter.

"You're so lucky," Marla said.

"I told you they were a wonderful group of kids." Sherry lifted the lid on the Icelandic pancakes.

Without an invitation Marla's hand plunged in and retrieved a chocolatey pancake roll. One bite later she pronounced Magnus a winner.

"I've changed my mind. Icelanders know good food."

"Icelanders love their dessert pancakes slathered with chocolate-hazelnut spread," Sherry said. "They prefer a plop of skyr on top. Like a creamy yogurt."

"What's your spin on this recipe? Does it really need improvement? Less is more, you taught me."

"I'm thinking of making my Icelandic pancakes savory, not sweet. A main course with a bent toward their preferences of what's available on that chilly island. The story to go along with the recipe will follow naturally."

"Do we need to grocery shop?"

"We need a few things, yes. You ready right now?" Sherry asked. Her sister was wearing overalls, a ponytail sprouting wild locks in all directions, and her signature flannel shirt.

Marla waved her hands across her torso. "This is as good as it gets. Let's get a move on."

On the way to the store something occurred to Sherry she hadn't yet addressed with Marla. "Did Dad mention anything to you about taking a cut in the salary he pays himself from the Ruggery?"

Marla fiddled with the passenger-side window control. "Maybe he felt like the cash he made from the sale of his inherited land minus the cost of post-flood renovations to the store gave him enough of a cushion for a while? Don discovered that in the books?"

"Yup. Doesn't seem right Dad would do that. I hope there's not a problem he won't talk about," Sherry said. She steered the car into the Au Natural grocery parking lot, pausing for a prime parking spot to open up.

"That's what we hired Don to shine a light on."

"If you're not worried, then I'm not either," Sherry lied. She side-eyed her sister, who was staring out the windshield, unwilling to elaborate.

The wait was worth the convenience of the parking spot. The hour was so close to lunchtime that as soon as they left the car, Sherry and Marla were immediately caught up in the stream of determined customers entering the store. As they neared the store's automatic doors, they were forced to duck to avoid being swiped by the decorative Valentine's Day mylar balloons waving about in the winter winds. The strategically located display reminded would-be romantics to stock up. Sherry clogged the customer flow when she untied one of the balloons from the makeshift archway.

"Might as well get an early start. In case Don needs a subliminal reminder of the big day. Want one?" She poised herself to untie a second balloon.

"That's okay. Maybe Grant will send me one. My cowboy has a romantic streak that appears once a year around this time," Marla said. She snatched two baskets from the stack by the door and handed one to Sherry. Sherry tied her balloon's ribbon to the hand basket.

"Let's split the list. Divide and conquer." Sherry ripped the written list in half and handed one piece to Marla. "Meet you in a few."

Sherry made a beeline for the meat case to find chicken pieces. She preferred the full-flavored dark meat of the boneless, skinless thighs. Reaching the desired package required patience while a man blocking her choice made his. Beside him was a couple ready to pounce on any space that freed up. The man touched three packages before selecting one to place in his cart. He didn't forgo his position. He made a second selection. Cooking for many. Sherry appreciated that. The couple edged in sideways and bumped the competition. Sherry saw her opening and made a move.

"Excuse me. I'll just grab my chicken and get out of your way. I know exactly what I want," Sherry said. Her patience was wearing thin.

The couple shot Sherry a look of indignation. The man holding his ground turned around with a smile.

"I'd know that voice anywhere. You're just the chicken parts expert I need." Ray studied the contents of Sherry's basket. His line of sight rose to the balloon. "Planning a romantic dinner?"

"Working on a recipe for the cook-off next week. Magnus Helguvson gave me a great idea. He's Thomas Helguvson's son. Icelandic pancakes stuffed with shredded chicken. Kind of a twist on chicken and waffles, northern edition."

"Sounds tasty," Ray said. "Since I've had the good fortune to run into you at my moment of indecision, let me ask you. Boneless, skinless thighs or breasts for stir-fry. Doesn't everyone like white meat?"

"Consider your audience. Are you playing it safe for the sake of not challenging someone's taste buds or are you willing to dive into the flavor and texture pool with an underappreciated cut and change someone's life forever?" Sherry asked, hoping she hadn't overdramatized the importance of adventurous cooking.

"Message received. I got it," Ray said. "Another question, non-food related. It's a firm plan, tomorrow Trooper will go to Harmony Lake. The weather forecast is cooperating. Sedgeman is back from vacation. The goal is to use all the investigative unit's resources to make sense of the scene."

"You're banking on all questions being answered?" Sherry asked with caution.

"You know I don't speculate and I don't gamble," Ray said. "Would you meet us down at the lake? Only for the initial stages of the search. We need to work on our own after that. You understand the sensitivity of the situation if a body is found."

An entire scene of activity flooded Sherry's head. She had only witnessed a search for a body from the comfort of her couch. Television conveyed a rescue scene as quick and efficient. Even glamorous. That was television, not reality. Her gut told her she may be committing to a painfully slow task. Still, she was invested in the process, for Patti's sake. After a moment of consideration, she agreed. "Okay. Text me the time."

"Will do," Ray said.

"You having someone special over?" Sherry asked as she scanned her remaining list. "That's a lot of chicken for one person."

Ray swerved away from the meat case to avoid an aggressive shopper threatening to use his cart as a battering ram if his path wasn't cleared. "Lilya, if she agrees. See ya." He got the last word in before Sherry could pose any follow-up.

Chapter 13

After leaving the meat section Sherry spotted Marla loitering around the cheese case. Cheese was not on the grocery list. "Hey. I ran into Ray at the meat case eyeing the chicken. He might have dinner with Lilya, the private investigator from Iceland hired by Nora Helguvson. Wonder what that's all about?"

"Is she attractive?" Marla got straight to the point. "He is a man, you know."

"Sure she is, and stylish to boot. The kicker is he's a stickler for never mixing business and pleasure." Sherry grimaced. "At least I thought that was the case."

"You suggested he look into Icelandic culture as part of the investigation, guess he took you up on that." Marla's casual tone took the edge off Sherry's curiosity. "I'd say, 'to be continued,' and trust him."

"I do, it's just that Lilya rubbed both of us the wrong way from the get-go."

As they made their way down the international foods aisle toward the checkout a stock boy on a ladder blocked their progress. His arms were full of pouches boasting colorful labels. He was precariously balanced while feeling for a lower step with his foot.

"Let me give you a hand," Sherry said. "Drop those in my basket." Rather than witness the stock boy tumbling to the floor, hands loaded with products, Sherry held up her half-full basket. The stock boy dropped the pouches a few feet before he was able to wriggle down the ladder safely.

"Thanks," he said. He gathered the pouches from Sherry's basket. "Would you like one? Dried fish, imported from . . ." The young man squinted through his glasses and searched both sides of a pouch. "Iceland. No wonder it's overpriced. Who knew we carried this item? I've never gotten a request for dried fish strips."

"And we're not requesting them either," Marla said.

"Not today, thanks," Sherry said.

"Last chance, we're pulling them from the shelves. They weren't selling at all. The expiration date was yesterday."

"I don't think so, but thanks for asking. Good luck," Sherry said as she walked away. "Why did I say good luck?"

"Beats me. Wishing him luck on his next ladder journey? Good luck selling an expired product?" Marla said. "You made the right decision not letting him convince you to buy that so-called fish. I like my fish fresh and moist, not dried and old. I'm happy Iceland is creative with their exports but that didn't look appealing whatsoever. Are you rethinking your recipe?"

"Don't worry. That's not what I'm making for dinner. My cook-off recipe is a more modern take on Icelandic cuisine."

After they brought the groceries home and organized them on the kitchen counter, Sherry and Marla took Chutney for a long walk. When they returned, they went their separate ways. Marla wanted to read a few chapters of her library book while Sherry researched Icelandic food folklore for the mandatory story to go along with her recipe. Finding her concentration waning, Sherry took to her comfort zone, the kitchen. She jotted down a tentative name for her recipe, Ponnukokur with Shredded Chicken, Peppered Gooseberry Jelly, Pea Pesto and Skyr.

Sometimes recipe contests preferred cute names like Cowboy Tater Tot Pie that hinted at the flavor profile and ingredients. The Round the World's Pantry—Cuisine and Culture Cook-off called for a title that hinted at the country of origin. Sherry's years of experience gave her the sense the judges wouldn't be as interested in a cook's recipe naming prowess as they were the cook's creativity with a chosen international cuisine. Finding the story to go along with the recipe was proving to be a challenge. Nothing was hitting her over the head. Maybe if Sherry began assembling the recipe she may have a better idea what to search for based on how the recipe came together.

"Mar, I'm starting the recipe if you want to help," Sherry called out. No reply. Two steps into the living room and the sight of her snoozing sister prone on the couch explained the unanswered call for assistance. "I'm on my own."

Sherry began the preparations by mixing up one bowl containing the pancakes' dry ingredients, and another the wet ingredients. After combining the two she let the batter set up while she warmed her seasoned iron skillet, the only pan she trusted to make the first pancake golden brown rather than a throwaway. She made two pancakes the size of a dessert plate. The pancake was going to serve as the round vehicle on which the savory ingredients would be transported to the judges' mouths. The other finalists, she imagined, might be using tortillas, or Ethiopian injeras pancakes, or arepas from South America, or crepes from France as the blank canvas for their fillings. The rounds could lay flat with a topping piled on or they could be folded in half or thirds to conceal the flavor explosion inside. Roti, farinata, blinis all could be competing against her ponnukokur. She had to make her pancake special, not complicated, and packed with Icelandic flavors.

The first pancake she lifted out of the skillet with her spatula rested on a plate in front of her. She could earn the title of Grand Prize winner along with five thousand dollars with a similar remake of this pancake. Time for final approval. Sherry studied the pancake for cracks and unevenness. Too pale. Edges too ragged. Improvement was needed. Pancakes don't like being rushed.

"What's going on in here?" Marla said as she entered the kitchen. "Something smells great."

"I got restless and had to throw together my pancake batter. I made a sample. No filling yet but I know what that'll be. It should only take thirty minutes or so tonight to put together."

"Can I cut off a bite?"

"Of course," Sherry said as she handed her sister a butter knife. The knife flowed through the thin, airy pancake. Marla pinched a wedge between her fingers and placed it in her mouth. The contentment on her face spoke volumes.

"Do you have a story?" Marla asked.

"I think I do. The pancake was speaking to me and I like what it said."

"In that case, job well done. The cook-off is Tuesday, right? At the new Southport Shores Hotel?" Marla asked.

"All of the above," Sherry said. "Tuesday's also Don's birthday and Valentine's Day."

"Is it meaningful that you chose a Valentine's Day balloon over a birthday balloon to decorate the table tonight?"

"I don't know what you're talking about," Sherry said. Without missing a beat, she added, "Do you think I put it in a good location?"

"Almost perfect," Marla said. "I'll fix one thing." Sherry followed her into the dining room where Marla lowered the balloon's ribbon a few inches. "At eye level no one will miss the message. Especially Don."

• • •

Hours later, the remnants of the creamy chicken-stuffed ponnukokurs were scraped from the plates. Sherry's brother Pep, sister-in-law Charlotte and baby niece Mimi were ecstatic about her cook-off recipe. The young family was one of her biggest supporters in all she did. In return she kept them well fed whenever the opportunity arose. Erno and his girlfriend, Ruth, were harder to read when it came to interpreting their judgment of her cooking. They appeared to savor each bite while taking the job of analyzing each component of the dish very seriously. Too seriously. They exchanged so many wordless glances between bites Sherry stopped waiting for input.

Sherry circled the table looking for any empty dishes to bring to the sink. "Any last words on how to improve the recipe?"

"I was so surprised with the flavor combinations," Pep said.

"The recipe was a reinvention of the sweet dessert pancake my student Magnus brought me on the last day of class. The pancake is roughly the same. I went with the savory chicken filling instead of the hazelnut chocolate filling. I want to prove the lowly chicken can be elevated by international methods."

"That chocolate one also sounds amazing."

"But it's already been done. Magnus said it was practically Iceland's national dish," Sherry said. "I went with chicken because the farms in Iceland are loaded with the tasty birds. I added a few veggies in the form of a pea pesto for color and flavor, potatoes, and dolloped skyr on the seam of the folded pancake, along with a peppered gooseberry jelly. The pièce de résistance is a background note of curry. It takes the flavor to the next level. A hint is all that's needed. Sweet, savory, spicy, tangy."

"Pep, you might want to put it on your food truck's menu," Erno said.

Sherry smiled at her father's suggestion. He was ever the glue that bound the kids' interests together.

"I'm not sure I can put it on the truck's menu without tweaking the recipe. I'd need to convince my customers the pancake is a toast, consistent with our menu's toast-topper theme. That being said, I'd say, sister dear, you've got a winner here."

Sherry absorbed every word. She was so grateful Pep embarked on his food truck business journey. He had credibility as her brother, but as a food service business owner he raised the bar. She could count on him for an honest opinion on any recipe.

"And our favorite niece, Mimi?" Marla asked. "How did she like the pancakes?"

Charlotte wiped her daughter's mouth with a napkin. An instant later, Mimi's crumb-laden hand was back up to her face. "Mimi loved the pancakes on their own, which was a nice way to keep her occupied. For a toddler she's an adventurous eater."

"I'd expect nothing less from my blood relative." Sherry's gaze shifted to Don.

"That was so good and really different," Don said. "Were you aware eating fermented shark is something that's done in Iceland? I'm glad you didn't go in that direction."

"I did come across that fact while searching for a recipe story. I wonder how fermented shark came to be?" Sherry asked. "I'll do some further research. Who knows? That might be the story I've been looking for. I made something new out of an old recipe. Inventions go both ways. It seems like an Icelander had the idea to make something new, fresh shark meat, taste old by fermenting it."

"I've never tasted fermented shark, but this meal beats what I'm guessing fermented shark tastes like," Erno said. Sherry's father turned to Ruth on his right. "Did you like it, sweetie?"

"The best. Sherry, you win," Ruth said.

"More high praise," Erno added. "Now that that's settled, how in tarnation are we going to solve the town crisis? I walk down Main Street and I'm accosted by every store owner and every pedestrian who's ever stopped into my store. That dag-blame-it *Coastal County Beacon* newspaper has set the town ablaze with its rhetoric. The editor has lived in Augustin for less than a year. He should go back to Iceland if he doesn't appreciate our bucolic ways. His son can stay here and finish school."

"Erno Oliveri," Ruth scolded. "You are Augustin personified but you need to accept we can't live in the past forever. Marina dredging and the proposed new concert pavilion will attract so many new customers to your store. What's not to like about that? The proposed cell phone tower needs to be built so I can make a phone call anywhere in town. If I'm the last to know something because I couldn't hear all the gossip, I'm going to blame the spotty reception on you."

Marla piped in. "And the town should install cameras at all major intersections and go from there."

"Eyes on everything I do," Erno said. "I can't scratch myself without it being public knowledge."

"The cameras aren't spying on us, they're keeping us safe," Marla said.

"Is the purpose of a newspaper really to prompt change? Seems dangerous," Erno said.

"All respectful and tasteful opinions without threat of censorship should be welcome. Unfortunately, the editorial page of the *Beacon* has become a battleground forum," Don said. He stood and collected a handful of remaining dishes.

"All in response to the lean of the progressive articles," Erno said.

"I haven't lived in Augustin very long, but I dare say, the debate is giving the citizens new life," Don said. He was wearing a sly smile.

"I might be on Dad's side until I get more time to digest the matter," Sherry said.

"Or until Dad leaves the room," Pep said.

"I make my own opinions," Sherry countered. "I just need to gather more facts." She followed Don into the kitchen. She whispered in his ear, "I've missed you."

"I know time with your sister is the priority while she's on the East Coast. We can make up for the lack of snuggles around Valentine's Day." Don's voice took on a husky quality that made the hair on Sherry's arm stand up.

"You're making me blush, young man," she said. She planted a kiss on his lips.

Don led her back to the table with his arm around her shoulders. In her hands was a dessert platter. Store-bought shortbread was passed around as plans for Saturday were exchanged.

"Marla and I will be at the Ruggery in the morning. Later I'm meeting Detective Bease at Harmony Lake," Sherry said. "Trooper and Officer Sedgeman, the dog's handler, will be conducting a search around the dock and the area grounds where Sigmund Helguvson may have entered the water."

"Amber's Officer Sedgeman? Her new boyfriend?" Ruth asked. "How exciting."

"Yes, Troy," Sherry said. "I call him Officer Sedgeman while he's on duty. Seems right."

"Why are you going down there?" Erno asked.

"Patti asked me to investigate the question of whether Sigmund was murdered or is living the good life, somewhere new, as someone new. Ray asked me to make an appearance at the lake to monitor the others' reaction to the proceedings. I'm not too hopeful I have much to add in this case." Sherry munched on a bite of the buttery sweet biscuit.

"Don't be too sure. You can't keep a good amateur sleuth down," Marla said with a laugh.

Chapter 14

Saturday mornings at the Ruggery were fast-paced as shoppers tended to come in as groups rather than the usual singles. When Sherry received the time to be at the lake from Ray she worried she'd be in the middle of a sale. She was right. It was eleven forty-five and she had to leave to get to the lake by noon, but just then a group of tourists from a sightseeing bus crowded the showroom. Sherry had to beg off. Amber was up to the task of fielding their numerous questions, but still, Sherry considered skipping the lake visit. Amber wouldn't hear of it. Sherry made her promise to call Marla to come in if need be.

When she arrived at Harmony Lake people were milling about without obvious purpose. Sherry called to the policeman holding Trooper's leash. She waited until he finished his word with Ray before she joined them at the foot of the lake's dock. Beyond them was a huge ice-covered lake. A thin mist layer hovered over the surface, indicating the rising temperature may be melting some of the ice. The surrounding trees were bare and wanting for color. There were so many monochromatic winter gray and brown tones at the park known throughout the county for its summer recreation, flower beds and arboretum-worthy ornamental trees. Sherry couldn't remember ever being at the location in the depths of winter.

When the two men parted Sherry recognized her opening. "We missed Amber at the Ruggery this week. Did you have a good trip?" She studied the man who'd caught Amber's eye months ago. Sherry and Don had yet to spend quality social time together with Amber and Troy. She respected Amber for being protective of her new relationship. Because he was a policeman, he seldom had much time for socializing, and when he did he spent much of it solely with Amber. She'd voiced some reservations to Sherry about what it would take for longevity in the relationship, but if she was happy for the time being, Sherry was thrilled for her.

"Hi, Sherry. She missed you, too. Yes, we had a very nice time," Officer Sedgeman said. His aviator sunglasses, square chin, and police cap perched on his head commanded respect as much as his deep crisp voice. "Why don't you call me Troy?"

Sherry grimaced. "Can I address you as Officer Sedgeman on duty and Troy off duty? Just feels right."

"Fine," he said. "Whatever makes you comfortable."

"Is Trooper up for the job today?" Sherry asked. Immediately she wanted to take back the casual question. Her nerves, in such an unfamiliar situation, had gotten the better of her. She looked down at the majestic Belgium Malinois with the soul-piercing glare in his eyes.

"Trooper will have reinforcement. Honor is here. He's a yellow Labrador retriever with full water cadaver search certification." The officer pointed to an SUV marked *K-9 UNIT* in a large bold font across the door. The imposing gunmetal gray vehicle also had *Connecticut State Police* emblazoned down the side. "We'll leave Honor in the car while Trooper works the dock."

"Poor Trooper," Sherry lamented. "He's being upstaged."

"The investigation needs to cover all bases. Land and water. Specialization has merits. Labradors are better suited for the water," Officer Sedgeman said. "Both breeds are trainable, trustworthy and nose smart, but the Lab has the extra edge of exhibiting a high degree of water comfort. Trooper has a role here," Officer Sedgeman said. He patted Trooper on the head. The mink brown dog with the elegant black tips on his ears, spine, and tail was surveying his surroundings. He sat at attention at the officer's side, receiving comments of admiration from anyone in proximity. His ears pricked when his name was mentioned, but at the same time he never took his gaze off the area in front of him, as if he were assessing his next move.

"My new boots will be ruined," Thomas said upon arrival. "This slushy mud is snow spackle."

Sauntering in along with Thomas, Lilya wedged herself next to Sherry. "Good morning, Detective. Good morning, Sherry."

Lilya wore a shiny black down coat and knee-high boots that were more appropriately suited to a runway than the day's sloppy conditions, Sherry noted. The difference was, unlike Thomas, Lilya wasn't complaining. She must have boots to spare if she didn't mind ruining a pair in the mud and ice. Ray's greeting to Lilya was barely audible. That absence of enthusiasm wasn't going to get him a dinner date with her.

"Trooper's going to locate the path Mr. Helguvson made from his car to his alleged demise off the dock," Ray said. "And Honor's on water duty. Thomas, did you bring something of Sigmund's?" he asked.

"Sure did. I'll get Sigmund's sweater. The one I brought I've seen him where all winter long," Thomas said. He disappeared around the police pickup truck.

"Sweater?" Lilya asked. "For the scent?"

"That's right," Ray said. "Trooper picks up the target scent off the garment and locks it in. Given the command to track he goes in search of the scent."

It wasn't long before Thomas reappeared from behind the police truck. "Here you go." He handed Ray a large plastic bag. "Let me add, this is a waste of time." Was that a smirk Sherry saw pass over Thomas's face? "A search on a desert island might bring more fruitful results."

True to style, Ray ignored the snarky comment. He tipped his fedora-covered head in the direction of the Lab being released from the police SUV. "Honor and his handler, Officer Glover, will wait their turn while Trooper performs his duties."

"Gold star for Augustin seeing the value of Trooper and a shared water search dog," Sherry said. "We're not always behind the times." Her gaze drifted toward Thomas.

He nodded his head in silent acknowledgment.

"If you all wouldn't mind taking a few steps back," Ray said. He directed Sherry, Thomas and Lilya to a location several feet from the dock, where they could view Trooper and Officer Sedgeman while not interfering with the tracking exercise. Before Sherry followed the others, she leaned in toward Ray.

"This is something of Patti's. After Trooper's tracked Sigmund's scent, would he be able to tell us whether Patti was on the dock?" She dug in her coat pocket and pulled out a tissue. The next step was to capture the licorice tin Patti had donated to Sherry nestled deep inside her coat pocket.

Ray accepted the tissue-wrapped candy tin. "Okay. After Trooper tracks Sigmund's scent."

The fact the request was granted with such ease left Sherry shocked. She decided not to press her good fortune by suggesting Thomas donate an article of clothing to the exercise in order to clear himself off the suspect list. Still, she couldn't resist a follow-up request to press a point.

"If she was, would he be able to tell us whether Patti could toss a full-sized human into the water?"

"I'm choosing to ignore that last request." Ray refocused on the surrounding activity. "Okay, folks. I'll need quiet while Officer Sedgeman and Trooper are working the dock and grounds."

Sherry secured a spot close to Lilya. A respectful silence swept over the onlookers. Lake ice shifting with a grinding screech was the only noise Sherry could hear. She watched as Trooper familiarized himself with the scent of Sigmund's sweater. The dog was given the command to track. His tail was wagging in an instant. His nose followed a path that led from the parking lot to the head of the dock.

"He's tracking a scent, but it could be anything," Lilya whispered. "A rabbit, another dog, a visitor from this morning."

"The scent he's picked up on is the same scent that's on that sweater. That was what his handler told him to pick up on," Sherry said.

"Thomas touched the sweater," Lilya said. "Doesn't that taint the results? The science of all this seems inconclusive."

"Another reason this is a waste of time," Thomas said.

"Thomas, did you walk on the dock today?" Sherry asked.

"Not today," Thomas said. "We just got here."

"Then Trooper shouldn't detect your scent on the dock. Now, if you were there within the last few days, well, then that's something to investigate," Sherry said.

Trooper's tail wag grew more intense as he fixated on a path toward the end of the dock. He began to whine and bark in a vigorous rhythm.

"Is he going to jump off the end of the dock?" Lilya asked with concern.

Sherry didn't know the answer. It sure looked like the dog might get carried away with his success and not give up the trail, no matter where it led. The momentum of Trooper's tail wag seemed enough to swing him over the edge if the footing was slippery. A moment later Trooper assumed a sitting position at the edge of the dock, overlooking the icy water. Officer Sedgeman carefully picked his way to the dog's side, slipping once or twice on black ice.

"He has a hit. He alerts his handler with a change in his body language. The wriggling, whining, those guttural noises he's making. You can't miss the change in his behavior. I learned all this from the last murder investigation I was involved in," Sherry explained.

Lilya's sights were fixed on the action on the dock.

"Good boy, good boy," the officer said as he ruffled Trooper's neck fur. He motioned a thumbs-up in Ray's direction. "Did you record the find?" he called back to Ray.

Ray lowered his phone from his eyes. "Sure did. Good job, guys."

The time had come for Trooper's reward. Once he was off the dock a swinging tug toy enticed him to join a rollicking game of keep away, putting the dog in carefree frisky mode.

"That was interesting," Thomas said as he passed by the dog enjoying his free time. He paused to study Trooper. "Even though all we learned is what we already knew. Sigmund was here, he was on the dock, and he went to the edge, if not over the edge and into the lake. He could easily have gotten out. Stunt complete. Maybe." He scratched his head. "Lilya, let's get down to the water's edge. The other dog is putting on a show down there."

"Sherry, are you coming?" Lilya asked. With one motion she slid down her snow mound to level ground with the balance and proficiency of someone who'd done the trick many times before.

"Go ahead. I'll be there soon," Sherry said.

When Lilya and Thomas were out of hearing range, Sherry caught Ray's attention. He nodded. Ray approached the tug toy game and called for a time-out. After explaining his change in plans to Officer Sedgeman, Trooper was led back to the dock with Ray bringing up the rear. Ray unveiled the candy tin and presented it to Trooper for examination. How Trooper flipped a switch from play back to duty was beyond Sherry. He was given the track command and retraced his steps around and along the dock. His tail remained stationary. His enthusiasm was there, but rather than becoming increasingly excited, Trooper went about his business in a sedate manner. He walked the dock twice and returned to his handler, head hung.

"Every search is a success," Officer Sedgeman said. "Even if he comes up empty." The tug toy was offered to Trooper and happily accepted.

"Good job again, boys," Ray said. "Let's get down to the boat." Ray carried the candy tin over to Sherry. "Patti wasn't on the dock." He placed the tin in Sherry's outstretched glove.

"Who else was here?" Sherry asked.

"We'll see," Ray said. "Come on." He wasn't interested in any more conversation about what could be. Ray turned and followed the trampled snow trail down to the boat launch. Sherry traced his steps before joining Lilya to witness Honor's performance.

"May I ask you what the difference is in duties between the dogs, Trooper and Honor?" Lilya asked as she examined Honor from a respectable distance.

Officer Glover squatted down to outfit Honor with a vest Sherry had seen other dogs at the Augustin Marina wearing as they boarded boats. Honor's vest was labeled *K-9 Unit Search*. On the bridge of the vest was a substantial handle.

"I was explaining to Sherry, Honor's a specialized cadaver dog," the officer said. "He can smell a human body or a body part one hundred feet under water." The pride in the officer's voice attracted a glance of pride from Honor.

"What's the handle for on his vest?" Sherry asked.

"In case he gets into trouble in the water and can't scramble back on board on his own. These dogs are tenacious in succeeding at whatever is asked of them, even to the point of overexertion. Or he may fall in the water. The boat we're using today is perfect for Honor to get as close to the water as possible, but accidents happen. The boat's rubber edging is slippery. Safety of the animal is paramount."

"And his difference from Trooper?" Lilya asked.

"Trooper's a search-and-rescue dog in an instance such as this," Troy said. "He's trained in tracking, criminal apprehension, bomb sniffing and narcotics detection. His nose is thousands of times more sensitive than a human's. This breed has been known to detect cancer in humans by the unique scent emitted. He is so good at what he does we decided to keep his training as is and let another superpower dog cover cadaver search. Dogs can feel stress like humans if too much is asked of them."

"How long does the water search and cadaver dog certification take?" Sherry asked.

"Honor needed one thousand hours of training for that cert. That's about a year and a half or more."

"Fascinating," Sherry said. "All these facts about our canine heroes never get old."

"Excuse me. I'm needed over there," Officer Glover said as he turned his attention to another officer unhitching the boat from a trailer near the water's edge. Sherry estimated the sturdy boat was about twenty feet long. The perimeter was covered in rubber. The dog would have an easier time resting his body on the supple tacky surface rather than a slippery, wooden, traditional boat deck. Ray trudged over, surveying the water in front of him.

"What an amazing dog, Ray," Sherry said. "Both dogs. Do they get along? Sometimes two alphas may have an ego clash." Marla's apt description of the sparring bulls crossed her mind.

"That's when the handler's experience will come in handy."

"Does his handler have to direct his dog through every inch to search?" Lilya asked.

"These dogs are so intelligent they're able to make decisions on their own. There've been many times Trooper, and I'm sure Honor, have sidestepped their instructions and gone rogue on a location when they know something is there that the handler doesn't have the ability to sense. When the handler is wrong, the dog must let the handler know. That's known as intelligent disobedience."

Lilya shook her head in amazement. "I may lose my job to one of these two."

Chapter 15

"The weather's cooperating," Sherry said. "The ice looks really thin in spots thanks to the warmer temperature."

"The boat's in the water, so that's a start," Ray said.

Off to Sherry's side, Lilya whispered in Thomas's ear. At the same time the boat's engine was fired up. Thomas uttered a reply, but Sherry couldn't make it out.

"Sherry, did you hear me?" Thomas asked.

"No, sorry. Boat's too noisy. What did you say?" Sherry asked.

"Did you hear about Patti's accident?" Thomas said.

"Accident? What happened? Is she alright?" Sherry's words grew frantic. "I haven't heard a thing."

Sherry searched Ray's expression for confirmation. He made a slight head bob.

"Seems she fell down the stairs at her workplace," Thomas said. "The security guard found her all tangled up with herself in the stairwell. She didn't remember much about how she got there. Only said she took the stairs because the elevator was out again. She's pretty bruised up and may have broken her arm trying to cushion her fall."

"I know she had a bad knee and was struggling when the elevator was out of commission the day we had our interviews. Temperamental elevator," Sherry scolded. Her words said one thing, but her harsh tone was meant for Ray, who she held accountable for not keeping her abreast of her friend's situation. Why was that? He was making a habit of doing that. He was so open with his findings not long ago.

"She was coming over here this morning at my request," Thomas said. "And Detective Bease's."

"We were very interested in her reaction to today's goings-on," Lilya said. "When the search concludes, she'd have to swallow the fact Sigmund's charade is over and everyone knows the truth."

"Or not," Sherry added with a sigh. She turned her attention to Ray. "You didn't think I should know about Patti's accident?"

Ray puffed out his cheeks. Sherry wasn't interested in making Ray squirm with discomfort so much as nudging him to consider she had feelings invested in the case. Job before social obligations was always Ray's modus operandi, but hadn't she earned herself a different set of rules?

"I'm not in charge of what you know and don't know, Sherry. If that's a problem I ask we sort this matter out at a different time and venue. I'm on duty. Work first." His gaze was hijacked by a car pulling into the parking lot. A moment later Gunnar and Carl slammed their car doors and joined Thomas at his side. Hearty greetings were traded.

Without a word Sherry questioned Lilya with a glance.

"They're here to support Thomas," Lilya said. "Quite a band of brothers they are. It would have served Sigmund well to have stayed in their good graces. They look out for one another."

"You don't think one of them had anything to do with his demise, do you?" Sherry asked.

"Food for thought," Lilya said without meeting her gaze.

"I like that expression," Sherry said. "Apropos for many occasions."

Ray walked the short distance to have a word with Gunnar and Carl. Probably filling them in on what had already occurred, Sherry imagined. After a brief conversation they dispersed and began the slippery walk to the lakeshore. As Ray passed Sherry and Lilya he told them the search was ready to begin. If they wanted to relocate, the time had come. Lilya took her cue and headed to where the men had formed a pack of onlookers.

"It's a little awkward for me that Carl and Gunnar showed up," Sherry said. "They're two of the three judges at the cook-off on Tuesday, but hey, I could run into them anywhere, right? Why not at a mutual acquaintance's search scene?"

"From what I've experienced with you and cook-offs, much stranger things can happen than running into a judge or two at a cadaver search," Ray said.

"I have a confession," Sherry said. "In all honesty, I'm coming round to the fact Sigmund would get himself out of hot water if he left his old life behind. He got plenty of people mad as hornets in his wake. Morphing into Sigmund 2.0 would buy himself some breathing room. The fact these guys would come to support Thomas is a strong indication how tight the bond is between them all. If Sigmund ran into trouble and alienated himself, maybe his recovery was beyond his capability."

"Lilya and Thomas are getting to you?" Ray asked.

"Their perspective is enticing," Sherry said.

"No sense speculating. We're here to dig up the truth. The truth may be at the bottom of this lake."

A few yards ahead Lilya waved from the top of a snow mound she had ascended. Sherry returned a wave. Lilya pointed to a neighboring snow mound waiting to be climbed for the perfect view of the proceedings.

"Are you still planning on a dinner with Lilya?" Sherry whispered. "The timing seems off until there's a break in this case."

"I'm not sure. I'm working on my recipe," Ray said. "No rush. Work comes first."

"I've heard that somewhere," Sherry said.

"Hold up, Glover," Ray called out. "Follow me. I need to see if Honor needs Sigmund's scent article to pick up on?" He began walking briskly toward the boat. Sherry didn't bother trying to keep up, her goal was to accept Lilya's invitation to climb a neighboring mound of snow. She reached the perch and staked her claim. Ray was still within six feet of her.

"You still have the sweater," Sherry said.

Ray kept his sights on the boat while addressing Sherry. "Glover said Honor doesn't necessarily need the scent. He'll pick up any decomposing odor, whatever the origin. That's his job today." He cupped his hands around his mouth. "Glover, you set to launch?"

"We are."

Ray scanned the attendants. "Everyone, figure out where you want to spend the next couple minutes. We are about to begin the water search. Once you're in position, freeze in place until Honor has completed his work. He'll either give an alert or we'll ascertain the victim in question isn't where we thought he was. The dog will get his reward treat for a job well done."

"I'll do most anything for a treat," Sherry whispered to Lilya, hoping to lighten the tension. The whisper traveled beyond Lilya. The expression on Ray's face implied her humor was mistimed. Sherry realized her hands were losing heat inside her gloves and her fingers were aching. She inhaled a long breath and watched Honor and Officer Glover board the boat.

"Glover, use every precaution for safety's sake," Ray called out. "Conditions are tricky."

"Yes, sir," Glover responded. "We're restricted by the ice thickness. The fact is, we don't need to go far out. I'll be on the stern with Honor. The engine will be idling unless we need to correct our course. Honor will detect a body if there is one down there. He can detect decomposition of human remains up to thirty meters under water from the boat's edge. Not necessarily the body we're looking for, but if one's down there, he is ninety-nine point nine percent capable of detecting it. He may lean overboard and lap up some water, that's just his way of confirming a find." Officer Glover leaned down to recheck the dog's vest.

"What if a body is found and it's beyond recognition?" Sherry asked.

"We have Thomas Helguvson here to ID the body if it's preserved. With the cold temps since the man's disappearance, the body should be well preserved," Ray said. He lowered his voice and stepped off his snow hill. He took a step closer to Sherry. "Monitoring Thomas's reaction to any find may prove invaluable. Your input on that matter is too."

"If I can, I will."

"You're dismissed before we pull anything up onto the boat."

Sherry cringed. "I appreciate that."

The lake's icy surface was becoming translucent with the warmth of the sun. Sherry had trouble distinguishing the ice thickness as the shades of grays and blues were varying. Unreliable guesswork was the best bet from her vantage point. If Sigmund's body had entered the lake at that location of the thinner ice circle, Honor had a distinguishable search area to isolate.

A moment later, Sherry lost confidence in her guesstimate when other discolored patches of ice became visible. Telltale bubbles trapped under thinner ice layers branched off in all directions. She wondered if the body may have drifted. Snow squalls, wind and temperature fluctuations may have played havoc on the selected search location. Honor's success was growing questionable. For Patti's sake, Sherry rooted for any solid outcome to bring closure for her friend.

The small boat's engine rumbled as the driver increased the power. A cloud of vapor rose from the rear of the boat. Paddles were balancing on the lip of the stern. Sherry considered they might be a better alternative to the engine for such a confined search. She supposed the motor was needed to power through any ice blocks. Honor sat poised on the bow of the boat. Officer Glover threw his arm over the dog's shoulder.

Sherry took inventory of the crowd gathered to witness Honor at work. Thomas and Lilya were within arm's length of Sherry, while Carl and Gunnar flanked their friends to form a wall of eager onlookers. Trooper and Officer Sedgeman provided support on the edge of the lake at the boat's launch point.

Ray called out to the boat, "All set," to which Officer Glover replied with a thumbs-up.

The hull of the sturdy, compact boat whined and screeched as it scraped through any ice it encountered. The squealing and crunching of the boat's hard rubber bumper against the ice gnawed at Sherry's ears. The driver wasn't taking the boat far. He was bisecting a circle of thin ice to widen the area of visibility. Ray explained all the action would take place within twenty-five yards of the dock. The driver used the lowest gear, alternating with idling, so as not to churn up the lake.

After a circle of cracked ice was formed by the bashing of the boat's hull, the driver cut the engine. The crisp winter air was still and the sound of the activity on the boat traveled with clarity. Sherry could decipher Officer Glover's command for Honor to enter search mode. Honor had his body crouched as if he were about to pounce. His front paws were draped over the side of the boat. His nose began to intently scour the water surface. A few minutes passed. The quiet was occasionally interrupted by ice crackling and Honor's nails scratching the rubber rim of the boat as he repositioned. If Honor had detected any human remains, Sherry had seen no alerts.

Something suddenly occurred to her. She addressed her question to no one in particular. "If all of you are here, wouldn't Sigmund's wife want to be here, too? I mean, she's the one who has the most at stake with the results."

"Nora didn't want to be here if Patti were here," Lilya said. "And she was supposed to come. Right, Thomas?"

"That's right," Thomas said without removing his sights from the boat activity.

"Nora knows about Patti?" Sherry asked, raising her voice as the boat's hull crunched through more ice. She knew the answer but to hear it from the source was reinforcement.

"Yes, she does. My job is to keep her abreast of her husband's whereabouts. She needed to know sooner rather than later, as there'll be more news to come," Lilya said. "His whereabouts and goings-on. Good and bad. In these situations, I almost always am the one to break the heart-wrenching news to the wife. She had her suspicions Sigmund had moved on from being the adoring husband she married, but the reality of locating and naming the other woman is always a punch in the gut."

Sherry studied Lilya's face for any clue she was overstepping her boundaries with too many questions. Out of the corner of her eye, Honor's bobbing and head motions caught her attention. He began to whine and fuss. He vocalized a series of high-pitched barks that sliced through the air. If he could form a word from his vocalizations, Sherry wouldn't have been shocked.

Chapter 16

"Sir," Officer Glover called out. "We got something here. We've got an alert. Looks like a hit." He pointed to Honor, who had assumed a statuesque sitting pose. His nose was lifting and lowering as he made sense of the smells assaulting him.

Ray raised his hand to halt the boat's movement. The driver cut the engine again. Ray snapped several photos with his phone. As hard as it was to tear her gaze from the unfolding scene on the lake, Sherry shifted her sights to the onlookers to note their reactions to Honor's victory celebration. With heads bowed, Lilya and Thomas were engaged in a whisper session. To their sides, Carl and Gunnar were shifting their weight from leg to leg, arms crossed on their chests. The face of each was screwed up into a grimace. Neither appeared eager to witness what could be a gruesome find. Sherry assumed, as friends of the deceased, both men may have suddenly reconsidered lending their support to Thomas today.

Ray moved toward the water, presumably to obtain a clear vantage point. "I'll be on the dock to get a better look." His first footstep on the wooden planks went out from underneath him. He landed on his rear end with a groan.

"Ray, are you alright?" Sherry called out. She was swift getting to the edge of the mud puddle he landed in. A policeman arrived to offer a second hand.

"Thanks. I'm fine," Ray said as he flicked globs of snowy mud off his pants.

"Let me help," Sherry said as she swiped at the back of his coat. Along with a dusting of snow, a bit of soiled paper dropped down from his coat. She removed her gloves and collected the paper from the top of Ray's boot, then wiped it clean on the snow. She held her hand in front of Ray's face. "Ray, this is a licorice candy wrapper. It was stuck to your leg."

Ray was distracted with the commotion at the water's edge. He lowered his eyes as if Sherry were speaking a foreign language he couldn't translate.

"Yes, Sherry," Ray said. "If it's important I need to know. Licorice? Not my favorite."

"I agree," Sherry said. She stowed the candy wrapper in her pocket.

"Sir," the officer said, "Glover is signaling me to get down there ASAP."

"I'll be right there," Ray said. He turned to face Sherry. "I don't think you want to be here for whatever Honor's come up with. Good chance it's grisly. The guys will put on their wet suits and proceed to the recovery stage. I'll let you know how it goes."

"Can you text or call me with definitive results when you get a chance?" Sherry asked.

"Count on it. I need to know if you saw any reactions of note from the onlookers. Red flags. We'll talk later."

Sherry turned back toward her car. After a few steps Thomas intercepted her.

"Leaving?" Thomas asked. Not far behind him Lilya's gaze was trained on his movement.

"Detective Bease said I was dismissed. Looks like Honor's done his job. Now I have something concrete I can tell Patti. She's been through so much I wanted to lighten her worries."

"I wouldn't rush. Maybe wait until the police confirm the findings. Honor can find any body, it doesn't have to be my brother's. Who knows what's down deep in that water."

"If I didn't know any better, I'd say you sound as if you know something more than you're willing to admit," Sherry said as she squared up to Thomas. "If you do, please let Detective Bease know so he isn't wasting valuable time."

"No, no," Thomas said as he studied his muck-spattered boots. "All I know is the character of my brother. Reinventing himself to pull the wool over our eyes would be consistent with his past shenanigans. I'd hoped he'd changed and matured when he moved to the States. He had a promising business plan in place, importing Iceland's finest food products to the U.S. Even though that wasn't going as planned, his support system wasn't going to let him flounder."

"Just curious, did your brother import licorice candies? I hear the flavor is very popular in Iceland," Sherry said. Her fingertips were on the wrapper in her coat pocket.

"You Americans don't seem to share the passion for salty black licorice that we have," Thomas said. "One taste of the sweet and savory intense flavor and I'm back in my *amma's* kitchen."

"Amma?"

"*Amma* is Icelandic for *grandmother*. The candy got us through some tough times. I have only great associations with the sticky, gooey gumdrops even though I admit I haven't eaten it since I was a kid. I'm sure if Sig wasn't already importing licorice he would have been soon. It comes in lots of forms and varieties. If he were as savvy as he claimed, he'd know which form fits the American taste for sweets."

Sherry nodded. "Any form might be a hard sell."

Thomas peered back down to the water and took in the scene. The boat was drifting across the ice circle while Officer Glover praised Honor enthusiastically. Thomas returned his gaze to Sherry. "I hope your friend Patti didn't have a hand in steering my brother in the wrong direction. It didn't take much for him to follow the path of least resistance even if it led nowhere."

Sherry wasn't interested in pursuing a conversation about Patti's involvement. She recognized how Thomas glommed onto a theme and wouldn't let go, much like his newspaper's views on "improving" Augustin. She didn't like the narrow-mindedness. If he had the notion Patti was guilty of murder, he may have the influence and tenacity to persuade others. As she reflected in silence, Gunnar and Carl approached.

"Thomas, Carl and I have an appointment we can't miss," Gunnar said. He never made eye contact with Thomas. The vagueness of his proclamation wasn't lost on Sherry. The men didn't want to witness what Honor had discovered. They had done their part in supporting their friend, but beyond that weren't willing to sacrifice cementing a nasty image in their brains. She felt the same way.

"Thanks for being here, guys," Thomas said. "You're both ride or die. I appreciate that more than I can ever express." The men tipped their heads in an unspoken understanding only a tight friendship can attain. "I fully understand."

"We'll see you at the cook-off, Sherry," Carl said. He softened the tone of his voice and faced Thomas. "I'm sorry to ask, but is the cook-off still on? No matter what the outcome of the day?"

"Did you see how excited Sig was about the wooden spoon and all its uses?" Thomas asked. "We have to celebrate his love of food and all that preparing it entails by absolutely holding the cook-off. He wouldn't want it any other way."

Carl pulled up the sides of his mouth into a semi-authentic smile. Gunnar kicked an icicle with the toe of his boot. The two men nodded in unison.

"Thanks for coming. I appreciate the support," Thomas said. "Fraternity of Bankless Brothers forever." He threw up a single wave. "See you later." Thomas headed back down toward the lake.

Sherry had been waiting for the opportunity to ask the judges a question.

Reaching out to two out of three of them was a good start. "Mind if I ask what mistakes Sigmund made in the past that may have made him an enemy so vengeful?" Sherry asked.

Carl and Gunnar exchanged a look Sherry couldn't interpret. Gunnar lowered his head, deferring to his friend to answer.

"Many years ago," Carl said, "Sig needed his first restart. He had messed up a journalism job so severely he ruined his reputation and credibility in that field."

"Thomas was lucky not to become collateral damage, being Sig's brother. You know, guilt by association. Lucky for him, he came out unscathed," Gunnar said.

"After that time, Thomas, being a good brother, propped Sig up with a substantial loan to finance a new career after years of dipping his toe in various dead-end careers," Carl said. "Sig really does, I mean did, have a passion for Icelandic foods. It made sense his career moved in a food-related industry."

"The problem was he didn't know his market," Gunnar said. "Not only who he would sell to, but where he was getting his product from."

"He should have studied your trending expertise, right?" Sherry said with a smile.

"Very spot on," Gunnar said. "Iceland has a, shall we say, unique set of tastes that may not be universal. But that's okay. Knowing your market is the job."

"We all lent a hand as best we could. He made of mess of that too," Carl said.

"Sounds complicated," Sherry said. "How many messes can someone clean up before the mess gets on them?"

"Hard to say." Gunnar backed away.

"Sherry, are you heading out, too? We can walk you to your car," Carl suggested.

"Yes, sure, thanks," Sherry said.

Carl and Gunnar trudged through the slop in silence. Tagging along, Sherry couldn't resist one more glance at the rescue scene. It looked as if the pace of the search had slowed to a crawl as care was being taken to ensure Honor didn't get too encouraged by his find and fall in. The dog was being coaxed back to the belly of the boat by a tug toy waved around by Officer Glover. Sherry could hear Honor being bathed in accolades.

"We'll see you Tuesday," Carl said when they reached the line of parked cars. "Don't worry. None of today's activity will have any impact on our ability to judge your food fairly and impartially. We discussed the matter."

"I wasn't even concerned about that. There is life to carry on with, outside of cook-offs. The two can be separated. See you then," Sherry said.

Inside her car, Sherry placed a call. "Patti, can I stop by? Are you home? I'm bringing you a meal. It's leftover from my trial run for the cook-off." Sherry groaned. "The cook-off's probably the last thing you're thinking about. I heard you had an accident."

"How many falls can one gal take in a week? I shouldn't ask. I don't want to subscribe to saying that bad things come in threes. Although this might be the third if you count the loss of Sig. I don't know."

"Don't think that way. The run of bad luck will end soon."

"Sure. I admit the cook-off's not at the top my list of concerns right now, but if you have a completed trial run for me, I'll he happy to try it. I'm starving. Yes, please stop by. It'll be nice to have a distraction from trying to make my bruised body comfortable. I've gone from a limp to using a walker, which is challenging with my banged up arm. I feel pathetic," Patti whimpered. "I would love some of your cooking. I'm not sure I can make the cook-off at this rate. It might have to send Hammy in my place."

"I need you there for moral support. Do your darnedest to get well."

"Believe me, that's my goal. I've been looking forward to covering the cook-off. The theme is brilliant. Challenge great home cooks to concoct their take on a recipe from a foreign cuisine along with a short story about the inspiration behind their recipe. You home cooks never fail to astonish me with your creativity."

"You're reminding me I need to type up my story."

"I remember when I had the ability to type." Patti groaned.

"You'll be better in no time," Sherry said. Although she had no idea what the diagnosis was.

"Do me a favor and let yourself in when you get here, please. I'm trying to stay as stationary as possible."

"Will do. But I don't think it's a good idea to keep your door unlocked for long." Sherry sucked in a deep breath as she mulled over her choice of words when presenting Patti with the progress in the search for Sigmund. She decided the words would come as needed, in whatever form the mood dictated. Sherry checked her phone for the time. "I should be at your place in twenty minutes. I just need to pick up Marla and Chutney. We're working at the Ruggery this afternoon. We'll go there directly from your house."

Chapter 17

Sherry, Marla, and Chutney arrived at Patti's townhouse on schedule. Sherry brought a heaping helping of last night's dinner leftovers. They found Patti on the shabby chic off-white couch with both legs propped up on pillows. Sherry was slow to react when Chutney wedged his canine body next to the puffiest cushion Patti wasn't propped up on. The light-colored couch and Chutney's not-immaculately clean paws were not a good fit.

"Don't even think about it, Chutney," Sherry said. Her dog lowered his head and made a beeline for the kitchen, where Sherry knew he'd make himself useful by vacuuming up any crumbs on the floor.

"Hi, Patti." Sherry's tone was upbeat but hard to maintain when she saw Patti's unfortunate state. "You look a bit worse for wear. Thankfully not as bad as I imagined. Your legs took the brunt of the fall?" Sherry asked. When Patti shifted her body Sherry spotted more damage. An arm wrapped in a bandage. "Your poor arm. Is it broken?"

"My legs are black and blue. Bad elbow sprain. I was lucky. Nothing's broken," Patti said. "And I have a good-size bruise on my back. I'm sure someone shoved me hard from behind."

Sherry shuddered. "You didn't see anyone in the stairwell with you?"

"No, not until Clem found me. Thank goodness for his safety rounds, which he's vigilant about. The assailant was stealthy. I didn't hear anyone, but I felt an intense push for sure."

"Why were you in the stairwell and not the elevator? It can't still be broken, can it?" Marla asked.

"I was working late last night. The cook-off will get my full attention next week whether I can attend or not. In either case, I had to put this week's work to bed." Patti squirmed to find a comfortable recline. The sudden squint of her eyes said she hadn't found one. "Yes, the dang elevator was out again. It worked for a while. I rode it up to the office in the morning. By the end of the day, it conked out again. It's been difficult on one bad knee to climb four flights of stairs since I slipped on the ice. I shouldn't complain. Our poor cleaning lady, Beatrice, can't even work because her cleaning cart can't make it up the stairs. I know she needs the money."

"Always thinking of others," Sherry said.

"Not always. I'm thinking about getting myself back to work. What am I going to do? Everything hurts. Sorry, I'm so rude. And cranky. Please, have a seat."

Sherry spotted the empty glass on a table next to the couch. "We'll fill your glass. Water?"

"Please," Patti said. "I owe you both, big time."

"And I brought you a meal. We'll microwave it before we leave. Be right back."

Sherry found Chutney in the kitchen sniffing for goodies on the floor. She filled Patti's glass with tap water. She returned the glass to Patti's side table, next to a photo. "Sigmund. Was this taken in Iceland?" She picked up the picture and studied the subject.

"No, that was taken right here in Augustin. At Harmony Lake. He loved the spot. Said it was an exact replica of the lake he grew up next to. He learned to skate and play hockey on it."

Marla nodded her head. "Harmony Lake does have that far north vibe in the winter."

"I wanted to frame the photo. Up until I heard about Nora. His wife," Patti said. She reached for the glass of water. "You two are the best." The strength of her voice diminished. "Thanks for the water. And the food."

"Our pleasure," Marla said.

"When did you hear about Nora, if you don't mind me asking?" Sherry said.

"I think I had the feeling in my gut before my brain could accept the truth," Patti said.

"There were signs?" Sherry asked.

"Sig's car, for one."

"His car?" Marla asked. "How so?"

"He had to delete a driver preference profile before he added me. I told you. I didn't even want him to add me. Why would I? I have my own car. I think he thought it was a sign of his commitment. I didn't."

"Maybe he just needed a safety net driver for some reason and the person he deleted didn't live close by anymore," Marla suggested.

"I saw the name as he was deleting it. It said Nora G. Unless that was his sister or a previous girlfriend, I was a little suspicious," Patti said. "It wasn't long before that name popped up again."

"How so?" Sherry said.

"I put the discovery of the prior driver profile out of my mind because when I asked him about his home life back in Iceland, he described a bachelor's life. I believed him. Until I saw him downtown buying a valentine's card last week. At Augustin Dry Goods."

Sherry nodded. "A store that carries everything for every need."

"I agree," Patti said. "The store doesn't look like much from the outside but it's a potpourri of treasures. They stock the best greeting cards. You go in to purchase picture hangers or an Augustin tee-shirt and come out with ten more items plus a wonderful birthday card or get well soon card. That's the beauty of our town. What you don't see at first glance is what you get, and more. You need to get to know the place to learn all that's offered."

"That reminds me, I need to pick up a birthday card and a valentine's card. For some reason Don's mother decided it was a good idea to give birth to him on a major holiday and cook-off day," Sherry said with a laugh.

"Count your lucky stars, I say. I won't be giving or receiving a valentine's card this year. I had already scrapped my plans to send Sig one I picked out. Know anyone who needs an unused card?" Patti pointed to a small paper bag on the coffee table at the foot of the couch.

Marla's gaze lingered on the bag.

"Take it. It'll be a long time before I trust again."

"Okay, thanks," Marla said as she scooped up the bag. "My hubby deserves a secondhand card for all he does." Her thankful smile briefly warmed the otherwise darkening mood.

"Why did you scrap your plans to send Sig a card if you saw him buying you one?" Sherry asked. "At that point you weren't one hundred percent positive he wasn't single. Were you?"

"At the store Sig didn't see me, and I didn't want to spoil his surprise, so I didn't approach him. He had his hand on a darling card adorned with a puppy and a cupid and hearts galore decorating the envelope. I was thrilled. The next day after we ate lunch together, I walked him to his car. After a proper goodbye, he got in and I noticed a stamped pink envelope decorated with hearts on the passenger seat. The same envelope he was holding at the store. The name on the envelope was Nora Helguvson. Nora G. from the driver profile, I deduced. My heart broke."

"I'm sorry," Sherry said. "What day was that?"

"The day I interviewed you and the judges for the podcast. I took a late lunch break with Sig after you all left."

"You mentioned having an argument with him," Sherry said.

"The tension between us had been building. He'd shut down about so many subjects. When I'd told him earlier his brother would be coming to my office while I recorded a podcast with the three cook-off judges, he boiled over. My intention was to promote a brotherly reunion of sorts. That backfired big time. I didn't like his attitude about my work, so I fought back. He wasn't making much sense at that point. I thought he had calmed down, but in the office he picked right back up again with Thomas."

"Trouble in one area of your life never fails to bleed over to the rest of your life," Sherry said. "No matter how much you pretend to compartmentalize."

"Lesson learned. Fool me once, shame on you, fool me twice, shame on me." Patti glanced at the paper bag in Marla's hand. "Any news about Sigmund's murder?"

"That's one of the reasons we stopped by."

"Yesterday, Thomas asked me to show up today at Harmony Lake for the body search. It caused me all sorts of anxiety. I don't hate Sig. I don't wish bad things on him. No one should die before their time. Then I took a spill, and I couldn't go in any case," Patti said.

"Thomas asked you specifically?" Sherry asked.

"The pessimist side of me told me Thomas only wanted me there to watch me squirm. He still thinks I had a hand in whatever's going on with Sig."

"I have breaking news on that front." Sherry's next thought was she didn't want Patti to get overly worked up and hurt herself. Unfortunately, there was no other way to do this other than dishing out the cold hard truth. "Detective Bease, plenty of police officers, and a land water rescue team are at Harmony Lake as we speak. I was calling you from the parking lot." Sherry paused, assessing Patti's reaction.

Patti shifted her position and steeled her back, but made no attempt at a reply, so Sherry continued.

"The Connecticut State Police cadaver dog, Honor, made a find just before I left the lake."

Patti perked up. "You didn't stay for the outcome?"

"No. Ray wasn't keen on me being there when the body was dredged up. Frankly, neither was I."

"That's it, then. No more foolish talk of Sig faking his death to avoid all the trouble he seems to be in." Patti's matter-of-fact assessment calmed Sherry's fear her friend might have an emotional reaction she couldn't quell. Patti closed her eyes. When she blinked them open, she calmly said, "I'm not off the hook, am I." It wasn't a question.

Chapter 18

"There's no way to sugarcoat it. Thomas thinks you had something to do with Sigmund's disappearance. Since he does, Sigmund's wife's private investigator has you front and center on the suspect list, too," Sherry said.

Chutney returned from the kitchen licking his lips. He parked himself at the foot of the couch. The dog's entrance created a necessary pause in the conversation. Sherry used the break to mentally run through the facts. Patti didn't know about Nora's existence much before Sigmund's disappearance. The elevator at the MediaPie building wasn't functioning late in the day Patti was injured. Coincidence? Why exactly did Thomas want Patti to be present at Harmony Lake during the search for any remains? Was his request for show because he knew her accident would occur prior to the search and, in her absence, she couldn't provide information she may be sitting on?

"I know he does," Patti said. "Who else was at the lake today?"

"Carl Carlson and Gunnar V., Thomas's good buddies, were there to offer support. And Lilya, the private investigator. Nora's private investigator."

"None of them would consider my innocence, I assume," Patti said. "Was Sienna there? The other judge?"

"No, not Sienna. Why do you think she would go?" Sherry asked.

"Just asking," Patti said.

"What's most important, now that the body's been found, is providing an alibi for the night Sigmund went to the lake and never returned, leaving behind his phone in shallow water, his coat torn and disheveled on the icy dock and a wooden spoon broken and bloodied," Sherry said.

Patti remained silent.

Sherry forged ahead. "That'll put an end to Thomas and Lilya's accusations."

"That night I worked late trying to edit the podcast, finding I was probably going to need to filter out the noisy argument from the waiting room that was bleeding into the podcast production. I was evaluating my options. I was nearly done when I got a text from Sig asking to meet him at Harmony Lake around seven p.m."

"But you were too busy to go," Sherry said. "If the guard at MediaPie can vouch for when you left, later that night, you're set."

"Clem can't help me because I did go down to the lake that night." Patti heaved an exhale. "I didn't see Clem when I left the building, which is unusual but not out of the realm of possibility. He must have been on break. I remember feeling unsafe in the empty building. When Clem's not around to log me out, procedures malfunction. I find the lobby kind of creepy that late in the day when only the sparse stragglers are around."

"At least you blew a hole in one of Ray's theories, that you intentionally tracked Sigmund's car to the lake with your phone in order to catch him in a setting conducive to murder."

"I was wondering how long that would take to get out, that he had me on his car app. I didn't want to be on the darn app at all, but he insisted."

"Okay, that can be explained," Sherry said, not defeated. "How long did you stay at the lake?"

"I didn't stay long because the footing was nearly impossible for me and my bruised knee to navigate."

"Did you make contact with Sigmund once you were there?" Sherry asked. "Did you talk to him?"

"I drove into the park entrance and parked in the visitor lot. It was so dark. The lot isn't lit. The moonlight was muffled. Clouds had rolled in and snow was beginning to fall. Very beautiful, but the whole time I had such an uneasy feeling in the pit of my stomach. I couldn't locate another car, but I know there are other small lots throughout the park," Patti said.

"What reason did Sig give you for meeting him at the lake that night? I mean, you'd had an argument, you'd seen the valentine *not* addressed to you in his car and he'd been making a fuss for some time. I'd think asking you to meet him at a dark isolated location wouldn't be ideal," Sherry said.

Patti sighed. "I'm a fool. He said he had something to explain to me that had to be done in person."

"But why so urgent? Couldn't the matter wait until the morning?" Sherry asked.

"Honestly, I didn't ask. In my heart of hearts, I knew we were breaking up and he was going to tell me he was married. I figured let it be where he's comfortable to tell the truth," Patti said.

"Awfully trusting of you." Marla shook her head.

"At the time I didn't give the fact I might be putting myself in danger an ounce of consideration. He's emotional but not violent."

Sherry took a moment to let Patti sort out her thoughts. Her friend was gazing off into the distance. When she focused again, Sherry continued. "Any other reason he needed to talk to you in person immediately that you can think of? Like maybe he was in danger and didn't know if he'd be alive the next day?"

"That's crossed my mind," Patti said.

"So, if you even considered that scenario maybe you can identify the source of the threat?" Sherry asked. At her side Marla was hanging on every word. She was leaning in so close to Patti she almost fell off the couch waiting for the reply.

"He had several problems. Hey, we all do, right?" Patti said.

"True, but luckily, it's not the norm to end up dead from them," Sherry said.

"Sig was in deep financial trouble. I wouldn't lend him money. A rule I have. I won't do it. He drank too much when the pressure mounted. He was working on that."

"Good rule of thumb, not to lend money," Marla said. "Hard to stick to. Was he angry about that?"

"Surprisingly he took my refusal pretty well. He was combative and pouty but that's nothing new. His business was on its last legs. He blamed the American palate, bad advice and lack of a dependable support system. It might have been where his decision to not share his life with me backfired. I may be a fool but I'm not an idiot. I wouldn't even consider lending money to someone so closed off. If he had any possibility left to repair his ties to Thomas, his brother would be his best bet and that's what I suggested to him."

"It still doesn't narrow down who might have had such a problem with him that murder was the only way out," Sherry said. "That's the missing puzzle piece."

"What did you do after you parked at the lake that night?" Marla asked.

"I waited in the car for a bit. I remember a thick burst of snow before the squall ended. I took a few steps, nearly lost my footing and bailed out. The lake has a sign posted, *No visitors after dark*. I don't break rules. Even for someone I care deeply about. Those weren't the only reasons I made a hasty retreat for the car."

"Why is that? What happened?" Marla asked.

"There was a car pulling out of nowhere while I was flip-flopping about being there. I was on my way back to my car. I caught a glimpse of the driver in some sort of sedan."

"Who was it?" Sherry and Marla spoke in unison.

"If I had to give an ID on the driver this very minute, I'd have to say it was Sienna Warren," Patti said.

"The cookbook author?" Marla asked. "The guest at your podcast?"

"The same."

"Why do you think it was her?" Marla asked.

"Her winter hat is distinctive. One I've never seen before. I asked her about it at the interview. Where I might buy a similar one. She said it was a gift and wasn't sure where to buy one," Patti said. "I think she didn't want to be twins so she withheld the information."

"I'd think since you could only see her head through the car window you can't be fully certain," Sherry said.

"I'm pretty sure. For all I knew Sig summoned her down to the lake, too," Patti added. "He might have told all his girlfriends the jig was up that night. I didn't want to play second fiddle if Sienna had just been with him. I was already in a funk over spotting the valentine in his car. Seeing her sealed the deal. I shouldn't be there. I turned the car around and went home, where I should have gone in the first place." Patti shook her head. "What am I saying? I was already second fiddle to his wife."

"Three's a crowd, you're right," Marla said. Another example of her sister's forthrightness. Sherry simultaneously admired Marla's honesty and silently admonished her lack of sensitivity.

Patti tried to straighten up. After one attempt she grimaced. Putting on a brave face was difficult when one's face is the only part of the body that wasn't screaming in pain.

"Do you think Sienna saw you?" Sherry said.

"She had to have seen me creeping over the snow."

A cascade of questions flooded Sherry's mind. She left them unasked. The timing was off. The person with the answers wasn't present.

Patti read one of Sherry's thoughts. "When I was outside the car, my head was bobbing up and down trying to sort out snow from ice under my feet while being careful to avoid low-hanging branches."

Sherry couldn't conceal her disappointment. With no clear alibi Patti was in trouble. "We'll figure this out."

Patti adjusted her posture again. Every time she did Sherry's stomach fluttered with sympathy pains.

"Sherry, I don't think you should participate in the cook-off. Look what happened to me. Someone pushed me down the stairs. Maybe it was Sienna. Maybe it was Thomas. It was definitely someone who does not have my best interests in mind. If they know you're my ally, you're a target."

"I'm not at all concerned," Sherry said. Her words spilled out before her brain had a chance to sort the facts. Her spontaneous positivity was a perk of Don's influence on her. It wasn't more than a few years ago being anxious about every uncontrollable detail in her life left her constantly exhausted. Don taught her to let go and enjoy. The energy she gained from that shift in behavior resulted in fewer headaches and more smiles. For him to flash through her thoughts at a time like this was an affirmation of her love for him. She realized she was smiling. The corners of Marla's mouth turned up. Could she know what Sherry was thinking?

"You should be. Sig's been murdered," Patti said. "His brother is the main sponsor of the cook-off. Did Thomas murder Sig? How about his wife? She sure had her motives. One way or another, anything could happen to you if the murderer thinks you're in any way involved in the investigation. And it won't be good. You'll pull out, won't you?"

"On the contrary, I need to take part. It's essential. I made recipe preparations to win the darn thing, and the connections to Sig's murder are too strong. There's a piece of the puzzle waiting to be discovered, I know it."

"Her mind is made up," Marla said. "I've seen her like this and nothing's going to stop her."

"I couldn't live with myself if I didn't warn you. Someone's out there with a weapon and I don't want you to get hit by the shrapnel," Patti said.

"Your mind should be on getting better," Sherry said. She maintained a brave face while her insides were icing over as she absorbed Patti's warning. "Marla and I are going to work at the store. On our way I'd like to stop at the MediaPie Center City Studios and have a look at the elevator, which seems to have a mind of its own as to when it does and doesn't work. Would you be able to contact Hammy and have him sign us in as visitors with the pretense Marla and I are picking something up for you at your office?" Sherry asked.

"Since when did you become an elevator mechanic?" Marla asked her sister.

"I don't know what you're looking for, but I'll do it," Patti said.

"I'm not sure what I'm looking for either, but I'll know it when I find it," Sherry said with a sigh.

"Now, how about warming up my meal before you go? All this intrigue has me starving."

Chapter 19

The *Coastal County Beacon* News Center was a pretentious building that caught Sherry's eye each time she strolled passed. When the media company moved in the bigwigs reimagined the building's staid brick exterior. The alterations resulted in a building void of the traditional colonial façade prevalent on most of the Augustin storefronts. What they came up with fit their business plan to a T. Sherry surprised herself that she had a growing admiration for the modern tilt of the structure. She had to admit, the building's bold attitude made a statement. Some referred to it as an eyesore. Her fear was that the height of the commercial building after additional floors were added, making it the tallest in Augustin, would attract copycats. Unchecked numbers of tall buildings would transform downtown's rustic character. A controlled dose of hustle and bustle was desirable, but to urbanize the historic coastal community was to crush its quaint core.

The thought dissolved when two television satellite trucks roared up to the building and parked at the curb. People were rushing in and out of the building's massive, mirrored glass doors, presumably executing all manner of media production. Her heart rate increased as she was caught up in the frenzy of activity outside the building, only slowing when she turned the corner toward the next block.

The buildings shrank in size and impression as she, Marla, and Chutney continued toward the MediaPie Center City Studios. The charm of New England's simplistic functional building design returned in full force as they neared Patti's workplace. The cityscape ahead of her was minimalistic and manageable.

Patti texted that Hammy was putting a package together and Sherry and company were on the security guard's list of approved picker-uppers. As the trio neared the building Sherry told Marla her plan.

"We're going up to the fourth floor to get Patti's package from Hammy."

The double doors swung open. The lobby was a monotone space with a scuffed marble floor and textured gray walls. A small area with cushioned seats invited a few visitors to sit but no one was taking up the offer.

"I can stay down here with Chutney," Marla offered as they neared the guard. She backed up a step toward an inviting high-backed armchair.

"I need you to come. Once we're up there, there's something I'll be looking for. I need your set of eyes, too."

They approached the block of a man in uniform. In front of him, two women in smart business suits were talking. The security guard was busy checking his clipboard and reading credentials worn around the visitors' necks. When the women were logged in Sherry stepped forward.

"Afternoon, ladies. May I help you?" the guard asked. He bent down to pat Chutney on the head.

"We're here to pick up a package for Patti Mellit," Sherry said. "She's on bed rest but you can't keep a good employee down. She needs some background material for her latest story. Her intern, Hammy, should have put us on the list." Sherry eyed the clipboard in the guard's hands.

"Of course. Hope she's doing okay. I was the one who found her in the stairwell. My rounds don't usually result in a discovery more substantial than a forgotten briefcase or lost set of keys. Finding a employee all tangled up in herself in the stairwell was quite a shock."

"She was lucky you were on the ball," Sherry said.

"She shouldn't have had to take the stairs from the fourth floor. The doggone elevator is giving us fits. The service company is coming this afternoon and I'm not letting them leave until they guarantee it's fixed."

Marla scoffed. "Wait. We have to walk up four flights? No elevator?"

Sherry expected the backlash was coming. "You can do it. You walk miles a day back on your ranch."

"Have you seen how flat Oklahoma is? Certainly not four stories high at any point."

"We'll be fine," Sherry said. Sherry glanced at the guard's gold nametag. "Right, Clem? Do you remember we were here for an interview with Patti earlier in the week?"

The guard chuckled. "Absolutely. I have a photographic memory. Nice to see you two again. You look fit as a fiddle. You should have no problem. Take your time and breathe. You should see the equipment the guys have to schlep up and down the stairs. It's a wonder there haven't been more accidents."

"I hope there's not another one today," Marla said.

"I could call upstairs and have Hammy bring the package down to you, if you prefer. He'll save you the trip."

Marla's head bobbed up and down at the attractive option presented.

"Thank you very much," Sherry said. "We'll take the stairs."

The guard scanned the list. "Sherry Oliveri, Marla Barras. Different last names but I'd be willing to bet the house you are sisters. Same pretty eyes."

"We are. That's right. Thanks for the compliment," Sherry said.

"Hold on to these temporary passes. I'll collect them when you come back down." Two passes were placed in the sister's hands.

On their way to the stairs, they walked by the elevator, which was cordoned off with yellow tape. The doors were closed and the lights above the frame, indicating which floor the elevator was stopped at, was dark. Feet away, the stairs' door was propped open with a chipped brick.

"How unceremonious," Marla said. She rested her foot on the brick. "There could at least be a lovely doorstop marking the only way upstairs. For inspiration."

Four flights later, they entered Patti's office.

Sherry caught her breath and greeted Hammy. "We thought we'd save you the trip down."

"Good day, ladies," Hammy said. "Nice to see you again. I'm getting the package together. It'll be a minute. Have a seat."

"Thanks, Hammy. I might have left my favorite pair of reading glasses in the waiting room last time I was here. There's a chance they fell between the pillows of the love seat I sat on. Would you mind if I take a quick look?"

Marla's breathing was still labored but she managed to gather herself and send Sherry a quizzical glance.

"Sure. Right through that door," Hammy said. "Continue through the studio, out the next door, and you'll recognize the waiting room. Call me if you need me. I'll have her package ready in a few. By the time you find your glasses."

Sherry led Marla and Chutney past Patti's recording studio's double desk. A boom microphone overhead presented an obstacle they were forced to duck under. Two desk microphones were positioned on either side to catch the quips and insights between host and podcast guest.

"The room is an intimate space, like a milking cow in a chute," Marla said. "You two must have been nose to nose."

"Nearly. The hardest part was figuring out how close or far I should be to the mic," Sherry said. "When I sneezed and hit my chin, I realized I was too close."

Marla laughed as she pulled the handle to open the next door. "One small detail. You don't wear reading glasses. What are we really looking for in here?"

"We're checking the garbage cans. I have a hunch a piece of gum or a candy wrapper might have something to do with Patti's accident." Sherry framed the word *accident* with air quotes. "If the office has been cleaned lately, we're out of luck, but Patti said the elevator's been out and the cleaning lady can't wrestle her cleaning equipment cart up four flights of stairs, so I'm betting the garbage cans are full."

Sherry checked the small garbage can in the restroom while Marla rummaged through the MediaPie logoed receptacle in the corner by the MediaPie logoed water bottles.

"Came up empty," Sherry said as she joined Marla.

"Nothing in there except bottle lids and some scrunched up tissues." Marla moaned. "They smell awful. You're not going to make me unscrunch the tissues to check for a wad of gum, are you?"

Sherry laughed, relieved Marla was with her to provide comic relief. "No, it's the wrapper I'm looking for. Keep your eyes peeled for wrappers. There are none in here. There's one more garbage can in the corner."

Sherry came close to colliding with Marla as each headed to the corner of the room. A moment later Marla raised her hand. She was waving a bunched up waxy wrapper pinched between her index finger and thumb. "This?"

Without a word Sherry plucked the wrapper from Marla's grasp. She flattened out the paper and read the words decorating the surface.

"I recognize that. It smells like what's inside the tissue," Marla said. "Carl Carlson said he was getting dry mouth from nerves while waiting for you to finish up your interview. I thought I had a Life Saver candy for him but I'd eaten them all on the plane ride. Can't expect the airlines to provide snacks. And they didn't. The candies really were lifesavers. I was withering away from starvation."

Sherry's heart rate ticked up as the adrenaline flowed. She rolled her hand over to speed up her sister's story. "And?"

"Anyway, Thomas came up with what he called 'one of Iceland's iconic treasures. Lakkris Nammis. Icelandic licorice gummy candies.' I remember the name because I joked that the words sounded like something a doctor should treat. I think my joke fell flat."

"That's it. Licorice. An acquired taste I never acquired." Sherry wrinkled her nose at the offensive odor wafting from the paper. "Do you know why licorice is so popular in Iceland?"

"I have to say, I've never given the matter much thought," Marla said with a smirk. "Tell me."

"I'll enlighten you," Sherry said with a matching smirk. "Licorice root was one of the only sweets Iceland has known until recently because of how difficult the island was to access for trading ships. Icelanders made almost all their candies with some form of licorice, because licorice root traveled well. They even use it to treat coughs and sore throats."

"Makes sense. To me it smells more like medicine than candy," Marla said.

"In the recent past there were tight restrictions on Iceland's imports in order to alleviate economic downfalls. Sugar and candy ingredients were even harder to get your hands on. Add that to the fact Icelanders have a taste for very strong flavors, like fermented shark meat and black pudding, which is sheep innards, the goodies most Americans wouldn't touch with a ten-foot pole if they found it on their dinner plate."

"How do you know all these factoids?" Marla asked.

"When I did research for popular Icelandic recipes the most amazing info came up. Not having access to a wide variety of sugary sweets is the least of their worries. Iceland is a tough place to make a living in many industries. Especially modern-day farming and ranching. Even modern-day tech can't solve climate issues and improve the island's extreme soil conditions. Living like your ancestors up there is a solution to that problem. Adaptation and surrendering to Mother Nature's whims. No surprise how short and limited the growing season is. The soil is volcanic. Many plants don't take well to the cold, wind and rain. Add to that, most of the native trees were harvested by the early pioneers, and what good soil there was is a bust now, thanks to erosion. These days greenhouses are popular and thriving, so that's something. There's more variety, although farming is still a tough way to make a living. End result—very limited local food choices. Solution—preserve what's available in the style of your ancestors and make the best of a tough situation."

"Old versus new," Marla said. "Sounds like a familiar theme playing out right here."

"The economy up there is still trying to support importing too much. Iceland does its darnedest to make do. If that means licorice is used in most every sweet, so be it."

"Back to why we've been searching for this wrapper," Marla said. She paused. "We found it. Now what?"

"I know for certain I smelled licorice in this room the day I was interviewed. Not when we first arrived, but after my interview. I remember commenting the smell reminded me of Halloween. Now I know why. Licorice was my least favorite candy when we trick-or-treated. It stunk up my plastic hollow pumpkin candy holder."

"That's right. Thomas supplied the candy. Makes sense. But why is that important?" Marla asked.

"Whoever put the wrapper in the garbage could very likely be the person who pushed Patti down the stairs. Maybe even the person who knows what happened to Sigmund Helguvson."

"I don't get the connection."

"Thomas said Sigmund was importing licorice candies from Iceland. Most likely one of the products that he misjudged as a popular choice for American taste buds."

"Fermented shark followed up by a licorice chaser. Yum," Marla said.

"You say Thomas supplied any candy takers here at Patti's office. Maybe a show of support for Sigmund. There was also a licorice wrapper on the dock at Harmony Lake this morning. Maybe from Sigmund, maybe from his assailant."

"Maybe Thomas?"

"Yet to be determined. I also have a theory about what jammed up the elevator and forced it to come to a dead stop on the fourth floor."

"The offending licorice?" Marla said. "Excuse me if I'm a little bit lost."

"If I'm right, I'll have the *what*, but not the who and *why*."

Sherry pulled her phone from her jacket pocket. She lifted her index finger to put the conversation with Marla on hold. She pointed to the "no cell phones" mandate posted on the door. "Yes, Ray." Sherry lowered her voice and checked that the door to the studio was closed tight. "I can't talk for long. Was a body found?"

Sherry listened to Ray's brief reply. He ended the call promising to keep in touch.

Chapter 20

Sherry's cheeks prickled with heat as she faced Marla. "They found Sigmund's body in the lake. Thomas ID'd it. He had a stab wound in his neck from what most likely was the broken end of the wooden spoon, and something substantial clonked him on the head judging by the severity of the head wound."

"He made someone awfully angry," Marla said.

"Someone, or more than one someone. It had to have been someone strong to heave him a couple feet off the dock into the water." Sherry glanced back at the wrapper in her hand before stuffing the paper in her coat pocket. "There's another piece to this puzzle I need to fit in. Let's see if Hammy's done packing up Patti's work."

When the sisters and Chutney returned to Patti's office, Hammy was on the phone. Chutney made himself useful by finding a crumb on the floor and scarfing the morsel up. The dog's nose then traced the source of the crumb back to a plated blueberry muffin on the desk, which Hammy must have been snacking on when interrupted. He set down his phone.

Hammy laughed. "Your dog's hired. Beatrice refuses to clean above the first floor until the elevator is repaired. Too many cleaning supplies to haul up the stairs. These old buildings don't even have a service elevator as backup. The darn thing's been out of service since the night Patti fell down the stairs. The Van Ardans have budgeted for a second elevator to be installed later this year. That's a relief."

"I'm with Beatrice," Marla said.

"Any luck finding your glasses?" Hammy asked.

"No luck. The glasses are probably in another coat pocket. Is that the package for Patti?" Sherry asked.

"Sure is. I was on the phone with her just now," Hammy said with concern in his young voice. "She sounds down in the dumps. Do you guys think she'll be okay? Losing her friend, then taking a wicked fall on top of that. That's tough." He handed Sherry the bulky envelope.

"She's got you here covering the work base," Sherry said. "That'll reassure her until she can return."

Hammy smiled. "Interns don't usually take the reins but I'm up for the task. She's the perfect mentor and prepared me well. I'll phone down to Clem you're on your way out. Be careful on the stairs. Don't be tempted to summon the elevator. It's stuck open on our floor, teasing us all." He forced a laugh that exuded exhaustion. "Nice to see you both. Let's hope for better circumstances next time. Let me get the door for you."

On their way to the stairwell, they came across the open elevator. Sherry made a turn.

"Can't we try it and see if it works?" Marla said. "Might be worth getting stuck for a few minutes in between floors."

"No way," Sherry said. Chutney was wary of the three-walled cubical he was facing. He backed away until the leash was taut. Sherry handed Marla the leash along with Patti's envelope. She stepped to the threshold, stopping short of entering the elevator's interior cab. To get a better view of the control panel she inched toward the casing of the doorframe, where the automatic doors were pocketed. From that vantage point she could see what she needed to see. Almost.

"I've had second thoughts. I don't think you should put your weight inside that thing if it's broken," Marla warned.

Sherry's left foot and hand straddled the gap between the floor and the inside of the doorframe. "I need a better look at the button panel." Sherry let the last word out of her mouth a split second before she lost her balance and fell forward into the elevator cab. An eerie hollow thud was followed by a lengthy whining shudder of the overhead cable mechanism holding up the giant metal box. Sherry held her breath as if her life depended on it. She wasn't positive staying still was a requirement to living another moment but was willing to give the measure a try.

When the cable's serenade ended, she exhaled. On all fours, Sherry crawled the short distance to the button control panel and walked her hands up the edge of the doorframe. The elevator sounded no more complaints as Sherry stood upright and examined the button marked with a four. She raised her phone up to the panel and took photos from various angles to get the shot. When she was done, she summoned the jeté technique learned from a year of ballet lessons in her teens. She leaped over the shaft gap to the safety of the hallway carpet. "The button was jammed with black licorice gum. I can see it, I can smell it."

"And the wrapper we found was from licorice gum or gumdrops or something grossly licorice." Marla stuck out her tongue. "I'd jam the nasty-tasting candy somewhere, too, if someone gave me a piece."

"Who unwrapped the candy and who was inventive enough to glue up the elevator button with it is the question," Sherry said.

"And why?" Marla added.

"To hurt or kill Patti makes the most sense," Sherry said. "We need to find out who was in this elevator the day Patti fell down the stairs."

"Unfortunately, probably tons of people. This is a busy place."

"Okay, then we're looking for a licorice lover," Sherry said. "One who was in Patti's office. One who has a big problem with Patti and Sigmund."

"Or someone who hates the stuff enough to jam it in an elevator button. I have an idea. Don't you think a security camera in the elevator may have caught the person with the sticky fingers?"

"Not necessarily. I don't think it would be hard to pull your puffy down coat over the control panel and hide your bad intentions," Sherry said.

Moments later the lobby was a welcome sight after climbing down four flights of stairs. When they signed out with Clem, Sherry left him with her two cents.

"I recall reading a local news report the elevator at the Augustin Manor Hotel was stuck, and after some investigation the service tech concluded a kid had jammed some gum in one of the buttons on the control panel as a naughty prank. An easy fix. You might want to recommend service look at the button panel. Just a suggestion."

"Interesting, thanks," Clem said. "I'm sure the technician will figure things out before someone else gets hurt."

Sherry hesitated before leaving Clem when a thought occurred to her. "Do you have a list of the fourth-floor office tenants I could have a copy of?" Sherry asked. "I'm hoping one of them found my reading glasses in the hallway. I misplaced them the day of my interview. I hear your cleaning lady, Beatrice, is providing limited service at the moment until the elevator is repaired. Otherwise, I'd ask her."

"Easy. It's a short list. Out of the five offices up there, Ms. Mellit and her intern keep three rooms—her radio studio, office and waiting room, as you saw. Mrs. Van Ardan has an office on the fourth floor. I don't see her here too often, maybe once a week. I'm not even sure what position she holds for MediaPie Corp. I do know she's an exceptional fundraiser for the charities her husband's company supports."

"And the fifth office?" Marla asked. "Who works in that one?"

Clem's face brightened with a toothy smile. "That space is reserved for the Van Ardans' dogs, Phoebe and Sugar. French bulldogs. And, of course, their nanny, Miss Melanie. The Mr. and Mrs. asked me to ring them when the elevator's fixed. The dogs did not enjoy the climb down when they were all here the day the elevator shut down again. That was also the day Ms.

Mellit had her unfortunate fall."

"Tell me, Clem. Would I be able to see the guest sign-in book from that day?" Sherry asked.

"I'm sorry. Those sheets go daily to storage in New York. I only have today's sign-in," Clem said.

"Do you remember when I came in for my interview on Patti's podcast. Not long afterward four men and a woman went up to her studio. Three were also on the podcast," Sherry said.

"Yes, I do. The woman was quite a head-turner. She showed me her cookbook. I'm not much of a cook and people who are impress the heck out of me. Doesn't hurt that she's a beauty."

Clem greeted a man dressed in a crisp pinstripe suit carrying a leather satchel. After the man signed the visitor log, Clem returned his attention to Sherry. "The day you and your sister were here, along with the other podcast guests, my bosses, Mr. and Mrs. Van Ardan, entered the building. They signed in and took note of Ms. Mellit's guests' names. They specifically asked me if the two men whose names were Helguvson gave me any trouble. I said, 'No. They were very cordial.' Because they were. To me."

"What do you mean, 'to me'?" Sherry asked.

"Those two were bickering like my sainted mother and her sister used to. Funny how they could switch off their argument the way family members can. When talking to me, they were most respectful," Clem said. He puffed out his ample chest. The buttons on his jacket strained to stay secured.

"What I wanted to ask you is, have you seen any of that group of men or the cookbook author go up to the fourth floor since?" Sherry asked. "Between that day and now?"

"Two men came back once. Mr. V. and Mr. Carlson. And Mr. Helguvson very briefly, a day or two later. No, I take that back. They all returned the day Ms. Patti had her accident. They had to rerecord some of the podcast for some reason. Ms. Warren was very put out when she arrived separately. She joined the men, who were still waiting in the lobby. Claimed the do-over was not her fault and she had lots of other things she should be doing. She wasn't the pretty lady I'd remembered from earlier. She was scowling and I let her be. I felt bad for Ms. Mellit, who was forced to come down to the lobby. The elevator was in working order at that point, so it wasn't as bad as all that."

"But, later in the day the elevator conked out?" Sherry asked.

"That's right," Clem said. "If I'm not mistaken, Miss Patti's guests had to walk down. Ms. Warren was in a much better mood at that point. I was worried her trek down four flights would put her over the edge. It didn't. She was fine."

Sherry took a moment to sort out her thoughts. Patti had mentioned there was no rerecording needed after she utilized her editing software. Maybe the pain meds had jumbled her memory. Or maybe she was executing a plan to return the suspect to the scene of the crime and didn't want Sherry to know.

"Excuse me, Clem," the man in the pin-striped suit said. "I'm sorry to interrupt, but there's a spill in the stairwell and it's very slippery on two of the steps."

"Yes, sir, Mr. Weathersfield. I'll get right on it," Clem said.

"I'm sorry, ladies. Would you give me a few minutes? Safety first." Clem hustled down the hall, opened a door and retrieved a sponge mop. He disappeared into the stairwell.

"Anyone seen Clem?" a woman asked. Her companion had a phone up to his ear.

"Just ask them where we sign in," the man asked with little patience in his tone. The woman huffed.

"Fine, skip it," he said. "The office is right over here." He waved the woman forward, bypassing any security requirement of registering their presence.

"Poor Clem. When it rains it pours," Marla said.

A few minutes later, Clem returned the mop to the closet and rejoined Sherry and Marla.

"We won't bother you much longer, just another question. Anything stand out about the men? Or Sienna? When the group returned that day?" Sherry asked.

"How so?" Clem asked. "Everyone has a quirk or two. You can't expect me to notice every one."

"Other than quirks, more like unprovoked anger, assertive attitudes that didn't seem to be warranted. Was the group cohesive or at odds?"

Clem blew out a breath, launched by puffed cheeks. "That's a tall order. Let's see. I mentioned Ms. Warren being cranky." He tapped his temple. "Accents? Does that count? Scandinavian if I had to guess."

"Any behavior you thought might be out of place?" Sherry asked, her words laced with a tinge of urgency.

"When Mr. Helguvson entered the building and joined the other men to sign in, the temperature went up some," Clem said.

"Now we're getting somewhere," Marla said.

"One of the men didn't want to sign the book, said he wasn't staying long. Rules are rules, so I had to play the enforcer," Clem said. He stood up a little taller.

"And Ms. Warren? Was she involved in any conflict that you witnessed?"

"Nope," Clem said with confidence. "Like I said, Pretty Lady was hanging back, tapping her boot toe while the roosters clucked over signing the dang book."

"You remember the Helguvson name. Do you remember all the names of the building's visitors?" Sherry asked.

"Hah! No. Their faces, though. Odd talent I have," Clem lowered his voice. "You know, I wanted to know why Ms. Patti had them as guests on her podcast. They must be celebrities, and I'll be darned if I could recognize any by sight. I went home and googled the names. Even yours. You are quite the decorated cook."

"She sure is," Marla said. "One of the best cooking competitors in the country."

"Anyway," Sherry said, "what did you find out, Clem?"

"I'm not just a pretty face, you know. I've got some techie skills. Was I ever surprised at who Thomas Helguvson was. Not like the celebrities you see on my wife's Hollywood entertainment shows, but more like a local celeb. No wonder the Van Ardans were on alert when they read the names in the log."

"So, you know the backstory?" Sherry asked.

"I learned it when I researched them at home. The Mr. and Mrs., as I call them, are the best. They love everyone. Even their closest newspaper competitors. Keeps them on their toes to have a new newspaper come to town, they say. I got me a copy of the paper and read it cover to cover. That Helguvson may have gone too far in my opinion. One too many negative Nellies against our lovely town. Just to make sure, I now have a subscription. I consider it job research."

Sherry smiled. "I understand."

"I'm not supposed to mention this outside the security detail, but the Mr. and Mrs. gave me strict orders to notify them if the Helguvsons ever returned. Told the other guards too. Harry works nights, Greg picks up the extra days. From the scuttlebutt I've heard, it's only Thomas Helguvson now. The other one met his maker. Imagine that. I saw him one day and he's gone the next. Life's not fair sometimes."

"I agree. Thanks for sharing, Clem," Sherry said.

"No problem," Clem said. "Folks around town are a bit up in arms these days over this, that, and the other. I'm sure that had plenty to do with the mood that afternoon. Ms. Patti was especially not herself."

"Hope to see you soon."

"Have a good day," Marla echoed.

"Say hi to Ms. Patti for me, please. Tell her to get well soon," Clem said as he held the door open for them.

"Absolutely," Sherry said.

"How fast does Patti need this work?" Marla asked, gesturing toward the envelope.

"She doesn't really need it," Sherry said. "She made up an excuse for us to stop by. We can hold on to it until our way home from the store."

As they rounded the building, Marla asked, "By the way, something you said back there. To Clem. The Augustin Manor Hotel elevator was pranked by a kid?"

"Sure was." She pointed to her scalp. "I have a storage compartment right up here filled with stories I've heard, just like that one. Never know when they'll come in handy. Unfortunately, I don't think the MediaPie elevator mishap was a prank. And there is a copycat out there."

Chapter 21

The frigid wind smacked Sherry in the face as she turned the corner. She adjusted her scarf to cover what skin was exposed. As she lowered her head against the biting chill, she noticed a flyer on the sidewalk. She picked it up with the clumsiness of insulated fingers.

Keep Augustin Ornery

Sherry showed Marla the flyer. The top edge was torn. "Wonder if the wind blew it down or an angry hand."

A few steps later they came upon a rebuttal tacked to a utility pole.

One Step Forward, Two Steps Back Is a Dance, Not Progress

Sherry searched the pole for a nail and secured the paper to create a side-by-side silent debate. "Let the people decide."

After a few blocks they were greeted by the Ruggery window display. Amber was the mastermind behind the Ruggery's window decoration and Sherry was so thankful for her creativity. The romantic setting on the other side of the glass was adorned with an area rug of hearts and flowers in the spirit of Valentine's Day. A floating Cupid wielded a bow and pointed an arrow toward anyone window shopping. Red ribbons and baskets full of oversized candies completed the diorama, with Amber's signature attention to detail. After seeing the care put into the window, Sherry knew most potential shoppers wouldn't leave the storefront without browsing the inventory inside.

"We're here," Marla called out as she and Sherry entered the store.

Chutney was unleashed and took off in search of his best canine friend, Bean. Chutney had been missing Amber's Jack Russell while the duo was away and sought to make up for lost time in a hurry.

"Dad?" Marla called out.

"Hi, ladies," Don said as he stepped into the showroom from the kitchen. "Erno ran to the bank. 'Back in a flash' is the last thing I heard him say. You've got me solo, in all my accounting glory." He checked his watch. "Although I'm only here for another half hour now that you two showed up."

"Hi, sweetie," Sherry said before planting a smooch on her man's lips. "Long time, no see."

"Listen," Marla said. "You two can spend as much quality time together as you like starting tomorrow night. Grant is coming into town to watch the cook-off."

"Grant's coming?" Sherry said. Her voice was charged with excitement.

"He's never seen you compete, and I've convinced him this is the one to watch."

Don cleared his throat. "I finally get to meet the man behind the Marla."

"Are you sure this is the cook-off you want Grant to see?" Sherry asked. "Unless Thomas Helguvson cools down his rhetoric in the *Beacon*, the event may be more of a shouting match between two opposing sides of town rather than a contest between home cooks. We're not even sure he didn't have anything to do with Patti's accident. I mean, he had reason to hold her responsible for his brother's murder."

"Absolutely," Marla said. "We're going to sit with Don and root for you, no matter what else is happening." She winked at Don. "Right, Don?"

"If you say so," Don said, his words supported by little conviction. He stared straight ahead until he relaxed his scrunched forehead. "Wait. I'm missing some details here. The investigation has taken a turn? Was Sigmund Helguvson murdered? I thought he disappeared or drowned."

"It's looking that way. Evidence around the scene points to a struggle, a blunt force blow and a water entry into a frozen lake," Sherry said.

"I wasn't aware of that nugget of information. Was his body found? Why didn't you tell me?"

"Give me a chance to tell you everything I know. We just got here. This isn't the kind of thing I like to text," Sherry said.

"Okay," Don said. "I see your point. Sure seems like passing on news in this day and age has become an instantaneous process, but I agree this is a sensitive issue. Why would you think his brother wanted to hurt Patti? And what's the scoop on Patti being in an accident? Living in Sherry's world requires a whole other level of trying to keep up."

"You're telling me," Marla said. "Buckle up, Don. Breaking a bucking bronco might be a smoother ride. By the way, better get used to the excitement level. This is your future staring you straight in the eyes." Another wink.

"Hi, guys," Amber called out as she entered the room from the storage closet. Her arms were filled with a mountain of wool bundles, mostly in beiges and grays. "The Gregory family's background color for their hall rug. It's going to be spectacular."

"Saved by the bell," Sherry said before exhaling a huff. "I was about to be thrown to the wolves for helping Patti."

"Not at all," Don said. "I'm behind you one hundred percent, as long as you're safe."

"I don't know what you guys are talking about. Who can fill me in?" Amber asked.

"Amber! First let me say, hello! I take it you had a nice trip with Troy?" Sherry said.

"Very nice. A few hiccups, to be expected spending so much time together in close quarters, but, all in all, we had a wonderful time. Now back to reality," Amber said and laughed. "Troy's first assignment back, Harmony Lake search to recover a body. I shouldn't have been at all surprised you were involved, Sherry. Troy told me he was going to see you there."

Sherry nodded. "He and Trooper did a great job this morning. Impresses the heck out of me. Along with another police dog, Honor, they found Patti's friend's body, Sigmund."

Amber drew in a deep breath. "That's tough. I hope Patti's okay. Did I overhear Don say Patti had an accident?"

"We haven't heard any details. You've come in at the right time. Sher, what about Patti's accident?" Don asked. "A coincidence? Timing seems fishy."

"There are no coincidences," Sherry said. "She was pushed down the stairs. Yes, fishy."

"Her friend Sigmund was murdered?" Don asked.

"Murdered. He had head trauma and a poke in the neck from something sharp. A wooden spoon perhaps." Sherry waited for Amber to soak in the news.

"A wooden spoon?" Amber asked after a minute. "How does that make sense?"

"Remember I told you Patti was interviewing me and some others for her podcast while you were away?"

"I do, but wait, before we move on to a new subject, you need to answer my first question," Amber said with a hint of frustration.

"Can I get in line? I have a few more," Don said with a sarcastic chuckle.

"We're getting there. Everything's most likely connected," Sherry said. She used her hands to accentuate the story's different components. "The topic of Patti's podcast was an in-depth discussion of a favorite kitchen tool. My choice was a wooden spoon." She mimed stirring and licking the spoon.

"The murder weapon? Uh-oh. You're now a suspect in the murder investigation?" Amber asked.

"What? Is that even a consideration?" Don asked.

"I'm not a suspect. Not as far as I know," Sherry said.

"Phew," Don said.

"Let me set the scene. The day of the podcast, Patti's boyfriend, Sigmund Helguvson, came along to the studio with his brother, Thomas, and three others who are serving as judges in the upcoming cook-off. The men are all buddy-buddy, kind of. Three of them have Iceland ties—the two brothers and a man named Gunnar V., who is a food-trend expert. And one of the judges was a cookbook author from Florida. The other was a man from Norway, Carl Carlson. He's a food columnist for the *Beacon* newspaper, which Thomas Helguvson is editor in chief of. Are you with me?"

"Barely, but yes," Amber said with a sigh.

"Sigmund—he's an exporter of Icelandic foodstuffs—wasn't being interviewed," Sherry said. "He was only fascinated with the podcast topic, so he brought along his favorite tool, which, like my choice, was a wooden spoon. Wooden spoons are very popular in Icelandic households, I've learned."

"He was proud of his knowledge of the spoon in his homeland and wanted to share his story with his girlfriend," Marla said. "Kind of sweet."

"That is sweet," Amber said.

"Sweet, except for the fact Sigmund's married and has been for years," Sherry said.

"Ugh," Amber moaned as one of the yarn bundles tumbled off the mountain. "Obviously, the next question is, did Patti know he was married?"

"I'm not sure I want to know," Don said. "To me, Patti's character is spotless. She's been such a fan of Sherry's and written glowing articles about my gal."

"Good question. Turns out, very recently she began to have doubts he was single. A valentine addressed to his wife confirmed her suspicions," Sherry said. "Now she's under investigation for having killed him. I need to prove she didn't. Unfortunately, she was at the wrong place at the wrong time. Sigmund summoned her down to the lake the night he was murdered and she went."

"You've established the wooden spoon was used as a weapon against him. But by who? Or is it whom? Did Sigmund have enemies that you know of?" Don asked. "Dumb question. He had at least one."

"He had a sordid past and pasts have a way of catching up to the present," Sherry said. "There's a list. His wife, his brother, Patti."

"Not Patti. You can't be serious about Patti," Amber said.

"If I didn't know her as well as I do, I'd say, sure. Why not?" Sherry shrugged.

"My guess is he discovered his wife was on to him taking a straycation with Patti," Marla said. "To have two vengeful women turn on you is enough to make any cheating man jump in a lake."

"Marla!" Sherry scolded. "Patti's certain he summoned her to the lake to explain the sticky situation, and who knows what else. Maybe express some remorse for leading Patti on?"

"Or maybe kill her?" Don suggested.

Sherry's mouth dropped open. "I never thought of that. Could be."

"Don may have hit the nail on the head. First of all, I doubt the philanderer felt remorse," Marla said. "How do you explain Sienna Warren being at the lake? How long was the waiting list to meet with this guy anyway?"

"And Sienna Warren is . . . ?" Amber asked.

"Besides being one of the judges in next Tuesday's cook-off, she's the cookbook author I mentioned and a friend of the Helguvsons. Thomas's newspaper, as the main sponsor of the cook-off, endorsed the judges, so she impressed him enough with her food knowledge to get the job," Sherry said.

"She was at the lake? The night Sigmund was killed?" Amber asked.

"Patti said when she arrived at the lake, she came across someone in another car. She was almost one hundred percent positive it was Sienna Warren because of a particular hat she was wearing."

"And why was she there?" Amber asked.

"Do I have to spell this out for you two? Sigmund was juggling girlfriends," Marla said.

"That's Marla's opinion and we have no facts to back her assertion up," Sherry said.

"Some men repeat their mistakes hoping for someone else to clean up their lives for them," Marla said. "Those are the ones to avoid. I say guilty as charged."

Sherry shook her head. "Innocent until proven guilty. Remember, Sigmund's not on trial here. His killer is, or will be if he's caught."

"From what you're spelling out," Marla said, "sounds like the creep's lucky to have lived this long."

"Your sister tells it like it is," Don said with a sly smile. "Grant better stay on her good side." Don grabbed his coat off the hook by the front door. "I'm putting in a few more minutes, then I'm pulling up anchor and tackling some errands. I'll see you both soon." He blew a kiss in the sisters' direction and returned to the kitchen.

"You said Patti went to the lake that night?" Amber said. "That's a problem." She was beginning to struggle with balancing the bounty of yarn skeins. "My arms are getting tired."

Sherry relieved Amber of some yarn. "Unfortunately, yes."

"That doesn't bode well for proving her innocence."

Sherry sighed. Her attention shifted to some commotion that caught her eye outside the display window. "The group looking in the window a few minutes ago is coming in."

"I'll take the yarn to the storeroom and unpack it. Call me if you need me, otherwise I'll be sorting and labeling," Marla said. She took the remainder of the Gregorys' yarn from Amber and set it on the sales counter.

Chapter 22

The group entered the store, announced by the tinkle of the brass bell over the doorframe. Amber greeted them one by one as Sherry expected she would. Her friend had genuine customer service down to a science. Amber pointed out Sherry as the daughter of the owner, and the group said their hellos. The sight of the trailing woman in the group took Sherry's breath away for a split second. Sherry skirted the sales counter to meet with her, bumping her hip on the corner in her haste. She grimaced with the fleeting pain.

"Lilya. How nice to have you come into the store."

"Hi, Sherry. Wouldn't miss out on a visit. Your store has quite a reputation," Lilya said. "Asking directions to get here opened up a Pandora's box of stories about your father, his rugs and a wonderful woman named Amber, who treats people as if they were family." Her gaze followed the group touring the store. "That strawberry-haired lovely must be her."

Across the room Amber's ears burned at the mention of her name. She side-eyed Sherry in hopes of an explanation as to how she knew the potential customer. Sherry responded to the subtle message. With a head tilt, she summoned Amber over.

"Amber, this is Lilya. She's a friend of the Helguvson family, who suffered a terrible loss very recently. She wanted to say hello."

"Nice to meet you," Amber said. Her head rotated back to the group waiting on her. "I'll take care of these folks while you two chat. Call me if you need me." She herded the group together and began a guided tour of the shop.

When the others were out of earshot Sherry returned her attention to Lilya. The woman had changed out of the shiny black coat she donned at the lake hours earlier. Her current coat was a colorful and expensive brand of après ski wear Sherry recognized from top fashion magazines. Very expensive. The private eye market must be hopping.

"Any rug in particular I can show you?" Sherry asked. She wanted the conversation ball in her court. On her terms. That way she could turn defense into offense if need be. If Lilya was bound and determined to pin Sigmund's murder on Patti, Sherry was ready to respond.

"Yes. I'd love to see what you showcase, after we have a talk. About Sigmund's murder."

"Lilya. I don't know any more than I did when I saw you earlier," Sherry said. She lowered her brows. "Isn't your job complete, now that you know Sigmund's whereabouts? You must have delivered the news to his wife. It may not be the outcome she saw coming, but it is what it is." Sherry twisted her mouth as if she bit her tongue. "I don't like that saying. It's so unspecific."

"My role has changed since I found Sigmund. I'm no longer working for Nora with the end goal of locating her husband," Lilya said.

"It wasn't exactly *you* who found him. The Augustin police Homicide Department found him. Led by Detective Bease." Sherry's words were clipped. Lilya rubbed Sherry the wrong way, although Sherry wasn't exactly sure why. Just a hunch the fashionable woman wasn't concerned about anything but her own glory. This was not the woman she wanted her friend Ray to be interested in dating. It was a moot point.

"Semantics," Lilya said. "Nora would like me to keep her abreast of the now murder investigation and even aid in the search for the killer in order to speed up the process."

Ray wasn't going to like this development. Sherry didn't either.

"By the way, it's always been a murder investigation," Sherry said. "Detective Bease never gave credence to Thomas's theory of a faked death."

Lilya shrugged. "He has a right to his opinion."

"Have you spoken to Detective Bease about adding yourself to the investigation?" Sherry asked.

"I wouldn't say I'm adding myself to the investigation so much as working parallel to his unit. No, I haven't spoken directly to the detective about my next move. I am a little worried about his reaction," Lilya said. "I don't think he likes me very much. Sometimes men don't know what to make of me in this male-dominated line of work. I don't dress the part of a PI, mostly because, well, most have an awful fashion sense. I enjoy *not* looking the part."

"Ray has come a long way with his fashion sense since I first met him," Sherry said as she pictured the crumpled, frayed fedora resting on Ray's head from years past. He had since upgraded to a newer untattered model. In those days his baggy khakis were consistently in need of ironing. He'd owned one tweed blazer that saw as much wear as the perma-scowl on his face. Sherry prided herself on the fact she may have influenced him to lighten his dour expression for the sake of coaxing witnesses to speak freely. Whether that was true or not, it was on Sherry's mind as she spoke with Lilya.

"I'll take your word for it," Lilya said. "Don't judge me by my appearance or my demeanor. Do take me as a full package. I'm very good at what I do. I may come across abrasive, stubborn, willful." She threw up her hands. "Guilty. I'm all that and more. This is a man's game and I'm changing the rules. Sorry if someone doesn't like it."

This woman was standing up for herself and Sherry was impressed. "You caught me. I admit I didn't know what to make of you either. I admit I prejudged you as one tough cookie, but not in the best way, without much basis. You've convinced me you are tough, and in the best way. I like that."

Chapter 23

"I know Detective Bease is your friend. Some might even say your confidant," Lilya said.

"Friend, yes. Confidant? Only when it comes to sharing recipe secrets. Any aspect of an investigation is his baby all the way. He shares what he wants to share and that's the bare minimum," Sherry said.

"Do you think the detective will be receptive to me cozying up to his investigation? I mean, beyond receptive. Will he treat me as an equal?"

The line was getting blurred. Sherry had her regrets Ray wanted to take Lilya out on a date while her goal was to get an inside track on the case. On the other hand, Ray was also blurring the lines if he pursued Lilya socially. Everyone's an adult, she decided. Let the chips fall where they may. "To answer your question, I can't speak for the detective," Sherry said. "My only advice is approach with caution. And respect."

"Maybe I'll accept his dinner invitation after all," Lilya said. Her coy expression was begging Sherry to react. "He got the impression my time here was over when the body was found. He texted me with an invite for the day of my choosing, before I leave. You could have knocked me over with a feather when he asked me. Like I said, I'm not at all sure he truly likes me for who I am."

Sherry grinned to herself. She thought she was concealing the smile, until Lilya told her otherwise.

"What's that look on your face, girl? Do you know anything about his invitation? You look like the cat that's hiding the canary in your mouth while saying you know nothing about the feathered friend's whereabouts. The invite certainly came as a surprise."

"Maybe I knew," Sherry said with a tip of the head. "You're single?"

"Absolutely."

"Just checking. For my friend."

"Do you know how hard it is to date in Iceland?"

"I have no idea but it's no picnic here in the States."

"Slim pickings up there. There are only three hundred thousand residents, and that in itself has led to the problem of who might be related to who."

"I never considered that. That's a big problem."

"Iceland has a dating app that we use to identify relatives we want to avoid getting tangled up with romantically. I've washed my hands of finding my special someone."

"Iceland is a special place on many levels, I'm learning. No worries. Ray is from the U.S. through and through. No problem there," Sherry said.

"You've convinced me. I'll accept. It might play in my favor. I'm sure he's thinking I have more information than I've put forward. I think he does, too. Besides, he's cute."

"Do you know more?" Sherry asked. "Because if I had to choose the guilty party at this very moment, Thomas is on my radar. You two seem quite well connected to one another."

Lilya's gaze drifted to the rug display showcasing moody winter scenes—snowscapes, foraging forest animals, winter root vegetable cornucopias. "Your store is a treasure. Do you ship as far as Iceland?"

"Of course. We'll ship anywhere a carrier is willing to travel. And thank you for the compliment. Dad is a wonderful artist and craftsman. A passionate believer in exposing anyone who'll listen to the history of hooked rugs here in New England."

Erno hummed a snazzy tune as he neared. "I couldn't help but overhear what may be my cue to begin my lecture."

"Dad, I didn't think you were here. You must have snuck in the back door," Sherry said.

"Sure did," Erno said. "And who do we have here?"

"I'm Lilya, an acquaintance of Sherry's. You must be Erno Oliveri."

"Proud to say I am."

"Nice to meet you," Lilya said as she shook Erno's hand. "I'd love to hear the story. My homeland of Iceland is a country of oral history. Thank goodness for that or we would never know half the time-honored traditions we practice today."

"Iceland? I'm not sure I've had a looky-loo from Iceland."

"Happy to be the first," Lilya said. "Beautiful treasures you have here, Mr. Oliveri."

Erno cleared his throat and realigned his seventy-year-old posture. "Please call me Erno."

"Yes, sir, Erno. I'd love to hear the history."

"Rug hooking in the form you see here became popular in New England and the Canadian Maritimes around the eighteen hundreds. What was interesting is the activity was labeled a country craft of poverty, unlike needlepoint and quilting, which were taught in elite finishing schools. Rugs to cover the floor and warm the house were unaffordable to many. Ironically, those with the least were the workers who made the rugs in factories. The workers were allowed to bring home scraps and ingenuity prevailed. The scraps were turned into beautiful works of art at home. Yarn wasn't even used in those days as it was too precious. It was needed for scarves and blankets. Today, hooked rugs are considered art, and rightly so. I'm lucky enough to preserve the tradition."

"Remarkable," Lilya said. Her gaze softened as she spoke the word.

"Erno," Amber called out. "We have a question for you when you're done over there."

"On my way. Thanks, ladies. Excuse me." Erno turned and strode over to Amber, resuming his upbeat hum.

"You're a lucky daughter to have such a gifted father," Lilya said.

Sherry nodded.

"If we can circle back to the murder investigation," Lilya said. "I have no doubt Thomas wasn't involved in his brother's death. Yes, Thomas was far from proud of Sigmund's behavior in the past. Sigmund worked with Thomas when they began as reporters for a local newspaper. Sigmund wanted to fast-track without putting in the time. He was caught not checking sources, and worse, plagiarizing a story from a competing paper. Following that failed career, funding any subsequent venture for his brother became a full-time expense for Thomas. Sigmund had shown a new side since marrying Nora. He was motivated to find opportunities outside of Iceland, talked of a fresh start with renewed commitment. Thomas had hope for a lasting turnaround. The talk had yet to translate into successful action."

"Was Patti Mellit one of those opportunities?" Sherry said with a tinge of sarcasm.

"A most unfortunate situation. A backslide for sure," Lilya said.

"Maybe there were more dalliances you and Thomas are aware of?" Sherry pictured the scene Patti described at Harmony Lake involving Sienna.

"Maybe." Lilya sighed.

"Sigmund was trouble," Sherry said. "Why didn't Patti see his type coming a mile away?"

"No sense looking back. He maybe should have considered the faked death plan," Lilya scoffed. "I have an idea. You're interested in finding the murderer because your friend is a suspect. Since many hands make for lighter work, doesn't it make sense for us to work together. If you're open to the idea I won't have to approach Ray at all about tagging along with his team. That way business and pleasure have a wedge between them."

Sherry scanned the room for anyone who may have heard Lilya's proposal. Seeing no one who would scold her for putting both feet, rather than one toe dip, into the investigation, she agreed with a nod.

"If we take Thomas and Patti out of the equation, who do we have left to consider?" Lilya asked.

"I don't know why we would take Thomas out, but okay. You tell me. Nora? Very likely Nora. I'd be spitting mad if I were her. In Sigmund's case, if she was fed up with his shenanigans, she could be the devil he knew rather than the devil he didn't."

"Too obvious. My idea is to fish the murderer out somehow," Lilya said.

Was that a preview of what Lilya considered working together? If so, Sherry's job would be to keep her ideas to herself and agree to all Lilya's plans. She had to shore up her confidence. "Have you ever investigated a murder specifically?"

"No, but how much different can it be from pursuing a cheating husband or tracking missing finances. With you on my side we should be able to crack the case in no time," Lilya said. "That would be an outstanding notch on my belt."

Behind her Amber was making noises at the sales counter that Sherry translated as a request to join her in packaging up purchases made by the latest group of customers.

"I'll do my best," Sherry said. "If there's anything else you need, please let me know. I need to give Amber a hand."

"Mind if I take a look around?" Lilya waved a card she retrieved from her patent leather quilted purse. The gold link strap jangled as she maneuvered the bag off her shoulder. "Call or text anytime."

Sherry studied the card before closing her fingers around it. "Thank you. I will. And, yes, please take your time browsing, there's so much to look at here." She watched Lilya sashay over to the fireplace rugs. After Lilya settled in front of the area rug showcase, Sherry joined Amber.

"What was that all about?" Amber whispered. "You weren't showing her any rugs. Wasn't she a customer?" She handed a customer a small rug tied neatly with twine. "Do you need help getting to your car?"

"No, thank you. We can manage," the man said.

"Thank you for coming in. Please, come again." Sherry handed the woman he was with a bag she packed with a set of wool drink coasters made from the remnants of yarn skeins. Erno was adamant no product, scraps or otherwise, go to waste. "Lilya is the private investigator I told you about,"

Sherry explained. "She was hired by Nora Helguvson to get a handle on what her husband has been up to since he stopped checking in with her."

"What was he up to that left him at the bottom of Harmony Lake?" Amber asked.

Before Sherry could respond, Marla joined the conversation. "Imagine being Nora. Your husband waves goodbye one day and goes in search of a life in another country, promising to ring you up when he's found the pot of gold." Marla assumed a singsong tone. "Sure, dear, take all the time you need to find yourself. I'll be here awaiting your return dressed in pearls and serving a hot meal." She huffed. "What could possibly go wrong with that scenario?"

Sherry laughed. "How do you always manage to make me giggle like a twelve-year-old at the most inappropriate times."

"Part of my charm."

"Exactly."

"Lilya's a very fashionable detective," Marla said. "Times have changed from the cliché of the grizzled guy who grumbles if anyone offers their opinion on an investigation." Marla cringed. "Oops. I didn't mean your friend Ray."

"Maybe you did a tiny bit," Sherry said. "And she's not shy about offering her opinion, that's for sure."

"I bet she can open a lot more doors with her classy approach," Marla said.

"What does she want from you?" Amber asked.

"Lilya wants some help finding Sigmund's murderer. Nora has extended her contract with Lilya. Although one of us would be paid for their time and the other would be doing the work out of the kindness of her heart." Sherry slit a new box of yarn open and the turquoise and blue shade variations dazzled her. She breathed in the scent wafting above the cardboard flaps. The aroma of the freshly dyed lamb's wool was musty and earthy, just the way Sherry loved it.

"Did you tell her about the licorice findings?" Marla asked.

Sherry hemmed and hawed before answering. "I didn't. Because I'm not sure who the candy belonged to and who used it to gum up the elevator works. The same gummed-up elevator timed to be out of service so Patti would be caught in the stairwell, subject to attack. What I am sure of is folks from Iceland have more of a taste for that flavor than almost anyone." Sherry stuck out her tongue. "Bleh!"

"Wonder what else Patti knew that made her a target?" Marla asked.

"Once again you two have veered off on another tangent. Licorice? I shouldn't even ask how that plays a part." Amber's attention shifted to a couple meandering past the yarn bins. "Be back for details."

Chapter 24

Sherry watched as Amber returned to the couple she had been consulting with. The woman began waving her arms over her head. Amber seemed to be pleading with her, doing her darnedest to calm the woman down. At the same time, a blur of people congregated at the entryway, fidgeting and jockeying for position to be the first one out the door.

A moment later, Amber beelined to the door and opened it. The procession out the door was not orderly. A man pushing a woman out the door nearly knocked Amber down as he elbowed past her. Sherry hustled over to see what could be causing the commotion. She arrived too late to get a word in with the departing customers. The door slammed in her face.

"What was that all about?" Sherry said. "I've never seen customers up and leave so suddenly. A minute ago, they were schmoozing over choices for a mudroom rug. Next thing I know they nearly take me down zooming out the door."

"Mrs. Holladay said she received an urgent text from her teenage daughter about an emergency in the center of town. Emergency units were blockading the streets and that's where their car was parked. The daughter was at home and having a panic attack that her parents were in the midst of a catastrophe. The woman told her husband and out they went."

"Are we in the midst of a catastrophe? I thought I've been hearing sirens," Sherry said.

Marla sidled up to Sherry. "Is there a problem?"

Before anyone could answer, the door swung open with such force the brass bell overhead bleated out a metallic thud, rather than a gentle chime. Sherry jerked her head toward the sight of the man who flung himself through the doorway.

"Can I use your phone? We were evacuated so quickly I had no time to grab mine. I was in the men's room. No coat, no phone. I'm lucky I had time to zip my zipper."

Interpreting the jumble of anxious words made Sherry's head light. The surprise of who uttered them added to her shock.

"Thomas." She studied the disheveled man, who was missing the blazer of his suit along with any other outerwear in the winter cold. "Are you okay?"

"Yours is the only place I could think to run to. There's a bomb threat at the *Beacon* building and everyone's in hysterics. The road's about to be completely blockaded so they can get the blast containment tanks up to the building. Poor Brad, our security head, is running around like a chicken with his head cut off. I told him I'd call central security for a full report. The alarm system we paid through the nose for is so deafening I couldn't phone anywhere near the place."

"Bomb threat?" Marla said. She surveyed the store. "Do you think we're safe here?"

"Thomas, I would have never thought I'd see you here?" Lilya said as she strolled up to the sales counter. She scanned him up and down. "Why aren't you dressed for the cold if you're out and about?"

"Lilya, can I use your phone? I'll explain in a minute. Just stick in the password to unlock it for me, please."

"Unusual request, but sure," Lilya said. She fished her phone out of her pocket and placed it in Thomas's quivering hand. "You've had too much coffee today."

Blaring sirens from two speeding police cars pierced the store. The back of Sherry's neck prickled. Rubbing the irritation away wasn't successful, as hard as she tried.

"I wish that were the problem." Thomas stepped aside, phone in hand, to make his call. While his back was turned, Sherry explained to Lilya what Thomas had told her. By the time Sherry finished the explanation Thomas handed the phone back to Lilya.

He sucked in a deep breath and rubbed his forehead with the heel of his hand. "Someone has made a threat to my paper. That's not unusual, hazard of the trade, but this one is serious. The caller made very specific threats as if he'd cased the building in detail and knew specific points of vulnerability."

"A caller?" Lilya asked.

"That's right. Our security guard had the presence of mind to hit the record button when the caller made his demands. He called the police and they arrived within ninety seconds. Unfortunately, the cops listened to the recording and deemed the call credible. They could immediately ascertain the caller utilized a trace blocker and a voice scrambler. From there, a full security breach action exercise was deployed. First step, evacuate."

"What were the demands?" Sherry asked.

Thomas lowered his head and paced a small area of the floor. He came to a halt and lifted his chin. "In a nutshell, the caller said the building would be blown up if the *Beacon* continued to try to destroy Augustin and the neighboring towns with our rhetoric."

Sherry rubbed her forearms to quell the pins and needles crawling up from her hands.

A melodic tone swelled from Lilya's coat pocket. She retrieved her phone. "Hello? Yes, he's right here." She handed the phone to Thomas. "For you," she whispered.

Once again, Thomas turned his back and spoke in hushed tones. Moments later he handed the phone back to Lilya. "The 'all clear' can't be given for a while. It's a big building. Nothing's been found. I need to go meet with Brad. Thank you, Sherry, for welcoming me into your wonderful store. It's clear you're in a minority welcoming me at all."

"Of course, Thomas. I'm so sorry for the trouble. A threat of violence isn't the right way to handle differences of opinion."

"First finding Sig's body, now this. What's that American saying? Three strikes you're out?"

"I doubt this incident has anything to do with Sigmund's murder," Lilya said. "A rotten coincidence, bad timing. When it rains it pours."

"You have to admit you may have brought this upon the paper with the rhetoric you print daily," Marla said. What Sherry thought, Marla vocalized.

"I understand your sentiment, yes, indeed," Thomas said. "I'm beginning to regret coming on so strong in my newly adopted hometown. The printed word is a powerful tool. Not to be taken lightly and not to be misused." He exhaled a somber breath. "I need to right my wrongs, take a page from Sig's handbook."

"What does that mean?" Sherry asked. "From all I've heard Sigmund was the furthest person from someone aspiring to right their wrongs."

Thomas glanced over to the front window. What would normally be a sidewalk filled with passersby peering at the Ruggery's display window was empty. Thomas sighed. "I did this. I'm probably to blame for enabling my younger brother prolonged downfall."

"Why would you say that?" Sherry said. The thought passed through her mind that it was easy for the oldest sibling to blame themselves for not rescuing the younger ones in the family. Being the oldest herself she took any of Marla and Pep's missteps harder than she took her own.

"Lending a relative money comes with consequences. Always. At the time I thought I was giving Sig a boost up at a low point. Instead, he saw the loan as a limitless funding source. We had so many arguments over money. Maybe I took out my frustrations on Hillsboro County. My newspaper gives me a platform and the power to reach a big audience."

"But why take such an inflammatory stand against our town?" Marla asked. "That's borderline bullying. You get to shout out what you advocate from a mountaintop while those that disagree with you don't even get to shout unless they own a media outlet."

"The Van Ardans are too nice to take on a hard opposing stance in the *Nutmeg News*," Sherry said. "And they're getting criticized for a lack of pressure thanks to you. Progress is great but shoving it down folks' throats is literally hard to swallow."

"I'm ashamed of what's going on out there," Thomas said. "I take responsibility. I have reasons to not want to live in the past. My family's past has been painful. I wanted to get rid of the past and taking that stance made me feel I was helping everyone jump into a bright future."

Sherry caught Marla's glance. Her eyes were widened with either fear or skepticism. Either way, Marla wasn't boarding the train Thomas was engineering.

"It might be too late for regret," Marla said. She cupped her ear and leaned into a new set of sirens barreling down the street outside the store.

"Let's hope not," Thomas said. "I'm teetering on the edge of losing some of my best employees because I thought it was a good idea to push the envelope. One is one of my oldest and dearest friends."

Sherry fashioned a guess. "Is that employee a judge in the cook-off?"

"I've said too much. I won't lose him. The Brothers have suffered enough loss. Things will change. It was too late for Sig but not for the rest of us." Thomas reached for the door handle to let himself out, only to brush shoulders with Penny Nagle.

"I'm so sorry," Penny Nagle uttered breathlessly. Not sorry enough to avoid bumping Thomas off-kilter. He righted himself and took a step forward. Despite his efforts to leave, Thomas was contained at the door as Penny refused to step aside. "Oh, it's you!"

"Yes, got to go." Thomas dropped his head and plowed forward out the door.

"Tony, I'm in here with the Oliveris. Hurry up."

Sherry winced as the volume of her bellow assaulted her ears. She held the door as Tony raced to his wife's side. The open door let in the blast of another emergency vehicle's siren.

"Shut the door, shut the door," Penny directed. A tear was running down her cheek. "The police came into our store and ordered us to get out. Our whole life is in that store. How can a madman take that away from us?"

"Penny, it's going to be okay," Tony said. His tone wouldn't convince anyone he believed in his sentiment.

"Was your store targeted specifically?" Marla asked. "We heard the *Beacon* building was the bull's-eye."

"The police were short and sweet giving up any details when they blew in," Tony said. "What they did share was a caller named our store as one of the reasons Augustin will shrivel up and die. For that reason, we were under a bomb threat." The disgust on Tony's face summed up his feeling toward the situation. "Now they're in our store tearing the place apart in search of any explosive device. Might as well be one. Unless they leave the place as they found it, we'll be closed for a while cleaning up. All because we wouldn't change the name of the store to fit the youngsters' whims."

"This is all the *Beacon*'s fault. And that man," Penny said. "Why don't they go back to where they came from and rattle someone else's chains." Another tear streamed down her face.

"The town is so polarized both sides of the debate are being terrorized," Tony said. "We're just trying to make a living. Leave us be."

"Take a seat in the kitchen. I'll make you two a cup of tea. No sense stressing anymore. It's out of our hands. If the police haven't stopped in here, I'm assuming we're safe," Sherry said. She pointed to the kitchen.

"I'll make the tea," Amber said. She surveyed the store. Her gaze stopped on Erno across the room. "Erno? Would you like to join us in the kitchen?"

"Sure would. Sherry, you know where to find us," Erno said as he followed Amber and the Nagles into the kitchen.

Sherry texted Don about the goings-on. He didn't respond, which was a good indication he was busy with one of his interests rather than glued to his phone awaiting updates. She sent a second text urging him not to worry. The phone in her hand buzzed. Rather than seeing Don's name on the screen she saw Ray's. Not exactly Ray's. A few days ago, in a moment of levity, she assigned him in her contacts as *Sherlock*. She entertained the thought she should return the name to Detective Ray. For the time being she was amused and left the name as is. She clicked on his text.

You and yours okay?

Yes, thanks. How serious is this?

Serious enough. All clear will be given soon.

Bomb threater can't choose a side. Or is he tipping his hand it's not about the argument, it's about something else like deflection from the truth.

Gotta go.

Ray!

She set the phone down on the sales counter and glanced out the window. She couldn't hear any sirens and there certainly hadn't been any explosions from the *Beacon* building or the Ruggery would have suffered the rattle. The buzz of her phone shook her from her thoughts. Patti's name topped the text.

I can't tell you what to do. I'd like you to keep your head down until the cook-off. If you're still competing.

I hear you. And yes, I am.

Chapter 25

Sherry's computer calendar grid was so full of appointments on February 14 she had to expand the view to see all her reminders. She zoomed in on Don's birthday reminder. Of course, she knew his birthday fell on the day of the cook-off and Valentine's Day. For weeks she'd been trying to figure out how to make each event the best it could be. The day arrived and the realization set in that something would have to suffer.

She had hoped to talk to all three of the cook-off judges before today, thinking one of them might be able to shed some light on Sigmund's murderer's motive, but had never gotten the chance. Now she had to hope she would get a chance to talk to them at the end of the cook-off.

Sending a text message with emojis and an appropriate GIF would put a pin in Don's birthday celebration until later in the day, while showing him she cared to send her love first thing in the morning. They had decided not to spend the previous night together in order to concentrate on Tuesday prep. Her Valentine present to him was a surprise intimate dinner she'd put together later in the day after decompressing from the cook-off. No rest for the weary.

Sherry could have used Marla's help getting ready for the cook-off after breakfast. She wasn't available because she was picking Grant up at the airport. Marla wasn't thrilled about the early-bird flight Grant booked but he didn't want to be away from the ranch for very long. The saving grace was the cook-off supplied all the ingredients and equipment necessary for Sherry and the other finalists to complete their recipes. That was the kind of contest Sherry loved. Marla's help would have been appreciated nonetheless.

Sherry was excited to see the cook-off venue. The Southport Shores Hotel had only been open since late autumn. Word had it that the events center of the hotel had a spectacular meeting and reception space with ample room for the twenty-five finalist cooks' workstations and ovens. She realized cook-offs had grown in popularity to such a degree sponsors would pay for luxurious venues such as the Southport.

Being a local, Sherry didn't take advantage of the travel and accommodation package gifted to the incoming cooks, but the cook-off reimbursed her for any travel expenses and food purchased to test her recipe. She could also attend a contestant breakfast and lunch. She never tired of the special treatment she received for having her recipe chosen as a finalist. Plus, it was one step closer to the grand prize of ten thousand dollars if she could only sway the judges with both her perfected recipe and the associated story she had settled on. Enough daydreaming, the time had come to join the other cooks at breakfast.

Southport, as the name suggested, was southeast of Augustin, and ranked in the top ten highest incomes per household in the Northeast. Sherry could see where the income was spent as the houses grew larger and more opulent the closer she drove to the hotel. The hotel itself was brand spanking new. If time permitted, Sherry had the desire to walk the grounds and see the gardens in their winter attire, something the cook-off literature boasted as a huge draw to visitors. If this was the future of her county, modern and upgraded, she could get used to the notion.

"Sherry?" Thomas called out as Sherry walked up to the hotel's entrance. "You coming to breakfast? I'm hoping to introduce as many of the cooks as possible to the judges in the casual setting. In about twenty minutes." He was dressed in burgundy corduroys, a camel-color blazer and black sneakers. When he was within a few feet he continued. "You've spent time with Carl and Gunnar, at the lake. How about Sienna?"

"No," Sherry said. "I didn't talk to her at Patti's podcast interview session. I was hoping to chat with her at some time. She sounds like a very interesting foodie."

"Good, then I'm so glad you're here. My wife is bringing Magnus later. During his school's lunch break. He's so excited. He says you're using a story about the Yule Spoon-Licker. I can't wait to see everyone's expression when they hear what Icelanders believe in."

"I appreciate your optimism, but only five cooks chosen by the judges get to tell their story. My first job is to impress them with my recipe, then hopefully I'm in the final five."

"True. Everyone begins with an equal chance. I'll see you inside." Thomas picked up his pace and passed Sherry. He disappeared around the side of the hotel, possibly to another entrance.

After finding herself in the flashy hotel lobby, Sherry followed the signs for the contestant breakfast. She'd been to many contestant meals associated with cook-offs and meeting the other cooks was always a highlight.

There were nerves and excited anticipation throughout the room. Some contestants were too revved up to eat, while others made a contest out of cashing in the free food vouchers to their uppermost limit. Interacting with the judges was an interesting wrinkle in the process. Many times cook-off judging was blind, and Sherry never saw the judges until after the contest.

She turned the corner at the end of the lobby and was met with a collection of people shuffling around the sign that identified the breakfast room. She greeted the first person she neared.

"If you're a contestant we'd like you to consider withdrawing from the cook-off," a bearded man wearing a baseball cap said.

"Why would I do that?" Sherry said. Her voice broke as she struggled to understand the remark.

"The sponsor of the cook-off is dragging Hillsboro County through the weeds. He wants no trace of heritage or tradition, and is driven by the almighty dollar. Supporting him is destroying everything our predecessors worked so hard to hand down to us."

"Yup," another person added.

A third chimed in, "It's true."

"Save our county."

"Sherry, is everything okay?" Thomas said as he wedged his body through the circle of people enclosing Sherry. Behind him was a female officer from the Southport police.

"I'm going to have to ask you to wait outside the hotel unless you have a ticket to the breakfast or cook-off," the officer said. "This is an event. It will continue as planned."

"I'm happy to have you all buy tickets and watch the cook-off," Thomas said. "I think you will be pleasantly surprised how the sponsor has been listening to the town with open ears."

"Huh, I doubt it," the man wearing the baseball cap said in a huff. He followed the direction of the police and left the area with his group.

"I'm sorry, Sherry. I thought we had this under control," Thomas said. His face was blushed pink. "The monster I created is lurking everywhere."

"Tell me, Thomas. Has it been worth it? Your paper has come on so strong I don't know how the wound will heal. This may be my last local cook-off because my hometown is crumbling before my very eyes. If the town goes, my family goes with it. We're going to have to start over somewhere else that promotes the kind of town values we've known forever. That doesn't include remaking everything old into the latest and greatest in tech, innovation and luxury." Sherry imagined her face was as red as Thomas's. She inhaled and saw stars. "I'll see you inside." She turned her back on the man and made her way into the room that boasted aromas of maple syrup, fresh muffins and sausage.

Throughout the forty-five-minute breakfast Sherry made small talk with the other cooks at her table. All were most interested in hearing anything the judges had to say, as was promised in a brief welcome speech given by Thomas. Toward the end of the meal Thomas had all the cooks present stand up and introduce themselves. Carl, Gunnar and Sienna then said a concise hello and a two-sentence summary of why they took their responsibility of judgment to heart.

Sherry came away with the impression there was little chance any of the three judges murdered Sigmund. They were confident, professional and exuded a fire for all things food. The thought passed and Sherry was back in the moment. On to the next task. Winning the cook-off.

The breakfast crowd dispersed, some well-fed, some running on multiple cups of coffee alone. Sherry had seen one woman return to the coffee stand at least five times. She hoped the woman's recipe didn't involve much slicing with a steady hand. Sherry checked the time. One hour until the contestants were to line up as a group for a photo, followed by a parade entrance into the convention room. It was common that the cooks would have a few minutes to orient themselves to the tiny cook-off station they were assigned to, once they found their name plaque. At the Round the World's Pantry Cook-off, that wasn't the case. It was up to the sponsors and organizers to have read the submitted recipes thoroughly in order to supply the cooks with whatever was needed to execute their work correctly.

As Sherry peered through the double doors she knew she was reliant on the cook-off gods to cast good luck over her station. She used the remaining time to make small talk with the other cooks and tour the hotel's amenities. After forty-five minutes the cooks were summoned to convene in the hallway.

"Cooks, line up, please," one of the women wearing multiple credentials on a lanyard around her neck called out. "Here are your aprons. Please line up according to your assigned number. One through twenty-five."

A man grabbed Sherry's forearm. "You look like you know what you're doing. Do I tie the folded apron around my waist like the pros on TV do, or put the loop over my head and let the apron hang down to my knees, like my granny did?"

Sherry laughed. She'd never been asked for apron dressage advice before. "Anything goes," she said. "Guess it depends on the message you're trying to convey."

"Ha, that's right. Thanks." He proceeded to loop the apron over his head and tied a bow in the back. "I learned every kitchen trick from Gran Gran, so this is for her."

Aprons on, photos taken, the parade into the convention hall began. Two by two the cooks walked up the center aisle of chairs filled with eager audience members. She spotted the bearded man, who was still sporting his baseball cap. He was respectfully applauding the cooks as they found their way to their assigned cook stations. Sherry located number fourteen and began a concentrated search of all her tools, equipment and ingredients. Relieved all was as it should be, she scanned the audience for familiar faces while awaiting the "Ready, set, cook," announcement.

Marla and Grant were sitting about ten rows from the cooks' elevated floor. The cooks' area was cordoned off with a velvet rope. The ovens were spaced in a diamond pattern, leaving no view of a cook obstructed. Sherry knew the judges, as well as the media, would be traveling around the room for interviews and to inspect the techniques of the cooks, as was always the case at cook-offs. Overall, Sherry loved the interaction with members of the media, the sponsors and the judges. She felt it upped her game and kept her on her toes. It wasn't always that way. Her first cook-off was nerve-wracking, to say the least, and the memory flooded back every cook-off since. As a cook-off virgin her quivering hands and rapid heartbeat that took forever to settle left her exhausted when the cook time was up. The memory was cemented in her head and replayed when she spotted her father in the audience. Unlike her first cook-off, the terror evaporated and was replaced with adrenaline.

Erno was seated next to Ruth. Don was at the end of the row, next to Charlotte and baby Mimi. Charlotte mentioned she may not make the full ninety minutes with Mimi on her lap but Sherry didn't care. It only took one minute of Mimi's apple cheeks and angelic eyes beaming her way and she was stoked to represent the family. Was Don signaling something? Sherry had exchanged waves with him and now he was pointing forward. Sherry followed the path of his index finger. Patti. Patti was making her way to a reserved section of seats in the front row of the audience. A smile tugged at Sherry's mouth. A good omen her friend was well enough to attend.

Chapter 26

"Cooks. May I have your attention, please." Thomas walked across the space between the seats and the cooks' stage. "Welcome, everyone, to Round the World's Pantry—Cuisine and Culture Cook-off. Now that's a mouthful." He laughed, as did most in attendance. "Twenty-five talented home cooks will be preparing a recipe they have chosen to reinvent. Five will survive the first round to reach the final round. The chosen five will have a brief story behind their recipe they feel inspired their recipe. Over to my right"—he glanced in the direction—"sorry, my left, your right, are the three judges. Let me introduce Sienna Warren, cookbook author, celebrity chef and international food enthusiast." He led a round of clapping while Sienna stood.

"Our second judge is Gunnar Vilhjálmsson. Another mouthful. Gunnar is a food trend expert who studies popular trends, gives expert predictions the industry listens to intently and has come to heavily rely on." Thomas initiated another round of applause. "Our third judge is someone *I* rely on to give my readers reliable food information, recipe tips and all manner of good advice when it comes to what we should put in our bodies. Carl Carlson."

"Wonderful set of judges," the cook next to Sherry said. "If we can impress them we've done a great job."

"I agree," Sherry said.

The judges sat at a table to the side of the huge cooking platform. Thomas wished the cooks good luck and the countdown to the cook-off commenced. The audience participated in the final five-second countdown before Thomas announced, "Ready, set, cook." The digital clock on the back wall reset to ninety minutes and began to tick backward.

In the brief time she was given, Sherry's pre-cook-off check of her ingredients and equipment went, much to her relief, smoothly. She was glad she'd taken thorough inventory because she reinforced the steps of her prep as she did so. With the clock ticking sometimes her nerves were rattled and thinking wasn't as clear. Time to begin. Her first step was to prepare the pancake batter so that it could set up while she moved on to the pesto and gooseberry sauce. She would then combine the ingredients for the chicken filling, leaving only the dish assembly for the last few minutes for the desired freshness the judges would taste. At home she had only practiced the exact order of recipe steps once, choosing to focus more on getting each component of the recipe correct. At her previous cook-offs she learned nothing ever goes as planned and flexibility becomes part of the process no matter how good the intent for precision. Better to get the components correct and work with any slipups accordingly.

The Icelandic pancake, ponnukokur, consisted of the usual suspects—eggs, milk, flour, butter and salt. It was the proportions Sherry had to balance correctly to achieve a consistency of a thin elastic crepe. The perfect vehicle to transport a luscious, shredded chicken filling to the judge's mouths. The crepe-like pancakes made for an eye-pleasing presentation shingled on a platter. All was going swimmingly until the media began to filter onto the cook floor. At the same time the temperature in the room was rising as contestants were preheating their ovens. Fifteen minutes into the contest she peeled off her light sweater to be more comfortable.

Commotion was building as cooks, who were stationed within eight feet of one another, danced around to get to their refrigerated ingredients housed behind the rows of ovens and prep tables. If a microphone was plunged in a cook's face during a crucial decision-making moment, it could mark the difference between a lucid decision and fuzzy thinking. Shooing away the interviewer was out of the question, as the sponsor's desire for publicity trumped all.

As Sherry whisked the pancake batter to a creamy smoothness she saw the first reporter approach out of the corner of her eye. Maintaining proper technique was essential as the judges would also be passing through at any time, too.

"A little more wrist," the reporter suggested.

Sherry's eyebrows sprang up as the bold suggestion was considered. Tapping into her best behavior Sherry replied, "Thank you."

"Just kidding, you're the best whisker around."

Sherry lifted her gaze from the pancake batter. "Patti. I thought you were some know-it-all who'd rather be cooking than writing."

"No way. I know when to stay in my lane. I won't bother you for long. I need a quote for my cook-off article. The *Nutmeg News* and the *Beacon* are going head to head here and I'm all for showing up the competition. I have an angle that I think will give my article a leg up." Patti read the notes on her pad.

"Fire away," Sherry said. "I'm going to dice the vegetables until you're ready." Sherry pushed the pancake batter bowl aside, leaving some chopping room on her uber-compact block table. She made a knife choice based on the small size of the carrots. She'd once cut her finger at a cook-off with an unfamiliar oversized knife that was razer-sharp. She had grazed the edge of the blade during a silly error of overcrowding her equipment because her table was so small. Since then, she'd learned to tidy up her prep table continuously as she traveled through her recipe. The extra time spent on it kept not only her workspace clutter-free but her mind as well. Choosing the size of the knife was as important. No accidents. Knock on wood.

Sherry's gaze rose from the carrots. Patti was reviewing her notes as if forming the right words would produce an interesting answer. Sherry was never sure what she said was at all noteworthy. She'd also learned taking back a written word was impossible. If Patti's question could steer her response in the right direction, Sherry was thrilled for the assistance. While her friend took her time, Sherry savored the extra moment to get her dice cut uniform, something that may win her points during judging.

"Okay," Patti began. "The theme of this cook-off is fascinating on many levels. Were you aware one of the judges, Carl Carlson, came up with the theme after Thomas chose him to judge? It was also Carl's idea to have the *Beacon* hold the cook-off in the first place."

Sherry stopped cutting. "I had no idea. Good for him. Thomas should be very grateful to his food editor." She resumed making her carrots into tiny coins.

"Here's my two-part question. First, about the cook-off theme. If I had to summarize it in four words, I'd say what's old is new. Do you agree?"

A carrot dice propelled itself off Sherry's knife. She stopped cutting again and caught Patti's eye. There was a sparkle to Patti's gaze.

"Yes. I agree."

"My second question is, does the Sherry twist I know you've incorporated into your recipe right here reflect the past, present or future of food trends?" Patti asked.

"I'd like to hear that answer," a soft voice said. Sienna sauntered up beside Patti and lent an intent ear.

Rather than risk a knife slip, Sherry remained silent in order to finish with the carrot she was making perfect cuts of. She continued to the shallots and celery. Dicing them to match the carrots, she had the basis for her veggie-chicken filling. She set down the knife with an experienced cook's efficiency. Blade facing away from her body. Her hand was steady, but inside her chest her heart was pounding. "Hi, Sienna. Thanks for stopping by."

The two women on the other side of Sherry's table traded nods.

"Let's see. My recipe is based on a traditional Icelandic recipe for a dessert. I've transformed it into a savory main course while still honoring the integrity of the region's preferred flavors. Namely, chicken in an herby, creamy sauce with root vegetables. The Sherry twist—a background note of curry."

Patti tapped her notepad with her pen. "Chicken, herbs and a touch of curry. None of those is a modern trend but maybe all together you've struck modern gold."

"Old meets new and they shake hands," Sherry said.

Sienna remained silent. Saying anything might tip her hand as to Sherry's chances. Sherry searched the judge's face for any change of expression anyway. The woman was stone-faced.

"Thank you, Sherry. I can't wait to taste the end result," Sienna said. She flowed on to the next cook station a few feet away.

"Was that awkward?" Sherry asked. "You knew you'd see her here."

"No, not awkward," Patti said with resignation. "If she had something going on with Sig, she's in pain too."

"Unless . . ." Sherry picked up her knife before continuing, "Unless she . . ."

"Good morning," Thomas said as he shimmied by the cook next to Sherry. "I'm checking on everyone's progress. Did we supply you with everything you need?" He made a point of checking Patti's notepad. "Am I interrupting an interview?"

"We're done," Patti said. She flipped her notepad upside down. Assuming they had already greeted each other sometime in the morning, any pleasantries were bypassed. "Good luck, Sherry. Thomas, would it be alright to get a quote from each judge after the results are in?"

"Fine with me," Thomas said. "I will mention you'll be seeking them out. Carl is writing an article for the *Beacon*. May the best writer win."

"How can I compete with the writer who's also the contest judge? He really has the inside track," Patti said.

"Remember, you said you had an angle. Stick to it," Sherry said. "Trust yourself."

Patti mumbled something Sherry couldn't interpret before she moved on to the next cook. Sherry glanced up at the countdown clock. Plenty of time left if she used it wisely. She made an impromptu decision to save the prep of the pesto and fruit sauce until after the chicken filling was complete. That way freshness was guaranteed. Time to slice the boneless chicken thighs into strips for fast cooking. Reorganizing the remaining recipe steps in her head, she was lost in thought until she realized Thomas had yet to move on.

"Sherry, I'm in so deep I don't know where else to turn. I almost canceled the cook-off because I've made such a mess of things. My brother's been murdered. My paper is selling well, but at what cost. I get threats of violence and worse every day. I can't change the past, but I can stop the runaway train in its tracks. I think."

"You can't change the past," Sherry said. Did he mean he wished he hadn't killed his own brother and pushed Patti down the stairs because she may be on to him? "I need to get back to cooking."

"Of course you do," he said. "You're the one to beat. You're the reason we have such a big audience attendance. You probably didn't mean to but you're saving my reputation by being here."

Sherry lowered her head and returned her attention to cooking her vegetables. She sautéed them in an oiled pan until the edges were browned. She removed the veggies from the pan and stored them in a bowl for later use. Time for the chicken. When the strips were cut, she heated more oil in the sauté pan. Adding the chicken to the pan, she browned the strips on all sides and lowered the heat while she combined her sauce ingredients. The strips shouldn't be swimming in too much sauce. She wanted to see and taste the chicken in each bite of folded pancake. The herbs must pop with freshness and be evenly distributed throughout the filling.

The cream sauce involved deglazing the pan with heavy cream, cream cheese, a light hand of curry powder, garlic, sea salt and thyme. Chives would be added after removal from the heat, for the pop of oniony, garlicky freshness. Chicken filling complete and removed to a bowl, she set aside the fragrant creamy goodness for later use. Making the pesto was as easy as pulsing peas, garlic, basil, parsley, Romano cheese, pine nuts, and olive oil in a mini food processor. Done. The gooseberry sauce was even more straightforward. Gooseberries, orange juice and sugar simmered until the berries were soft. Done and done.

Sherry's next trick was to get the pancakes to behave in the hot pan. Browning the edges while retaining a moist, almost elastic texture was what Sherry had practiced. Pancake number one was the naughty child. It wouldn't brown until it was tough as nails, so the firstborn had to step aside. Pancakes two through six developed perfectly. The thin crepe batter was assembly-line fast to cook, once the temperature was leveled off. Sherry removed each pancake and stagger-layered them to create a shingled pancake mountain.

Sherry checked the clock again. With more than twenty minutes to go Sherry's best choice was to place the pancakes in a warm oven with a breathable dish towel tented over them. When the clock indicated ten minutes remaining, she would assemble the dish on the serving platter to assure the judges were treated to a scrumptious warm stuffed pancake. Until that time came, her next step was to locate the refrigerated skyr that she would dollop on top of the crepes a moment before presentation time. She checked the foot traffic to the refrigerator containing her creamy, tangy skyr. The path was clear until she found herself face-to-face with the two judges who had yet to visit her station.

"Sherry Oliveri," Carl said. He picked up her notecard-size sign to read the recipe title printed below her name. "Ponnukokurs. Growing up in Norway, I had those dripping with chocolate hazelnut spread. In Norway they're called pannekakers. The tender eggy pancakes exist all over Scandinavia. You're making them savory. Genius."

"I still make ponnukokurs, or pannekakers, depending on where you're from, every Sunday. I experiment with different fillings, but my favorite is Nutella and mascarpone cheese combined with roasted bananas," Gunnar said. His eyes lost focus as he must have transported himself back to Sunday brunch, featuring his ponnukokurs.

"That sounds amazing," Sherry said.

"What was your inspiration?" Gunnar asked.

Was there a right or wrong answer? Sherry pondered. She remembered Carl would be submitting an article for the *Beacon*. Her words may live on in infamy. Choosing them wisely was important.

"I have a fun story behind my recipe, and just in case I make it to the final five, I don't want to give away any spoilers."

The men nodded, indicating she'd piqued their interest.

"What I can say is I met a wonderful child from Iceland who introduced me to one of his family's favorite treats," Sherry said. "He also loves ponnukokurs. If he tasted your favorite he'd say you're going to have one very happy Spoon-Licker visiting you. You do use a wooden spoon, I'm assuming?"

"Of course," Gunnar said with a smile.

"Another example of the past creeping into our recipes," Sherry said. "That's one of the main attractions of cooking. Bringing a simple recipe, pancakes rolled around chocolate hazelnut spread, and elevating it. Pleasing the Spoon-Licker."

The men swapped gazes.

"You've been talking to Thomas, I see," Gunnar said.

"That's how I feel. Recipes are never devoid of a connection to the past."

"I agree one hundred percent, Sherry," Carl said. "That's what the theme of my cook-off recap article is going to touch on. If Thomas doesn't like it, it will be my last article for the *Beacon.* It might be anyway."

"She needs to get back to work. Us, too. We've got some tremendous recipes to judge. I am incredibly excited to see how everyone handles the last minutes," Gunnar said. "Thanks, Sherry."

Carl sighed and followed Gunnar to the neighboring cook's station.

"What was I just about to do?" Sherry asked herself. She watched another cook open the refrigerator behind the ovens. "Get my skyr. That's right."

"Here you go," the cook said as she handed the container to Sherry. "Your yogurt."

"Skyr's not a yogurt, it's a creamy Icelandic cheese. They've been eating it up there for a thousand years."

"I have never heard of that," she said. "Good luck."

"Thanks. Maybe I'll start a new trend," Sherry said.

Chapter 27

In the final three minutes of the cook-off Sherry wiped her hands clean. She gathered up her white platter loaded with expertly shingled ponnukokurs filled with creamy chicken filling and topped with a smear of gooseberry sauce, a spoonful of pea pesto and finished with a dollop of skyr. The other cooks had either brought their recipes to the judging table or were in line to be up next. Everyone wanted to be in the final five, the ones chosen to relay a story that would put their entry over the top and their name on the grand prize check. All that was left for Sherry was to deliver the goods.

When she returned to her station she exhaled and began a light cleanup. The audience helped the timekeeper count down the final ten seconds of the cook-off. The applause that followed gave Sherry an energy boost she needed to not plop down on the row of chairs located near the refrigerators.

While Sherry was waiting for the judging to be over, she let the events of the morning wash over her. Had she let the periodic interruptions wreak havoc with her recipe prep's flow? She didn't think so. Out in the audience, Don waved to her. Marla was giving her the thumbs-up. She spotted Erno, who was seated next to Ruth, then Charlotte and Mimi. One of her best showings of family attendance. Fifteen minutes went by while the audience murmured and conversed. The cooks were exhausted and only managed small snippets of chatter among themselves.

The three judges, who had disappeared out a rear door to confer, returned to their table. They were provided with microphones.

Thomas positioned himself in front of the audience. "Ladies and gentlemen. The judges have reached their decisions as to the final five cooks. Before I read the names, I would like to hear from the judges. Sienna? How difficult was your decision this morning?"

Dressed in a turquoise cable sweater and a pearl-studded hairband adorning her auburn hair, Sienna commanded attention when she stood. Impossibly trim, she appeared more like a catalogue model than someone entrenched in the food industry. The audience hung on the silence prior to her much-anticipated words.

"Thank you, Thomas. I've had the best time here this morning tasting the cooks' creations. Our taste buds traveled round the globe. The cook-off was aptly named, Round the World's Pantry. We judged on creativity, adherence to the chosen culture's palate and, probably the hardest for the cooks, ease of preparation. Most cultures pride themselves on long, slow cooking for a deep complex flavor that is nearly impossible to recreate in ninety minutes. Let me tell you, mission accomplished. So much so, our job was indeed most difficult." Leaving the audience gasping, Sienna sat back down.

"Well said, Sienna. Next up, Carl Carlson. Sienna told us how hard the decision to narrow down to five was. Can you tell us what surprised you most about the recipes? No spoilers, please."

Carl stood. The legs of his corduroys were bunched up and he spent a moment pushing them back down below his calves. The judges must have made an effort to coordinate because he too was dressed in a pastel pink cable sweater. The vibe was young and sporty even though he was most likely in his mid-forties.

"Good question," Carl said. He took the time to scan the cooks and the crowd before returning his gaze to Thomas. "Thank you for coming, everyone. Even those who may not have come for the sole reason of watching home cooks battle it out for kitchen supremacy." He paused while a ground swell of muttering rippled across the room. "I was most surprised how well the cooks launched their own versions of classic recipes. It's a lot harder than it sounds when you're being judged for that specifically." He held his sights on Thomas, who puffed out his cheeks.

"Thank you, Carl." Thomas waited until Carl slowly and deliberately lowered himself to his seat. "Last, but not least, Gunnar V."

Gunnar sported a yellow sweater with a black turtleneck peeking above the neckline. He was handsome and ruddy. When he stood, he revealed a rounded belly, attesting to his enjoyment of a good hearty meal.

"My question for you is since you make your living following and even predicting food trends, did any of today's cooks show you a trend you weren't familiar with?"

Sherry saw the audience as a whole sit up straighter in their chairs. This was a question they wanted answered. An inside track on the flavor or ingredient of the moment might put their own cooking one step ahead of the uninformed.

"No spoilers, right?" Gunnar asked.

Thomas nodded.

"Yes, is the short answer." Beyond that Gunnar wasn't willing to elaborate.

"Thanks, Thomas. Maybe after the contest we can discuss your findings more."

Gunnar sat back down. The audience showed their appreciation with a round of applause. One of the most animated clappers who caught Sherry's sights was Magnus. He and two women had made their way from the back of the seats to the front row. That was a perk of being the sponsor's son, and one of the women, Sherry guessed, was his wife.

"Okay, folks, the time has come," Thomas said. He pulled a sheet of paper out of his back pocket. "The five cooks the judges felt most represented the theme of the cook-off and should move on to the story round are the following. I'm reading the names in no particular order. Please hold the applause until all five have joined me up here. Thanks. Would the following cooks please join me at my side." He ran his finger down the sheet of paper. "Linette Sampson, Jessica Tillagio, Fran Brown, Sherry Oliveri and Wendy Klockenbrink." He paused. "Looks like the men in the group need to step up their game."

A breath later, Gunnar called over from the judge's table, "*Mister* Fran Brown."

"Excuse me," Thomas said. "I retract my statement. The men have been represented after all." The audience chuckled. "Please come up if I read your name and bring your story if you have it on paper."

The woman who was Sherry's neighboring cook hugged her as Sherry left her station. She wished she had a moment to freshen up in front of a mirror, but luckily no points were deducted for frazzled hair and a shiny face. Thomas shook each hand and reintroduced the cooks, giving each a few minutes to deliver their story. Sherry was third up. The two stories before hers involved the introduction of wheat to Greece and the legend of how tofu was invented in China two thousand years ago. Both stories highlighted a past that made the present possible, and Sherry knew the cooks were on the right track. Her turn came when Thomas handed her the microphone. A deep breath later, Sherry began. Her paper quivered in her hand as she read her story.

"Pardon my pronunciation of some Icelandic words," she began. "I took a risk preparing an Icelandic recipe today. I didn't have a connection to the cuisine personally and I had to dig deep to be inspired. This story did the trick for me." Sherry peered up from her paper and saw eager faces in the audience.

"Let me start by introducing one of Iceland's most controversial national dishes, at least to Americans. Hákarl is fermented, rotten shark, with a putrid smell and horrifying taste." The response from the audience reminded Sherry of the few times Chutney wretched up his lunch. "The dish is a culinary legend. Many Icelanders treasure it," she said as she glanced at the judges. Gunnar granted her an approving head bob. "Despite its ammonia-rich smell. But why eat it rotten? The Greenland shark is poisonous when fresh, with its very high content of urea. You don't want to eat that. It's toxic. Fermentation gets rid of all the poisonous substances. The downside is, when you open the package, bad odor explodes in your face. The solution: if you put the fish on a plate by a window and wait a while till it loses its scent, it's known to be tasty, filling and nutritious. In an unforgiving environment, putting up with some stink is how to survive. Where am I going with this story about an ingredient that is so foreign to my recipe?" She didn't wait for a reaction.

"Well, it's not as foreign as one might think. For one important reason. When I learned about fermented shark's place in Icelandic history I was intrigued. It might be new to me but it's been around since the age of the Vikings. The fact that such an ancient dish still exists and is considered a delicacy in its original form inspired me to honor one of the oldest cultures by taking one of their other national dishes and putting a modern savory twist on it. I didn't put a twist on fermented shark. You can't change perfection. But, I'm beyond happy to represent a recipe that's a combination of old and new—the essence of Iceland's cuisine." Sherry lowered her paper and handed the mic back to Thomas.

"Thank you, Sherry. You've given us lots to chew on."

The remaining two stories also captivated the attention of everyone in the room. Sherry was having the time of her life marrying stories with cooking.

"You cooks brought your A-game," Thomas said. "Time for a few minutes of judges' deliberation. Cooks, if you wouldn't mind returning to your stations, you may have a seat."

Chapter 28

Sherry watched the clock. She had enough time to use the ladies' room and place a call to Ray. He would have to track down the wooden spoon to give her an answer to the question she posed, but surely it was safely stored with the other murder scene evidence.

Ten minutes dragged by before Thomas walked out with the microphone in his hand. "I'll begin with the three third-place winners. Yes, not one of the five final finalists goes home without a prize. One thousand dollars each to the following: Sherry Oliveri, Wendy Klockenbrink and Jessica Tillagio, please step up to receive your prizes. And thank you so much for your wonderful recipes and stories.

Sherry's shoulders rounded a touch as she made her way to Thomas. The risk she took preparing an Icelandic recipe hadn't paid off to the degree she'd hoped. Third place out of twenty-five contestants was very good, she told herself as she bypassed those whose names weren't called, but her standards in cook-offs were high. She'd let some distractions take her mind off her work and the consequence was some aspect of her recipe didn't meet the judges' standards. Or was the problem her story? She shook Thomas's hand and accepted an envelope with the *Coastal County Beacon* imprint on the top left.

"Nice job, everyone. If you wouldn't mind standing beside me." He directed Sherry and the other two to line up with him. "Now for the second-place winner and the grand prize winner. I'll present you two together since calling one name spoils the ending. Come on up, Fran Brown and Linette Sampson." He paused while both cooks wound their way around the cook stations to reach the front of the judges' table. "Sienna, would you mind naming the second-place winner?"

Sienna stood and reached across the front of the table for the mic. "Yes, thank you. The second-place winner did a wonderful job showcasing the Greek pancakes called *tiganites* in a savory recipe with shrimp, mushrooms, herbs and delicate chives. Her story of how a Greek physician invented the foundation of the recipe two thousand years ago to promote healing for those with an unbalanced diet was eye-opening. Congratulations, Linette. We have lovely plaques for the winners, which we are engraving with the names as we speak."

Thomas waved an envelope as Linette approached the judges. "Enjoy," he said as he handed over the envelope. "Carl?"

Carl rose from his seat and was handed the mic. "Before I present the grand prize to Fran Brown, I would like to speak for the judges on the winning entry. Peruvian empanadas with green sauce were a delight, all three of us agreed. The right texture of the round dough wrap, the filling of ground beef and olives was sublime, and the fresh herbal sauce put the recipe into the next stratosphere of flavor depth. Right, judges?"

Sienna and Gunnar beamed in agreement.

"The story Fran chose to share was one of a centuries-old cookbook being the first written record of the empanada. Seems there's been an adherence to the theme of the past enduring and thriving in the present when it comes to recipes. Right, folks?"

The audience applauded. At the same time, a few choice phrases were called out.

"Stay old, Augustin."

"Keep your wrinkles, Augustin."

"Thank you, folks," Carl said. "Fran Brown, please accept your check as the grand prize winner of the Round the World's Pantry—Cuisine and Culture Cook-off."

A hearty cheer went up for Fran.

"Congratulations and thank you again for coming to the cook-off this year. Can't wait to see everyone next year." Thomas had a word with each finalist, reaching Sherry last.

"I've had my eyes wide open here," Thomas said. "I thought maybe the person who killed my brother and the person who made a bomb threat to the paper might be one and the same, and might be bold enough to show up here. I think the vocal group was your run-of-the-mill agitators. Nothing to be concerned about."

Sherry studied the man's face. He was so cool about some very serious circumstances. Too cool. "Would it be appropriate if I had a word with the judges?"

"About the contest or about Sigmund?" Thomas asked. "Never mind, ask them whatever you want. The investigation's completely stalled as far as I'm concerned. I wish he had just run away and not gotten himself murdered." The first demonstration of emotion Sherry had seen from the man since she'd met him.

"Now's as good a time as any," Sherry said. As she turned away from Thomas she muttered, "I think I hit a nerve."

The judges were separating from a conversation huddle. "Your recipe was delicious," Gunnar said as Sherry neared.

"I wanted to thank you all," Sherry said. "I've been in a lot of cook-offs and this one has been one of my favorites. I know the timing was rough with all the extracurricular activities going on. It must have been hard to focus." She didn't want her comment directed at solely one person, so she shifted her sights from Sienna to Carl, landing on Gunnar.

"Add to that, Carl and I are in the middle of contract negotiations at our other jobs," Gunnar said with a sigh.

"Nothing to negotiate with me," Carl said. "I'm moving on. The workplace has gotten too volatile. I go home with a headache every night. The fact that I had such a heck of a time convincing Thomas this cook-off was a fantastic idea to sponsor reflects how far off our two mindsets are. I gave notice that I was leaving the paper."

Sienna was inspecting her manicure while the men were talking.

"Sienna, are you in town for long? Detective Bease mentioned you lived in Florida."

"Did he mention I was to stay around a few more days because I was pinpointed as having been at Harmony Lake the night of Sigmund's murder?" Sienna said. "You know who else was there?"

Sherry's eyebrows shot up. Another nerve hit. "Patti Mellit."

"Yup. She threw me under the bus so fast my head is still spinning. And I thought I did her a favor being on her podcast."

"The detective is sorting out the facts. I wouldn't take it personally. He's covering the bases." Sherry fidgeted with her apron, struggling to untie the strings. "This darn thing. Must be in a knot." Instead of offering assistance, Sienna walked away.

"Need help?"

Someone attacked the knot before waiting for an answer.

"Thanks, I couldn't quite get my fingers in the loop," Sherry said. She twisted her neck to see who was undoing her apron. A woman with fuzzy blonde hair, hardy rose-hued complexion and pronounced square shoulders brought the apron string forward.

"Happy to assist," the woman said. She was accompanied by a blonde boy.

"Magnus. Hi. I'm so glad you made it. I wish I had won for you but third isn't bad," Sherry said.

Magnus was almost leaning on the woman next to him.

"Hi, I'm Sherry. Magnus was in a gardening class I taught at his school."

"I heard. He couldn't wait to come over and say hello. I'm Nora.

Thomas Helguvson's sister-in-law and Magnus's auntie."

How noticeable was Sherry's jaw drop, she wondered. She snapped her mouth shut while processing the shock of the introduction. Too much time passed before she spoke. "Nice to meet you. I'm so sorry for your loss." Sherry scanned the crowd for Patti. No sign of her.

"Thank you," Nora said.

"Ms. Sherry, you didn't use the Spoon-Licker story? Why not? I bet you would have won if you did," Magnus said. He wasn't making eye contact and his lower lip was protruding.

Sherry lowered her exhausted frame to Magnus's eye level. "I had to be the one who found the story I used. I appreciate your help, but it was important I used the story I used."

"Sigmund would have appreciated your story. The idea behind the import-export business he was banking on here in the States was to promote the legacy of Icelandic national dishes. I don't think he listened to good advice. He sure made of mess of the venture and his chance at success."

"Uncle Sig was about to start working with my dad at the paper," Magnus said. He lifted his head and shined a half smile.

"It wasn't what he wanted but his try at entrepreneurialism bombed," Nora said.

"Bombed?" Sherry didn't expect a reply, but rather was testing the reaction waters based on Nora's word choice and the *Beacon*'s recent event.

"Last I heard from him he was in negotiations with his brother. Waiting for an opening at the paper. In the food section, of course. It sounded like a strong possibility. I suppose Thomas got tired of bailing Sig out. Add to that, Sigmund's viewpoint was the opposite of Thomas's. Hiring him would have been a complete disaster."

"You're not saying . . ." Sherry began. She swallowed her supposition.

"Why not?" Nora said. "Sig didn't know boundaries. He may have asked for help one too many times. I was hoping he'd chosen to fake his death and live happily ever after as someone else. I would have gotten used to the idea of starting over, myself, alone. But he had to go and get himself killed. Another plan gone awry."

Nora put her arms through the sleeves of her coat. She retrieved a cable-stitched, pom-pommed hat out of the coat pocket and pulled it down over her blonde hair. The wild ends tried to escape being subdued, giving Nora the look of a wind-blown adventurer. "Magnus needs to get back to school. It was nice meeting you." She secured Magnus's hand in hers and led him away.

After two steps, Magnus turned and waved.

"That's the hat I saw at Harmony Lake," Patti said as she sidled up to Sherry. "I thought it was an Icelandic brand. Who was that lady? A friend of Sienna's? They have the same hat."

"Whoa, whoa, slow down," Sherry said. "That was the hat you said Sienna was wearing the night Sigmund was murdered?"

"The falling snow sparkled along with the metallic yarn threads. Through her windshield I could see the letter *I* insignia patch on the front. Didn't get as good a look at the wearer," Patti said. "For all I know it could have been that lady. Who was that?"

Sherry twisted her mouth as the words refused to come.

"Oh, no," Patti said. "That was Nora." She paused as she scanned the room. "What did she say? Did you talk about me?"

"I absolutely did not," Sherry said. "Her nephew, Magnus, was in my gardening class this past week. He dragged her over to say hi. That's all." She dipped her head toward her shoulder. "Well, she also lamented the fact Sigmund made a mess of his life. And hinted she wouldn't be surprised if Thomas had something to do with his murder."

"His sister-in-law thinks he's guilty?"

The crowd was thinning. Sherry lowered her voice, as it could carry. "I don't think she's certain. There are others to consider."

"Like herself?"

"Maybe," Sherry said.

"I don't suppose you asked her if she knew Sienna Warren? Maybe Sigmund gave a hat to each of them so he could keep better track of his herd." Patti managed a weak laugh. "Maybe that was going to be my Valentine's Day present. Speaking of valentines, yours is waving at you."

To Patti's right, Don was beckoning Sherry. Marla, Grant and Erno were bunched around him.

"It's his birthday, too."

"I'll let you go," Patti said. "Your day has barely begun."

"Can I ask you one more thing?" Sherry said. "Why did you tell me you didn't have to rerecord parts of the podcast when, in reality, you had the three judges return the same day and rework the necessary spots?"

Patti grimaced. "You're a darn good sleuth. That's why I asked you to lend me a hand. I also figured the time would come when you put two and two together and I'd be busted for a white lie."

"But why? I'm only trying to help you. Clem, your doorman, was easy access to the answer of whether the judges returned that day."

"They were fighting in the green room while waiting for your interview to end. I heard them. I recorded them. They were fighting with Sig, and I had the evidence. Yes, I could have fixed the material with my editing software, but I wanted them to know I caught them all squabbling. It's normally nothing to be concerned about, except one ended up dead."

"That's right. What you couldn't have known is you risked your life calling them back into the studio if one was the murderer who thought you could ID him or her," Sherry said.

Patti groaned. "I suddenly realized after Sig's accident at the lake I'd be putting you in terrible danger if I involved you. I regretted ever asking for your help. Ignorance is bliss and I wanted bliss for you. If you didn't think I had them return to the studio you wouldn't narrow one of them down to being my assailant. All leads point to that. I wanted to take over the reins of discovering who, so as not to endanger you."

Sherry gave Patti a hug. "You're the best. But don't do that again," she scolded. "I need to know everything you know." Sherry's gaze bore down on Patti. "Is there something else you need to share?"

"Isn't that enough? Sienna and Nora share a taste in hats and men. The three judges may be suspects in Sig's murder and one may have pushed me down the stairs. And you say Nora thinks Thomas is at the top of the list. Oh, wait, Detective Bease has me on the suspect list. Proves I'm not doing such a good job at sleuthing. Can I hand the reins back to you?"

"We'll get this sorted out," Sherry said. She hoped that wasn't a hollow promise.

"The town might implode before anyone can get to the bottom of Sig's murder," Patti said. "Your man's shoulders are going to give out if you don't hustle over to him. See you soon." Notepad in hand, Patti headed toward the exit.

Don was gesturing for Sherry to meet him at her workstation. Sherry pointed to her purse and complimentary tote full of cook-off sponsor goodies resting on her prep table. A moment later she found Don leaning on the oven.

"Hi, my lovely winner." He planted a kiss on her lips. "Great job today."

"Thanks. Sorry I didn't win grand prize with all my favorite cheering section on hand."

"You're always a winner in my book," Don said with practiced enthusiasm. "What happened to this?" He held up a wooden spoon snapped clean in half.

Chapter 29

"I have no idea. I didn't even request a wooden spoon today. I don't know where that appeared from." Sherry scouted the remaining crowd. She spotted Thomas chatting with a group of lingering cooks. Not far from him, Gunnar and Carl were entertaining a reporter and photographer. She couldn't locate Sienna among the people milling about. She did notice the bearded man with the baseball cap approaching Thomas.

"Want me to put it in your goody bag?" Don asked.

"Sure," Sherry said. "Someone must have thought it was mine and returned it to my station." Which made no sense at all, but Sherry didn't want Don alarmed.

"Marla and Grant really want to have dinner with us," Don said. "Let's go back to the original plan of combining Valentine's Day with my birthday and invite the whole gang. We'll order out."

"I think that's a great idea," Sherry said. "I was going to surprise you with a special dinner. Turns out I'm pooped."

"Good, because I've already given everyone an invite while we were waiting for you."

"Hey, Sher," Marla said as she gave her sister a hug. "That was so exciting. Best cook-off ever. Right, Grant?"

A handsome man with unshaven facial scruff, dressed in blue jeans, flannel shirt and toting a shearling jacket slung over his shoulder, moseyed up to Sherry. "Hey, Sherry." Grant crowded out Marla to bear-hug Sherry. "You're a hog at the trough when it comes to cook-offs."

"I think that's a good thing. Thanks, Grant."

"After smelling all that food all morning I sure have a strong hankering for your grub tonight. What time should we trek on over to your house? Marla and I hope to spend some quality time together before that. I haven't seen her all week." He winked at Marla, who uncharacteristically went mute. She feigned the use of a fan to cool herself after her husband's provocative suggestion.

"I've missed Marla's cowboy," Sherry said. "I'll have some good Valentine's Day grub for you tonight. And birthday grub for you. Might not be homemade but it'll be good." She grabbed Don's hand. "I need to get home and start preparing." One more look inside her goody bag assured her the broken spoon was in there. "Where's Dad?"

"He got a text from Amber about an order and went back to the store,"

Marla said. "He said to tell you, 'Great job as always,' and he'd see you later. He'll be bringing Ruth tonight."

"I wonder if Amber can come for dinner," Sherry said.

"With her friend?" Marla asked.

"She'll be there," Don said. "It's my birthday."

"Wow, you really have put the word out. Thanks, honey."

Sherry and Don were among the last to leave the room. Thomas and the many helping hands who coordinated the contest were busy running from location to location organizing an exit plan for all the equipment. Fran Brown was granting interviews with the media by his oven, a position Sherry found herself in often. Her gaze lingered on the commotion surrounding Fran for a few moments.

"How you feeling?" Don asked.

"I took a chance with my recipe. Maybe Gunnar thought I was pandering to him and Thomas by choosing an Icelandic recipe."

"Sienna's not from that region of the world, is she?" Don asked. "I thought you mentioned she lived in Florida."

"That's right."

"Was your recipe more about helping Patti out than winning?" Don asked.

"What's that saying, nice guys finish third?" Sherry asked as she turned her attention to Don.

"Something like that. What did you think would happen? The murderer would rush out and admit guilt because of a certain recipe? I don't really get your motive."

"It was a long shot, I admit. I thought the story associated with the recipe might flush someone out, yes."

"The story was about eating rotten shark. Kind of turned my stomach if I'm being honest. How was that going to flush someone out? Oh, and there's a joke there but I'll resist," Don said with a sly smile.

"Thomas," Sherry said. "I wanted a reaction from Thomas. His brother, Sigmund, started an import-export food business. Dried fish strips were one of his items. I saw the package at the grocery store. The stock boy there was removing them from the shelves because Americans don't quite know what to do with the strong flavor and chewy, to say the least, texture. Another failure of Sigmund's and another punch in the gut to Thomas, who was one of his financiers."

"Do you think Thomas murdered his brother?"

"He had his reasons. This was a chance to get a reaction. If he lost his composure once he sure as heck will do it again."

"And did you see any telltale reaction after your story?" Don asked. "Besides a gag reflex from me?"

"Nope. Not a one. From Thomas." Her words slowed to a crawl and lingered on "Thomas."

"Someone else?" Don asked.

"Maybe," Sherry said. "Time will tell."

"One more small snag in your plan. What if you never got as far as the final five? You couldn't tell your story at all if you hadn't made the final round. Did you have a plan B?"

"First of all, I'm offended you would even suggest I wouldn't make the finals," Sherry said, steeling her posture as rigid as she could manage. "You're right. I had no plan B."

"I always work with a plan B. If something doesn't go by design, I make other arrangements. That's what makes a good sea captain."

"Why do I get the impression we're not talking about the murder investigation anymore?" Sherry said with a broad Valentine's Day smile.

Don's eyes rose to the ceiling and he shrugged. If a halo sprouted over his head, Sherry wouldn't have been surprised. Something was fishy and it wasn't just the fermented shark.

Chapter 30

"Happy birthday, dear Don, happy birthday to you!" The chorus of well-wishers wrapped up Don's birthday serenade with the presentation of a cake topped with glowing candles.

"Thanks, everyone," Don said. "Best birthday ever. Chicken Cordon Bleu, Caesar salad, roasted potato wedges, asparagus. All my favorites. I'm a lucky guy." He blew a kiss across the table to Sherry.

Marla pushed back her chair and collected the dessert plates from the kitchen. She placed the stack in front of Don and whispered in his ear. Something was up and Sherry's imagination took flight. That was until Don shook off Marla and she returned to her seat, seemingly dejected. The table went silent.

Don raised his glass of beer. Everyone followed suit, including baby Mimi, who lifted her sippy cup.

"Sherry," Don began. "I wanted to thank you for coming into my life and making every aspect of it better. Especially mealtime. I know today hasn't been the best of days. You were robbed of the grand prize at the cook-off, and whatever sleuthing scheme you were hoping to succeed at didn't materialize. We love you and you're always a winner to me."

"What's he talking about?" Erno said. "Sherry doesn't expect to win every cook-off."

The room exploded with laughter.

"Get to the point," Grant called out. He curled his tongue under his teeth and produced a hog-calling whistle. Chutney and Bean came running.

"We're all here now," Erno said.

"I've never seen so much suspicious behavior," Sherry said. "Amber, you'll tell me what's going on, won't you?"

"I don't know what you mean. Back to you, Don," Amber said.

"I asked Erno for your hand in marriage and he's given me permission," Don said as he walked around the table and kneeled at Sherry's side. Erno's head bobbed up and down in agreement. "Sherry, will you marry me?"

"What? You schemer. You managed all this, got everyone together under false pretenses and, and . . . yes!" Sherry yanked Don off the floor in a feat of superwoman strength. "Yes!"

"Oh, I forgot this." Don wriggled out of Sherry's embrace and dug in his pocket. He presented a box.

"Open it," Marla called out.

Inside the box was a sapphire and diamond engagement ring, which he slipped on her finger. "Phew, it fits."

The cheers were so loud the dogs sought refuge elsewhere. Congratulations followed, as did Don's coconut cream birthday cake.

Later that evening, Sherry confided to Don she had a sneaking suspicion something was up but she didn't dare pin her hopes on what she wished for. "Why else would you all suddenly decide you had to see one of my cook-offs all together. It was as if I had announced my retirement, and you know that's not happening any time soon."

"Could have been for my birthday, you know. It doesn't always have to be about your cook-offs." Don tapped into his limited acting experience to imitate a sullen pout. "Let me get to those dishes, I'm a year older and I need to conserve my energy for other things."

• • •

"How does it feel to have a fiancé?" Amber asked.

Sherry opened the register and slipped a copy of the sale she had made in the proper drawer well.

"Not much different. Except I have some new hardware." She waved her jewel-adorned hand. "We're not even ready to set a date until after the summer commuter season. Don's hoping to extend the season with new boat radar and safety gizmos, so this is another trial year basically. No rush."

The brass bell jingled over the Ruggery's entrance.

"Good morning."

"Thomas. I hope there's not another bomb threat at the *Beacon*," Sherry said. "You wouldn't say 'good morning' if there was."

"That's right. All is relatively calm for the moment," he said.

"You remember Amber? She can assist you if you're looking for any particular rug type or even if you have no idea what you're shopping for." Sherry's relief that there were no more bomb threats translated into a chuckle.

"As much as I'd love to work with Amber, I came to have a word with you, Sherry."

"Sure," Sherry said.

"I'll be in the back," Amber said. She gave Sherry a second glance and received an "It's okay."

"I'll get right to the point," Thomas said. "Kids can't keep secrets for very long and Magnus is no exception."

Sherry's brows knit together as she tried to comprehend where this was going.

"Magnus said he left you a message on your cook station yesterday. A wooden spoon, from our family's collection, snapped in half."

"Why would he do that?" Sherry asked.

"He wanted you to use his story about the Spoon-Licker Yule Lad in your presentation to the judges. He thinks you would have won if you did and he was frustrated with you. He's very sorry and would be here in person if he weren't at school."

"Please don't be hard on him. I know he's had a tough year adjusting to the family's relocation. And the goings-on with the *Beacon*. And the passing of his uncle. He was worried about you and his mom."

"I've really made a mess of trying to promote some change in the county," Thomas said.

"I have to agree," Sherry said. "Everyone's paying the price for what could be your ego getting in the way of what started out as a good idea to have a competing paper in the county."

"Ego?" Thomas asked. "Huh, maybe. I was riding high for a while. I had my three amigos along with my success. Carl was getting great reviews writing for the food section of the paper. I nudged him to put a modern spin on his content and he begrudgingly did. Gunnar has made a name for himself identifying food trends. Sig was doing okay. He was talking about giving up his business and joining the paper. I wanted to reunite us for the sake of—well, you're right. For the sake of my ego. I've invested so much in our fraternity I couldn't suffer failure if we all went our separate ways."

"How does Sienna fit into the scenario? I'm aware she and Sigmund knew each other," Sherry said. Thomas held her gaze, never flinching.

"Yes, Sienna and Sig had a special relationship," Thomas said. "One I would never exploit for the purpose of advancing my career. She meant a lot to him in the short time they knew each other. Let's leave it at that."

"But Patti. She was dragged through the mud by Sig." Sherry bunched up her hand until her knuckles were white. "You knew she was going to get hurt and you did nothing about it. I'm sorry, but there's not much I like about you except the son you produced."

"I didn't know anything about Patti until just recently. I promise you. Sig had gotten word that Nora had hired a detective to find him. That meant Lilya would uncover his time spent with Patti. Seemed like just a dalliance to me and Sig had more responsibilities than to get involved with a lovely woman friend he enjoyed spending time with."

"Responsibilities?" Sherry prompted. "And you're not even taking Sienna into consideration?"

"Sienna can take care of herself," Thomas said in a dismissive tone. "Sig was in debt, to me, to the Bankless Brothers, probably to Nora, and his new business was out of the honeymoon phase with investors and not showing any upward tick in profits. None, zero."

Time to pounce. Thomas no longer directed his conversation at Sherry. He had turned inward and was talking to himself. His tone softened and his posture sagged. Over his shoulder a concerned Amber was making faces at her friend. The unspoken message was, "Call my name if there's a problem happening."

"Did you kill your brother?" Sherry blurted out.

When Thomas lifted his gaze, a tear was rolling down his cheek. "I didn't. But I think I know who did. Your friend Patti."

"Thomas, she didn't and we have to find out who did. I am one hundred percent certain she did *not* kill Sigmund." Sherry had had enough of the conversation. "Amber?"

"Yes, Sher. Do you need my help?"

"I'll get out of your hair. And I'll let Magnus know he's forgiven." Thomas let himself out without so much as a farewell. Sherry wasn't offering one up either.

"Do you believe him? That he didn't kill his brother over lost finances and general all-around annoyances?" Amber asked.

"A devil's advocate, that's what I need. But, yes, I do."

• • •

The day cruised along smoothly. Erno checked in by phone only to receive a scolding from Sherry about not taking full advantage of removing himself from the store on his days off. Twenty minutes before closing the doorbell tinkled and in walked Ray. Sherry met him at the front of the store.

"Good afternoon, Sherry," the detective said. "Congratulations on your cook-off win. With an Icelandic-inspired recipe, no less."

Ray was bundled in a down coat the size of a queen-sized bed comforter. He wore a knit ski hat so all-encompassing only his eyes, nose and mouth were visible. No forehead, no cheeks, no hair.

"Did you just come from the slopes?" Sherry asked.

"You haven't been outside lately, I'm guessing," Ray said. He lifted his hat off his head, leaving a haphazard mop of hat-hair exposed. "The temperature has dropped about twenty degrees. It's zero out there. And the wind is picking up. Winter's barking and I'm dressed for it."

"Hi, Ray," Amber called across the room. "You look adorable."

Disarmed by sweet talk, Ray fumbled for words. "Th . . . thank you." He watched Amber return to the storage room. "Do you have a minute?"

"Sure," Sherry said. She glanced up at the clock. Ten minutes to closing time. "Want to have a seat? I should stay out here but we can pull over a kitchen chair." Leaving him no time to respond, she crossed the showroom and dragged a wooden chair out of the kitchen.

"Don't scratch these beautiful antique floors," Ray warned.

"No worries. All the furniture is padded under the legs." She steered the chair behind the sales counter, where it came to rest. "Have a seat."

"Thanks." Ray lowered himself into the chair. "I want to pick your brain. Thomas is off my list."

"Mine, too," Sherry said. "I believe him now. I didn't a few days ago but I do believe he didn't kill his brother."

"Besides your belief he has an alibi," Ray said. "The night of the murder Thomas was at a cook-off organization meeting at the Southport Shore Hotel. I didn't just take his word for his timeline I substantiated his claim with surveillance video from the hotel. The time stamp is the issue. Pinpointing exact time of death is difficult due to the water temperature's ability to preserve the body tissues."

"Okay," Sherry said. "So, not necessarily a solid alibi."

"Sigmund Helguvson left some collateral damage in his wake. His wife, Nora, for one. But she isn't high on my list. Why would she hire a detective to prove he faked his death? She wouldn't profit on him doing so, unless she was planning on taking him to court for any laws he may have broken. Doubtful. That's expensive and time-consuming for not much return."

"Unless hiring Lilya was an elaborate scheme to detract from his murder, before, during and after."

"You know something," Ray said. "Care to share?"

"I have a nagging feeling Lilya knows more than she's letting on. She wants us to join forces, when the fact is she has more access than anyone to the people in Sigmund's inner circle."

Ray selected a pen from a ceramic jar. He clicked the mechanism to release and retract the point, over and over until Sherry put her hand out to stop the annoyance.

"You've already joined forces with her, haven't you," Sherry said. It wasn't a question. She knew. "Have you gone out on a date?"

"We've set the date, not gone yet. You know I don't mix business and pleasure," Ray said. "That's why I'm here. Lilya's on her way over and I wanted to make sure you're okay with having her stop by."

"Of course. I have to say I'm surprised. You've never been one to pair up in your investigations. You trust her that much?" Sherry asked.

The doorbell jingled and in strolled Lilya. Her face was red except for her cheeks, which were blotched with white. "Goo affernoo." The words were delivered with frozen lips.

"Come in, get warm," Sherry said.

"Thanks for coming, Lilya," Ray said.

Lilya pulled off her downy white hat. Possibly cashmere. Static electricity from the store's heat gave the airy yarn a life of its own. She tested the pliability of her lips. When they moved freely, she spoke. "I think my face is thawing out. It is so cold outside. I couldn't find a parking spot close by and the wind is whipping."

"Take my seat," Ray said.

"I think I'll stand to stay warm for a few minutes, thanks anyway," Lilya said.

"If everyone's comfortable, I'll get right down to brass tacks," Ray said. "Sherry wants to find Sigmund's killer so her friend Patti can have some closure. Some say Patti's the murderer. Nora would like to find her husband's murderer. Some say she's guilty. Thomas Helguvson has an alibi. Do his friends Gunnar V. and Carl Carlson?"

"Why do they need an alibi? Why would they want Sigmund dead?" Sherry asked.

"Gunnar started working for the *Beacon* today," Lilya said. "In the job Thomas promised Sigmund. Food and home section editor. The announcement is on the front of today's paper."

"Rewind a little. Thomas had promised the job to Sigmund?" Sherry asked. "I knew Carl was threatening to vacate the job. He told me at the cook-off. He couldn't continue to align himself with the paper's content bias. Sigmund wasn't on board with the modernization of the county either, from what I knew. I guess as Thomas's brother he earned certain allowances others didn't get. Still, something isn't lining up."

"Nora claims Sigmund was fully invested in his import-export business because he wanted the U.S. to experience what old-school Icelandic eating was all about. He was all about bringing the past back alive to gain appreciation again," Lilya said. "Only problem was, the cash had nearly dried up. And Icelandic exports may be a hard sell. One of the last communications he had with Nora was, unfortunately, a plea for funds, which she wasn't willing to send. The communication dwindled after that, she said."

Sherry puffed out her cheeks. "Dried fish strips are a tough sell in today's fast-paced culture. He was waging an uphill battle for customers. But still, it doesn't make sense he would cash it all in for a job he didn't have faith in. Unless Thomas made him an offer he couldn't refuse."

"They're an acquired taste. For selective palates," Lilya defended.

Ray scrunched his forehead.

"At Patti's office the men were in the midst of a disagreement," Sherry said. "She even had to redo part of the interview because the recording picked up the bickering."

"I wonder if they were having a blowout about who gets what job, who's leaving their job, who owes who money?" Lilya suggested.

"Unfortunately, Patti edited out the words before anyone else was able to listen," Sherry said. "She said they would have had to have been amplified to be understood, if that was even possible, coming through a wall like that."

After a pause, she added, "It couldn't have been over the wooden spoon Sigmund brought to Patti's podcast that day. The opposite. My sister, Marla, said when they were talking about the wooden spoon and handing it around the room, tempers were soothed."

"What do you know about Carl Carlson and the Gunnar fellow?" Ray asked after his long stretch of sitting in silence, absorbing the back-and-forth between Lilya and Sherry.

"I made it a point to talk to them after the cook-off," Sherry said.

"For what reason?" Ray asked.

"Two reasons. One, to get a handle on what they thought of my entry, and second, to see if my story behind my recipe had struck a chord with them, or Sienna."

"I don't need to know about the entry, but did you strike a chord? And what would that chord be?" Ray asked.

"My story was about the popularity of eating rotten fermented shark meat in Iceland."

"Ooph!" Ray sucked in a long breath and slammed his eyelids shut.

When he opened them Sherry plowed ahead.

"Sienna's not from Iceland so I don't think she had an emotional connection to the quirky eating habits of the residents. Carl mentioned he felt strongly about preserving the past, whether it's a popular idea or not. Keeping the past alive through recipes is very important to him. The main reason he was talking about leaving the *Beacon*. He wasn't willing to capitulate."

"And Gunnar?" Ray asked.

"Gunnar flip-flopped as if he were undecided. Blew with the wind," Sherry said. "Maybe the story choice was where I lost points with him."

Ray began clicking the pen button again, a sign he may be growing impatient with the ambiguous proceedings of the meeting.

"Nora and Sienna had the same pom-pom winter hat," Sherry said. Ray stopped clicking.

"Do you see importance there?" Ray asked. "You're not giving me much to work with."

"Patti said she saw someone in a car at Harmony Lake the night Sigmund called her to meet, presumably to tell her he was married."

"Right, she told me," Ray said.

"After meeting Sienna at the podcast, Patti was certain Sienna was the woman driving out as Patti was driving in. At the cook-off she learned that Nora had the same distinctive hat hailing from Iceland. So, was the driver Nora leaving after getting her just desserts, and not Sienna after all?"

"This is getting so complicated," Lilya said.

Chapter 31

"Nora may have been at the lake? Not Sienna?" Ray asked.

"Sienna was there," Sherry said. "She told me as much after the cook-off."

"And where does Sienna fit in? A love triangle?" Lilya said.

"Nora has more reasons than ever to take matters into her own hands. Talk about too many cooks spoiling the broth," Sherry said. She saw Lilya rub her temple. "Are you sorry you extended your contract with Nora? You may not have very good news for her, that she is high on the suspect list."

"Somehow I have a feeling she already knows," Lilya said with a glance in Ray's direction.

"Lilya, has Nora ever mentioned licorice?" Sherry asked. "Have you ever seen her eat a licorice candy or smelled it on her breath?"

"If I had a dollar for every right turn this conversation has taken, I could retire tomorrow," Ray said. "You've mentioned licorice before. Where are you going with this?"

"Lilya? Have you?" Sherry persevered. If Ray could be impatient, she could, too.

"I'm a licorice admirer myself. Actually, more like licorice tolerator. I grew up on the candy and its health benefits, so I respect the stuff. Let me think. I recall one time when Nora and I had our first meeting in my office. Like any good Icelander, I have a bowl of individually wrapped licorice candy sitting in a glass bowl on my desk. I handed her the dish and she took a candy. That's the only time I saw her eat any candy whatsoever."

Ray checked his phone. "I gotta go. Sherry, I'd still like to take you up on that wooden spoon offer."

"Absolutely," Sherry said. "Everyone should have one in their arsenal."

"And we almost have an answer to the inquiry you texted me from the cook-off about the wooden spoon that stabbed Sigmund," Ray said. "Lab work takes time."

"Is Sherry involved in making me dinner? In that case, let's hurry it up and schedule a date," Lilya said with a wink. Ray, caught red-handed mixing business and pleasure, reddened.

"Nope, it'll be all my handiwork. Have a good evening, ladies." Ray covered his head with his hat, zipped his coat up to his neck and let himself out.

"He's a nice guy," Lilya said as she prepared herself for the bitter cold looming outside the door by putting on her gloves and wrapping her scarf artfully around her neck. "It's fun to make him blush."

"He's one of the good ones," Sherry said.

Lilya nodded with the slightest of head bobs.

"Thanks for stopping in," Sherry said. Her gaze followed Lilya as she left. "Amber, how's it going?"

A text came in on her phone as Amber called back all was well.

Any chance you could stop by my office after work today? I'm doing a group interview about the cook-off, the more the merrier. LMK.

"Hey, Sher," Amber said as she approached the front desk. "Your dad has chosen the most luxurious pastels for his spring collection. I'm hypnotized by the nature tones. Would you mind double-checking I assigned each to the correct bin number? Some have the subtlest variations. I know he'll spend hours rearranging them if I can't assure him you lent a second opinion."

"That's ridiculous," Sherry insisted. "Dad never second-guesses your expertise, but I'll do what you ask anyway."

"Thanks. If you'd just eyeball my sorts that's all we need. I'll swap you for front-of-the-house duty. We only have a few minutes left until closing anyway."

"Sure. I need to send a fast text. Patti wants to do a group cook-off interview when I'm finished here. I'll tell her forty-five minutes I'll be there." Sherry poked at her phone with one finger to construct the text. She hit the *send* key and made her way back to the storage room.

Walking in the room, her senses were dazzled by the cozy smell of fresh lamb's wool. Earthy, musty, grassy and slight caramel notes all tickled her nose and brought a grin to her face. Seeing the gorgeous colors her father's artists dyed the virgin wool, she was transported forward to the spring months that promised blooming flowers and budding trees.

"I need to buckle down," Sherry said to herself. She took a deep breath and soaked in the surroundings. "I've got a job to do."

Thirty minutes later she completed the task, only switching two yarn bundles to a more precise color description.

"All done," she announced as she joined Amber. Amber's Jack Russell was hot on her heels. "I moved two skeins. That's it. And you know how I knew where they belonged?"

"Because you've grown up with yarn surrounding you every single day?" Amber said.

"No. There was a bulb out in the track lighting and the darker than normal room gave your eye the notion that the color was something it wasn't." Sherry thought for a moment. "I wonder if the darkness played a trick on Patti's eyes and she didn't see who she thought she saw?"

"I'm not sure what that means about Patti, but if you're concerned, it's worth checking out," Amber said. "I've got a dinner date. I need to freshen up and drop Bean at home. Mind if I head out?"

"Get going. I'll lock up. Have a great time."

Before she switched off the store lights, Sherry sent out another text.

I'd like a meeting with you soon. I have some ideas. No time to fill you in by text.

If Ray could be short on time, she could, too. Leave 'em wanting more was an invaluable adage her father taught her when she was interviewing for her first job. She still took the words to heart after all those years. Ray would have to sit on her words until she had time to get back to him.

To make the frigid twilight hour borderline unbearable, the wind was relentless. The darkening sky was clear. No clouds meant no atmospheric heat trap and the cold reigned unchecked. Sherry was glad she'd left Chutney at home in the capable hands of her neighbor Eileen. His tiny body couldn't withstand the frigid onslaught. She picked up the pace to generate some body heat. Despite her efforts, by the time she was within a block of MediaPie, her fingers were numb, her eyes were watering, and her nose was running.

"Good afternoon, Clem, or is it evening?" Sherry said as she greeted the doorman.

"Ms. Oliveri," Clem said. "So nice to see you."

"Nice to see you, too, Clem."

"Miss Patti gave me your name so you can go right up. I'll log you in," Clem said.

"Thanks. Clem, I have a question."

"Shoot."

"The night Patti had her accident. I know she didn't want to report the accident as a possible assault because she never saw the person she assumes pushed her. I'd like to help her figure out what may have happened. Do you think the person who pushed Patti may have logged in the book and didn't log out—maybe you were off your post because you went to the utility closet or men's room for a moment and he or she scooted out of the building?" Sherry asked.

"Could be," Clem said. "We have a symbol for those that miss logging in or out, you know, just in cases like this."

Sherry's eyebrows lifted. "The symbol is written in the log, and then what?"

"Well," Clem said, "the offender makes a list called the Incomplete Log-In Blotter. Supposed to be red-flagged by security central, especially if there's a robbery or some such mischief."

"Would a police investigator be able to get his hands on that blotter for the day of Patti's accident?"

"Yes, ma'am. That's what it's prepared for. I'll put in a request on behalf of the Augustin Police Department. Who shall I say is the officer requesting?"

"Detective Ray Bease. Thank you, Clem. He can be reached at the police station if they need to double-check the legitimacy." Sherry made a mental note to give Ray a heads-up the call may be coming in.

"I'll see you when I'm leaving. I don't want to make the blotter," Sherry said. She made her way to the elevator after stopping at the ladies' room to freshen up.

"Hold the door," a male voice echoed from down the hall.

Sherry stuck her finger on the *door open* button. A moment later Gunnar joined her for the ride up. "What floor are you going to?"

"Fourth floor. Thanks. Glad this thing is working," Gunnar said. "How was your day?"

"Good, thanks," Sherry said as the door slid shut. She punched the number four. The button didn't stick, much to her relief. "How about you?"

"First day on my new job," Gunnar said. "At the *Beacon*. Here I am in enemy territory. For a joint interview by the two newspapers."

The door opened before Sherry could digest the implications of what Gunnar had said. "Joint interview? Is that what this is?"

"Sure is. The brainchild of Thomas and the Van Ardans. Patti Mellit and I are sharing the byline."

"Well, I'll be darned," Sherry said.

At Patti's office door she rang the buzzer to be let in. She was met at the door by Thomas.

"Hi, Sherry. Gunnar. Patti's fiddling with the recorder so I'm the doorman. Come on in. We're waiting on Sienna and Carl. Sherry, you're the hand-selected contestant representing all the others."

"If you're trying to scare me you're doing a good job," Sherry said, following that with a shaky laugh. "Why wouldn't you get the Grand Prize winner to speak on all the cooks' behalf?"

"To be honest, I asked him. He was hightailing it out of town back home to Arizona. He can't stand the cold. Can you imagine?"

"On a day like today, yes," Sherry said. Inside the office she removed her coat and set it aside. "So, this article is a united effort between the *Nutmeg News* and the *Beacon*? That's amazing."

"Sure is. We aren't enemies anymore, we're friends who may agree to disagree on things like how far to take modernizing the county. I'm reeling in my viewpoint, not entirely but a fair bit, to right some wrongs I've created. The townspeople's passion is what has hit me the hardest."

"Sherry, hi," Patti said as she came in the room. "Thanks for joining on such short notice. This chance began to materialize at warp speed. I didn't want the flame of enthusiasm to burn itself out."

"You mean you wanted to hurry this meeting up because you didn't want Bev Ardan and me to change our minds," Thomas said with an impish grin.

"Something like that," Patti said. "Now we're only waiting for Sienna and Carl."

On cue there was a buzz at the door. Patti let Sienna inside. Hellos were said before Sienna shared that Carl wouldn't be joining the interview. The disappointment on everyone else's face brought down the positive mood in the room.

"Did he give a reason why he wouldn't be coming?" Thomas asked.

"He texted he no longer was employed by the *Beacon* and his stint as cook-off judge was up yesterday," Sienna said. "He felt no obligation to carry on. He also said something about the fact the cook-off was his idea from the get-go and Thomas never gave him a lick of credit for the success."

Thomas lowered his gaze the way a child caught red-handed stealing a cookie before dinner would. "He's been unhappy for a while. I'm not surprised. We can get this done with you three, no worries. Gunnar, you're acting as writer and interviewee."

Chapter 32

"Let's take seats in the studio, if you all wouldn't mind. It's a tight fit so I hope everyone showered," Patti said with a laugh. "Follow me. I'm going to set the mics to pick up our conversation. Free-flowing banter is best. I'll toss out some questions and whoever wants to jump in with an answer, please proceed." As soon as everyone sat down, she adjusted the boom mic to loom over the group. "Be careful. This guy is lethal."

"Is this for a podcast as well?" Gunnar asked. He opened a notepad and poised his pen to capture any spoken gems.

"I'm taping what's said for the ease of selection and transcribing. But if I had everyone's permission, I would consider it for a podcast as well. I have questions, you have questions. Both newspapers will be well represented. The topics will be varied. The aim is to strike gold with everyone's input."

After a few minutes of mic adjustments, knob futzing and seat sorting, Patti gave the signal the interview was underway. She introduced the participants and the proposed theme.

"Today I'm sitting down with two cook-off judges, Sienna Warren and Gunnar Vilhjálmsson—I hope I did your last name justice—one cook-off contestant, Sherry Oliveri, and the main sponsor of the Round the World's Pantry—Cuisine and Culture Cook-off. What began as a cook-off where food is celebrated as the world's common language morphed into a chance to knit back together an unraveling community through the power of food and heirloom recipes. To get the ball rolling, I'd like to ask the cook-off's main sponsor, the *Coastal County Beacon*, today represented by editor in chief Thomas Helguvson, how successful was the paper's first cook-off?"

"Thanks for having me today, Patti," Thomas began. "Extremely successful. I couldn't have asked for a more dedicated team to work with. Today, I'm in wonderful company with two of the cook-off's hand-picked judges and one of the most talented amateur cooks in the country. I only wish my third judge, Carl, was able to attend, because he gets full credit for coming up with the idea to back a cooking competition right here in the wonderful town of Augustin."

"Smooth," Sherry said under her breath. To her right, Gunnar gave her a side-eye glance, as if he heard what she said.

"Gunnar, you replaced Carl as the new editor of the Food and Home section of the *Beacon*," Patti said. "Any hard feelings between you two, you and Carl?"

Gunnar shrugged. "It was his choice to leave the position. I wasn't Thomas's first choice for the job, mind you. Sigmund Helguvson was going to replace Carl, who had given his notice two weeks ago."

"I wasn't aware he'd given his notice," Patti said with a sigh. "I think you have the credentials to be a fine Food and Home section editor."

"Thanks. I'll do my best," Gunnar said.

"Since we have Sherry here, a contestant who made the final five round, would either Sienna or Gunnar, or both, be willing to tell her why her recipe entry and associated story behind the recipe came in third place rather than taking the Grand Prize?"

"Patti, you're really putting them on the spot," Sherry said. Her cheeks warmed. She wasn't sure she wanted to hear what they had to say.

Sienna and Gunnar traded quizzical looks.

"I'd be fine with telling Sherry some of the reasons, but I'm not giving away all my secrets in case I'm asked back." Sienna smiled in Thomas's direction.

"Great," Patti said. "Let's start with the recipe. Sherry made the bold decision to transform an Icelandic recipe into a Sherry recipe. Facing a judge with Icelandic ties, no less. It was either a smart move or one with too much risk. What do you say, Sienna?"

"I didn't even give that a lick of consideration. I judged her recipe creative, manageable, eye-pleasing in its presentation and the flavors were wonderful. It had a good amount of wow-factor but not quite enough. That's where I dinged her. That's all I'm willing to say."

"Gunnar, what would you like to add? If you have any insight on behalf of Carl, feel free to add your two cents," Patti said.

Gunnar raised his head, keeping only Patti in his sights. "I followed the judging criteria and Sherry came in third. With her recipe and her story." He paused. "I'd like to reprint Sherry's cook-off story in our joint article. It's not only about the power of food, it's also about when to leave something well enough alone, even if it's offensive to some."

"Like fermented shark?" Patti asked.

"Yes. Sherry, your story made a point about leaving a recipe that has no chance for improvement alone and choosing one which has possibilities for greatness. The same can be said about people. People who get more opportunities than they deserve, and repeatedly squander the chances, often at the expense of others, are as offensive as smelly shark meat," Gunnar said.

"Are you talking about Sig?" Patti asked.

Gunnar shrugged. "It does seem to apply. I bet the story will resonate with a lot of readers who have someone in their life who'd rather drag people down with them than strive for improvement. Interesting Sherry would use the cook-off to relay the message, knowing who her audience would be."

"It might be only you who is getting that message," Sienna said.

"Think about it. If Thomas had left Sigmund to handle his snafus we wouldn't all be in this mess," Gunnar said. "And if Thomas had let Carl do his job to his own standards, he'd still be employed at the *Beacon* and I'd be working alongside him rather than replacing him."

Thomas fidgeted in his chair, rolling it backward until he wasn't under the boom mic any longer. "Turn the mic off. I have something to say off the record." His words, delivered with the tone of a man on a mission, sent goose bumps up Sherry's arms.

Patti rose from her chair and flipped a few switches. The blinking green lights on the console beside her halted their dance and became a steady red.

"Are you sure you're not recording this time?" Sienna said. "Thomas said 'off the record.'"

"I guarantee," Patti said.

Sherry wasn't convinced and avoided her friend's gaze.

"Gunnar, you're right. I did empower my brother. Only I saw it as trying to nudge him in the right direction." Thomas lowered his head. "I thought we were on the right track, especially with Sienna's help."

"How well did you know Sigmund, Sienna?" Sherry asked.

"I'll answer that. I introduced them," Thomas said. "When Sienna told me her story beyond her cookbook authorship, I thought they were a perfect match."

"But he's married," Gunnar said. He made a quick glance in Patti's direction.

"And I'm spoken for, too," Sienna said.

"It wasn't about romance. Ever," Thomas said.

"It's okay, I'll explain," Sienna said. "When Thomas was interviewing me for the judging position, I shared I was five years sober. My recovery depends on me owning my truth. Thomas immediately asked me if I would become Sigmund's sobriety sponsor. He'd been struggling lately, and AA suggested changing sponsors."

"Sig never mentioned any of that to me," Patti said. Her shoulders sank. "He had a lot of secrets. That can wear a person down."

"Sienna, you were at the lake the night Sigmund was killed. You admitted it to me after the cook-off," Sherry said when she recognized Patti was struggling to stay engaged.

"I was," Sienna said. She lowered her head.

"Sienna didn't kill Sigmund," Thomas said. His face tightened and his jaw muscle flexed.

"Are you sure? Maybe Sigmund was ambivalent about being sober and tried to take it out on her and she was forced to defend herself. I'm sure Sienna is quite proficient with the many uses of the wooden spoon, even as a weapon," Sherry said.

"You don't really believe that theory, do you?" Sienna asked. She donned a slight smirk, challenging Sherry to continue.

"No, not really," Sherry said.

"I have a witness to everything I did at the lake from arrival to departure, so I'm not worried. That night I got a text from Sigmund saying he was going to Harmony Lake to meet with Patti and tell her the truth about being married. He ended with 'I'm going to need some liquid courage, forgive me.' I couldn't let that happen under my watch. I called Gunnar and Carl for backup, but only Gunnar was available."

Gunnar tipped his head. His humility was admirable. "I didn't owe the guy anything. On the contrary, he owed me. I just didn't want to see him go down this way, even after all he'd put the rest of us through. The most important detail Sienna hasn't shared is Sigmund told us at the lake it would be a lot easier if he could reinvent himself somewhere no one ever knew him. Right, Sienna?"

"He did say that."

"And then what?" Patti asked.

"He saw Patti drive into the parking lot and shooed us away," Sienna said. "I left."

Patti made a guttural gasp, as if her throat had closed tight and she was struggling to breathe.

"It *was* you," Patti said.

Sienna nodded.

"Both of you didn't leave?" Sherry asked.

"I couldn't leave him in such a vulnerable state," Gunnar said. "Maybe he would end it all by jumping in the icy lake or something, he was so desperate."

"If you're trying to make me feel guilty, I don't," Sienna said. The pinch of her lips said otherwise.

"If I were Thomas, I'd feel guilty, too," Gunnar said. "For many things."

"You don't sound like someone who's appreciative of being given the chance to work for a prestigious newspaper," Thomas said. "I hope I haven't made a mistake in the guise of salvaging a friendship."

"Look," Gunnar said. "It's no secret you and your brother were at odds over money, over the direction the *Beacon* is taking, over his dalliances. I'll support you until there's a concrete reason not to."

Sherry wriggled in her chair like the twelve-year-old students who had trouble sitting still during her class. Her comfort level was dipping. She wasn't sure she hadn't broken out in a sweat.

"I've had enough. This is going nowhere worthwhile," Thomas said. "Gunnar, we need to get back to work. Deadlines are looming, and just because your boss is your friend doesn't mean you don't have to burn the midnight oil on your first day."

"I agree," Gunnar said. "I don't think we're going to get anywhere today. I need to go back to work. I want to impress the boss."

Thomas slapped the table. "It's clear this meeting has taken place before its time. Let's try again when the wounds aren't so fresh. Thank you all for your time. Gunnar, I'm right behind you. I need a word with Patti."

Gunnar stood and left the room. Sherry could hear a second door open and shut.

"Thank you, Patti. The idea behind this meeting was genuine. The timing's off, I guess. Do you need me to walk you out?" Sherry raised her eyebrows to send Patti the message she'd stay with her if need be.

"I won't be long, but thanks," Patti said. "Would you mind telling Clem I'll be leaving in about five minutes, so he keeps an eye out for me?"

"Of course," Sherry said. "We don't want a repeat of any accidents."

Moments later Sherry was riding the elevator down to the lobby along with Sienna and Gunnar. They checked in with Clem on their way out.

"Short meeting," Clem said with a grin. The grin evaporated when the scowls of the trio smothered his jovial greeting. "I'll sign you all out."

"Patti will be down in five minutes. If it's any longer than that, would you mind checking in on her?"

"Of course. That's my job," Clem said.

"Good night, Clem," Sherry said as she followed the others out to the street. "Heading to the *Beacon* building or are you going home?"

"Back to work. My current home is the Augustin Manor Hotel. I try to spend as little time there as possible," Gunnar said. "I wasn't sure I'd be staying in the area and need to find a rental."

"The hotel's my current home, too," Sienna said. "I'm going to check flights back to Florida. This cold is beginning to freeze my brain. I hope Detective Bease understands I can't stay around any longer. If he has any questions, he knows my cell number."

"We'll drop you by the *Beacon*," Sherry said to Gunnar. They chose their path down the sidewalk, a beaten-down snow trail.

"This is a joke," Gunnar said. He approached a lamppost with two flyers attached at eye level. "Two sides of the debate. Both sides wrong." He tore the papers down, crumpled them up and tossed them in a steel receptacle. "Enough conflict already." His tone was rigid, unforgiving. He began to cough.

"You journalists are caught up in the clash. When the papers cool their heels, so will the community," Sherry said. "Are you getting sick?"

"Probably. It's been a sleepless week," Gunnar said. "Time to unleash the magic." He fumbled with a wrapper, using his unbendable gloved fingers to free the sucker inside. He let the wrapper drop to the sidewalk.

"Litterbug," Sienna scolded as she bent down to retrieve the paper.

"Old habits die hard," Gunnar said.

Sherry held out her hand to help in disposing of the candy paper. Instead of tossing it in the receptacle, she put it in her pocket. The familiar scent of the licorice sucker wafted in her direction. "You keep a supply of those with you always?"

"Another old habit I haven't even tried to kick, yes. A miracle for a throat tickle. The gummies last for a long time."

"Was Sigmund importing the candy here? I wonder how well it would have been received?" Sherry asked.

"I think he was," Gunnar said. "Another untested decision."

"Do Thomas and Carl like licorice?" Sherry asked. Sherry thought back to the moment Marla found a bundled tissue in the wastebasket at Patti's office, cringing at the smell. Someone wasn't keen on the flavor.

"Thomas is not a candy eater. He likes to supply it, though. Probably to support his brother. Last time I saw Carl eat a licorice was when he accepted a sucker from Thomas in Patti's office, so I guess he does," Gunnar said.

The *Beacon* building came into view two blocks ahead.

"Did you two hear about the crazy prank a child played while he was staying at the Augustin Manor Hotel? It prompted hotel management to post a sign next to the control panel of their elevator." Sherry recalled the article she'd read in the *Nutmeg News*. "It reads, 'Please Don't Dispose of Trash Anywhere Except Trash Receptacles.'"

"The elevator story?" Sienna asked.

Sherry nodded.

"We heard the story, remember?" Sienna asked Gunnar. "A kid jammed a chewed-up gummy bear into one of the elevator floor buttons and clogged up the whole system. He and his family are banned from the hotel for life. It happened the week before we arrived."

"I hadn't heard that story. Rotten kid. Needs better supervision. I'm going to say goodbye. Thanks for walking me this far," Gunnar said as they approached his new place of employment.

"At least you'll have company. I wouldn't want to be the only one working in this huge building after dark." Sherry looked up and noted how many of the windows were dark. "Thomas said he'd be joining you after he had a last word with Patti. Have a good night."

"Bye, Gunnar," Sienna said.

When he was safely out of sight, Sherry followed up on her question. "You think he knew the story of the kid and the elevator?"

"I'm certain. We were told the first time we met up in the lobby to go to a cook-off organization meeting. The concierge obviously was warning everyone to be vigilant so it wouldn't happen again. We both laughed at the ridiculousness of the kid's naughtiness."

"Gunnar didn't make it a secret he was unhappy with Thomas and Sigmund's relationship getting in the way of his career, did he?" Sherry asked.

"I know what you're getting at. You think Gunnar killed Sigmund," Sienna said. "Don't you think all clues point to Thomas or Sigmund's long-suffering wife?"

"Personally, I don't think Nora wanted anything more from Sigmund than to end the marriage properly and get on with her life."

Sienna sculpted an icy snow dome with the toe of her boot, the silvery pom-pom on her winter hat dancing left and right with her foot motion. After a few minutes she raised her eyes in Sherry's direction. "Maybe. I admit, I was thinking Thomas resorted to drastic measures to cut the cord on his brother's financial dependence until I heard what Gunnar had to say. Gunnar is a clever fellow." Sienna softened her voice. "I think the final straw was the wooden spoon. For one of the two."

Chapter 33

"It was a failure," Sherry said. "The proposed joint article was a bust. The wound is still too fresh."

"I'm sorry," Don said as he flopped his head back on a pillow. His hand was resting on Chutney, who lay on the couch between them. "It's early days yet. At least there was a beginning."

"I agree." Sherry mirrored Don's prone position. "I can't help but believe Sigmund's murder has everything to do with the animosity between Thomas, Sienna, Carl, Gunnar and Patti. The unsolved murder is fogging up the air and someone knows something they're not willing to share."

Sherry's phone rang. Don's eyes were nearly closed, and the sudden ring jarred his head forward. The caller ID showed an unknown number.

"Hello?" Sherry said.

"Hi, Sherry, this is Lilya, and Ray is also on the call."

"Hello, Sherry," Ray said.

"Are you together?" Sherry asked.

"Does that matter?" Ray asked.

"No, I suppose not," Sherry said. His avoidance gave her the feeling they were.

"We have a question," Lilya said. "Your sister, Marla, told Ray the judges' choices of which kitchen tool to talk to Patti about may not have been their first choice. Or that they had changed their minds for one reason or another. Can you confirm that?"

"That's what I heard also, yes," Sherry said.

"Do you know if any one of them originally had chosen a wooden spoon before changing their choice?" Ray said.

"My guess is Gunnar," Sherry said.

"Guess? A lucky guess or an educated guess?" Ray asked.

"I'd say an intuitive guess," Sherry said. "You've had the spoon analyzed for what foods may be on it, like I suggested, I assume?"

"We wanted to hear your confirmation. Yes, the results are in and they're brilliant," Lilya said. Sherry noted, on their end of the phone, the cooperative timing was flawless. No time was wasted on dead air, just as Ray preferred it. Lilya may be the perfect match for Ray after all.

Sherry heard paper rustling through the phone.

"Egg, milk, Nutella, mascarpone cheese."

"No banana?" Sherry asked.

"Yes, banana. I couldn't read my own scribbled notes."

"Check, check and check," Sherry said. She sat up straight, disturbing Chutney, prompting a curmudgeonly huff. "Everything on the list I gave you. And Sigmund's blood?"

"Check," said Lilya.

"We need to get over to the *Beacon* building in downtown Augustin right now. Thomas may be in big trouble. Meet me there as soon as you can."

"No, no, no," Ray scolded. "If Thomas is in danger, you'll be, too."

If she gave his statement a reply, that would open the door to debate. Sherry wondered how long until he realized Sherry dropped the call.

On the other side of Chutney, Don popped up and finished the job of destroying the dog's moment of contentment with his two favorite humans. Chutney relocated from the sofa to the rug.

"Whoa, whoa. Where do you think you're going?" Don asked. If he was expecting a different answer than the one Sherry had given Ray, he was mistaken. "You're jumping blindly into some sort of situation you told the detective was dangerous for Thomas. I can't lose you in the first twenty-four hours of engagement. I haven't even paid off the ring yet. In case you said no."

Sherry whacked Don with a throw pillow. "Pay it off." She grabbed her phone and her warmest down coat and scarf.

"I can't stop a tsunami. My only choice is to ride the wave," Don said. "Let's go."

• • •

Sherry and Don, side by side, shuffled down the sidewalk past the MediaPie building. She waved to Clem, who stood vigil inside the glass doors. He hustled to open the door.

"Be careful in this arctic cold wave. It can freeze the skin in ten minutes. Night is especially treacherous," Clem warned.

"Yes, sir," Sherry said. "That's the least of our worries." They scurried on a few more blocks until she reached the glass and steel behemoth that was the *Beacon*'s headquarters. Sherry could count on one hand the number of office windows lit up. She labored one last frozen breath before entering. Her gaze panned the spacious lobby, illuminated with impractical mood lighting. No doorman or security guard in sight. That was a problem. No Ray or Lilya either. After a short time of standing idle, Sherry led Don through the lobby in search of the office directory. She found the directory signage next to the double-wide pair of elevator doors. Thomas and Gunnar had offices on the sixth floor. Thank goodness the elevator was in service.

Another few moments dragged by before Sherry's impatience got the best of her. She muted her phone to keep the element of surprise on the table. She shouldn't have assumed both elevators were in service, because when she pushed the button to summon the doors to open, only one light out of two shone with availability. The other remained inactive, possibly reserved for daytime use. The bell rang, the metal door slid open, and Sherry and Don stepped into the spacious cubicle. The door shut and she was immediately overcome with the objectionable smell of licorice. Her senses rejected the earthy, burnt and curiously sweet odor and she shook off a shiver that traveled through her core.

She checked the button panel, not only with her eyes but also with her nose. If there was a jammed gummy embedded in any of the floor buttons, she would channel her inner Trooper and sniff the offender out. She scoured the buttons and came up empty.

"Would you like to explain what you're smelling?" Don asked.

"Licorice," Sherry said.

"Do you smell it?"

"Thank goodness, no."

Sherry pushed the button for the sixth floor. Before she exited the elevator, she checked her phone. No word from Ray or Lilya. They should arrive soon. She followed the hall sign for Thomas's suite, 602. The chance Gunnar went looking for Thomas in his office, rather than the other way around, was a hunch on Sherry's part. There was a fifty percent chance she should have chosen Gunnar's office, 604. Too late now. She raised her hand to knock on the door. As her hand recoiled with knuckles clenched, she heard a man scream Thomas's name. It had to be Gunnar. Thomas must have snapped. She was wrong. Gunnar was the one in danger. She heard a scream so blood-curdling she fell back a step. A shout blasted through the door and a woman shrieked for help.

"Thomas, no!"

Despite the shrill nature of her bellow, Sherry recognized Lilya's voice, sounding frantic. How did she get inside Thomas's office before Sherry? She stared at the door. Sherry's assumption that Gunnar was the murderer was premature. Thomas must be holding everyone hostage. Sherry dialed 911, whispered the necessary information to the dispatcher and declined to stay on the line as she was advised to do.

Sherry turned and surveyed the hallway. A fire extinguisher was about one-quarter of the way down the hall. All she had to do was kick the glass out to free the equipment, something she'd seen done on TV, but putting her boot through glass would come with consequences, she imagined. She was thrilled to see a tiny knob that opened the glass panel with the ease of two fingers. She freed the red metal device from its mount and pulled the safety pin on the top. Armed with the ready-to-use extinguisher, Sherry tried the handle of Thomas's office door. The handle released and the door opened a crack, with a cautious push of her boot. Seeing the back of a winter coat inside the door, she lifted the hose and squeezed the nozzle, blasting him in the face as she hollered to attract his attention.

"Not me! Gunnar!" screamed Thomas, his face in his hands.

"Not Thomas!" Lilya shouted. "Gunnar!"

Before Sherry could re-aim the nozzle, Ray snagged the extinguisher from Sherry's hands and soaked Gunnar's face with foam. He crumpled to the ground, desperately swiping at the thick layer of foam.

"Lilya, secure that window," Ray shouted. "No one's going to be thrown from the sixth floor."

"What? Who's being thrown from the window?" Sherry asked.

"Gunnar threatened to toss Thomas out the window because he was about to blow the whistle on him. He's making a habit of tossing bodies into deadly situations," Lilya said.

"Blow the whistle? It was Gunnar after all?" Sherry asked as she saw Thomas struggling to clear his face of the noxious chemical. She handed Thomas her scarf to wipe his face with. "So sorry."

"Gunnar admitted to me he had to kill Sig because he had stepped on his dreams one too many times. He felt there was no end in sight once Sig got the job here at the *Beacon*. The job he felt was his," Thomas said. "The stress and strain of financial ups and downs took its toll, and Gunnar wanted to clear his path of the obstacle he felt blocked his lasting success. My brother."

"You two followed these two here tonight and you weren't sure which one, if either, murdered Sigmund?" Ray asked. The astonishment in his voice brought a smile to Lilya's face.

"I'm with her," Don said. "Whatever she says goes."

"I had the culprit narrowed down to one or the other," Sherry said. "There was enough evidence for sure, it just needed to tip the balance in one direction over the other."

"The wooden spoon?" Ray asked. "Gunnar, was that your wooden spoon at Harmony Lake covered in milk, egg, Nutella, banana, and blood?"

Gunnar moaned.

"Was the licorice wrapper we found on the dock at Harmony Lake yours?" Sherry asked.

A groan rumbled from the heap of a man on the floor.

"Did you gum up the elevator so you could push Patti Mellit down the stairs before she uncovered your scheme?" Thomas asked.

Gunnar grumbled.

"The MediaPie security guard's Incomplete Log-in Blotter registered you logged in on a visit to the building the evening Patti was hurt. You never logged out," Ray said. "You were waiting for Patti in the stairwell."

"Good job, Clem!" Sherry cheered.

Gunnar lifted his foam-covered head. "It couldn't have worked out better. Your man, Clem, called Patti to come get her dinner delivery as I was about to give up on her leaving the building."

"You ambushed her," Sherry said.

"Patti knew too much. She recorded my argument with the brothers about the job at the *Beacon*. Carl was leaving, it should be my job. I was most qualified. Once again Sig stepped on my chance for success. Just like his idiotic import business rather than my suggestion we all go in for tourism. Which is now a billion-dollar business in Iceland." Gunnar struggled to finish his story.

"But why hurt Patti?" Sherry asked.

"Patti was on Sig's side. I chose the wooden spoon first. I was going to make it a new old trend for this year. I'm the expert on trends. Not Sig. Not you. He's stolen everything from me." His head sank back down to the floor.

"But murder?" Thomas asked. "Your days as Iceland's high school team wrestler of the year must have come in handy tossing my brother into Harmony Lake like he was a feather."

"My glory days. Proves I was always a team player. For what? The Bankless Brothers was a team of losers. It should have been called the Thankless Brothers. Being a member got me nothing but misery and debt. I saw my opportunity to eliminate the problematic member and I took it. I need a lawyer," Gunnar whined.

Chapter 34

"I bought both newspapers," Don called out. He slammed the door behind him. "Oops, didn't mean to scare you, Chutney."

The indignant dog removed himself from his sentry post facing the front door sidelights.

"Good boy. I appreciate you watching over the house while I ran to Augustin Dry Goods. Sher, the Nagles say hi."

"Thanks," Sherry said. She lightened Don's load by taking the *Coastal County Beacon* off his hands. She brought the paper to the couch and took a seat. "Renovation Plans Reached for Hillsboro County—Part One. The subtitle reads: for Part Two, please see today's *Nutmeg News*."

"They're not going to make us buy both papers every day to see a full story, are they?" Don asked. "We should at least get a subscription discount for all you did for them."

"I don't sleuth for pay," Sherry said with a laugh. "I was helping out a friend in need."

"I see a more united Hillsboro County in the future. Open minds are prevailing."

"People are coming to their senses since the cook-off," Sherry said. "Baby steps."

"How much credit do you give your last cook-off for naming Sigmund's murderer?" Don asked.

"A lot. For one, Gunnar shared his favorite filling for his weekly Icelandic pancake while we were chatting at the cook-off. It was trivial information except for the fact he stated his favorite kitchen tool was the wooden spoon. No one makes pancakes without a wooden spoon if they own one. Magnus's story of the Spoon-Licker and his delivery of a broken spoon to my cook-off station gave me the idea to check the wooden spoon used on Sigmund for signs of Gunnar's pancake ingredients. Ray's lab team found all Gunnar's favorite ingredients on the spoon used against Sigmund.

"Good work, everyone," Don said. "I've been known to be a spoon licker in my day," Don said. "But I've never used a wooden spoon as a weapon."

"Gunnar got the potato in his shoe."

"Okay, whatever that means."

"If I'm not mistaken, the look on Gunnar's face during the telling of my recipe story was cringy. One glance at him up at the judge's table and I was certain I struck a chord. I couldn't be certain what that chord was until I eliminated Thomas from the suspect list. That would only leave Gunnar."

"Why did Gunnar push Patti down the stairs?" Don asked.

"Simple answer is, he didn't want to get caught. Patti asked the judges to rerecord a part of the podcast not because it was necessary, but because she wanted the group to think she may have caught some incriminating talk on tape."

"Smart, but risky."

"She thought it was a good idea at the time. In reality, she couldn't make out much of what they were arguing about, but they couldn't know that."

"Patti put herself in danger," Don said. "See why I'm concerned when you jump into a murder investigation?"

"Patti's a good person. She didn't want to see someone else get hurt whether it was me or someone wrongfully accused, including herself. Her gut told her one of the judges may have been the killer. Gunnar wanted her silenced when he thought she had the goods on him. He also admitted there was a chance Patti witnessed the murder at Harmony Lake if she hadn't left when she said she did. He was getting paranoid by then. Patti had to be silenced. He also admitted to calling in the bomb threat against Thomas's newspaper. He thought creating a diversion from the murder investigation would buy him some time to come up with his next move."

"Wonder what put Gunnar over the edge?" Don asked.

"Tourism and the spoon."

"Explain."

"One of the reasons Thomas wanted to modernize Augustin in a hurry was because the Band of Bankless Brothers lost out on making it big after the Icelandic banks collapsed. Anyone who went into tourism, which was Gunnar's business plan, made it big. Import-export, not so much. Sigmund's business plan. Poor Thomas. Always trying to clean up Sigmund's messes."

"Sibling relationships are complicated," Don said. "And the spoon?"

"Gunnar wanted to talk on the podcast about the wooden spoon."

"You stole his thunder?"

"Not before Sigmund did. Gunnar didn't want anyone to think Sigmund gave him the idea to choose the wooden spoon. Sigmund suggested the spoon and the bad feelings Gunnar was already harboring against his old friend boiled over. Gunnar had enough of Sigmund usurping so many aspects of his life. Enough was enough."

"Is that your neighbor?" Don said as he stared out the picture window. "She looks hysterical."

Outside the house, Eileen was waving her arms overhead and shouting in the direction of Sherry's house.

"Maybe her cat escaped." Sherry heaved her tired body off the couch and opened the front door. "Eileen? Do you need me?"

"I heard he gave you a ring," Eileen called out. "Happy days are here."

"Thank you. We'll talk tomorrow," Sherry said as she threw Eileen an air hug. "Too cold."

"The news is out," Don said with a laugh. "By the way, it was nice to have Marla around. Maybe one day she and Grant will move back East."

"Maybe. As for now, you guys are all on probation for pulling the wool over my eyes all week long. And I thought the cook-off was the main attraction."

"And a proposal I didn't want your family to miss out on."

"Problem is, from now on, every time the entire family is all in the same place, I'm going to expect a nice surprise." As if on cue, Chutney began a barking tirade. "Who could that be?"

Don checked the door. "Erno. Come in. We were just talking about the family."

"Okay," Sherry said. "What's going on? I don't trust either one of you when you join forces."

"Hello to you," Erno said. "Stopped by to pick up the last of the books from the Ruggery. Don called and asked me if I would, so here I am."

"We could have brought them over, Dad," Sherry said.

"I asked Erno to stop by so we could ask him together about something in the financials. I didn't feel right about asking him alone. It's not my place. I'm only looking at the numbers, not the reasons why," Don said. "And frankly, Sherry is such a good mystery solver I knew she'd want to be involved."

"Have a seat, Dad. Can I get you anything?" Sherry asked.

"No, thanks," Erno said while he unzipped his coat. He sat in the armchair opposite Don and Sherry.

"You know what I'm going to ask, don't you?" Don asked. He held up the books he was returning to Erno. "Let me first say all the money is accounted for. Nothing is missing, merely misplaced. The bottom line is not affected in any way."

"You never found out why Dad wasn't receiving his full salary?" Sherry asked.

"Let me explain something," Erno said. "I'm not a spring chicken and I don't need my full salary at the moment, thanks to my recent inheritance. Rather than cause a whole shebang of debate, I've begun diverting a portion of my salary into an account I call—"

"Next Gen," Don said.

"I want to provide you two with a nest egg and a nice wedding, the way I did for Marla and Pep. Even though you're a little older than they were. I couldn't provide much on your first trip down the aisle," Erno said. "I had the others to provide for. But now, all things being equal, you three kids are receiving the same gift, just at different times. When you and Don started showing signs of getting quite serious, I opened the account again after cleaning it out for the other two when they married their significant others. Your mother wanted this and I'm glad I could see it through."

"Dad, I don't know what to say," Sherry said. She jumped off the couch and hugged Erno.

"You're one of a kind, Erno," Don said. "Not many would be so generous. Thank you. But please promise us you'll restore your salary. We don't need much more than a bouquet of flowers for our wedding."

"Wait a minute. Better run that by the bride first," Sherry said with a laugh. "Thanks, Dad."

"Hey, Sher," Erno said. "I've been meaning to ask you. Before Marla and Grant went back to Oklahoma, she asked me if I had an extra wooden spoon she could have. I said, why don't you ask the Wooden Spoon Queen herself, and Marla said you already had one promised to Detective Bease and she didn't want to drain your supply. Why the rush on wooden spoons?"

Sherry reached across Don and opened the *Nutmeg News*. "If what Patti told me is correct, it should say right here in today's column." Sherry searched the Food section and found what she was looking for. "She said it would be printed today." She ran her finger down the column. "Here it is: *What's Old Is New. The Resurgence of the Wooden Spoon in the Modern Kitchen.*"

Recipes from Sherry's Kitchen

Snappy African Groundnut Stew

2 sweet potatoes, peeled and diced
12 chicken thighs
½ cup mango chutney
¼ cup smooth peanut butter
1 10-ounce can diced tomatoes with green chilies

Preheat oven to 375 degrees F (190 degrees C).

Place sweet potato cubes in a medium baking dish and bake until just fork tender. Remove from oven and set aside.

Place chicken in a large baking pan, season with salt and pepper, and bake for 30 minutes.

Meanwhile, in a medium saucepan, combine the chutney, peanut butter and tomatoes with chilies and cook over low heat until it just begins to simmer.

After the chicken has baked 30 minutes, spoon the sweet potatoes and chutney sauce over the chicken and continue to bake 15–20 minutes more until bubbly and browned.

Icelandic Savory Ponnukukur Pancakes

5 eggs
2½ cups milk
1 teaspoon salt
1¼ cups flour
butter or cooking oil

Beat the eggs, milk, and salt together in a bowl until frothy. Slowly add the flour, whisking to incorporate until a smooth batter forms. Set aside.

Heat a nonstick or well-seasoned cast iron skillet over medium heat. Once the pan is hot, add a little butter or cooking oil to coat the bottom of the pan. Pour in just enough batter to coat the pan (about ⅓ cup if using a 10-inch skillet), and pick up the pan, tilting it to all sides so that the batter evenly coats the bottom of the pan in a thin layer.

Cook the pancake until set and the bottom is golden brown (30 seconds to a minute), then use a spatula or knife to carefully flip the pancake. Cook the other side for an additional 30 seconds to brown, then tilt the pancake out of the pan and onto a plate.

Repeat, using more butter or oil as needed to prevent sticking. Fill with creamy chicken filling (recipe follows).

Creamy Chicken Filling

2 tablespoons butter
½ pound boneless, skinless chicken thighs
1 teaspoon salt
½ yellow onion, diced
1 stalk celery, diced
1 clove garlic, minced
1 teaspoon mild curry powder
pinch cayenne pepper
½ teaspoon ground black pepper
¼ cup heavy cream

2 tablespoons cream cheese
2 tablespoons fresh chives, minced
pea pesto, gooseberry sauce, and skyr for topping

Heat 2 tablespoons butter in a skillet over medium-high heat. Sprinkle chicken with 1 teaspoon of salt. Cook chicken in skillet until cooked through. Add onion, celery, and garlic, and stir, sautéing until onion is just starting to turn translucent. Add the curry powder and cayenne and deglaze the pan with cream and cream cheese, stirring up browned bits from pan bottom. Remove from heat when chicken is coated and sauce is creamy. Sprinkle filling with chives. Top with pesto, gooseberry sauce and skyr.

About the Author

Devon Delaney is lifelong resident of the Northeast and currently resides in coastal Connecticut. She is a wife, mother of three, grandmother of two, accomplished cooking contestant and a recent empty nester. She taught computer education and Lego Robotics for over ten years prior to pursuing writing.

Devon has been handsomely rewarded for her recipe innovation over the last twenty-plus years. Among the many prizes she has won are a full kitchen of major appliances, five-figure top cash prizes, and four trips to Disney World. She won the grand prize in a national writing contest for her foodie poem "Ode to Pork Passion." Combining her beloved hobby of cooking contests with her enthusiasm for writing was inevitable.

When she's is not preparing for her next cook-off, Devon may be found pursuing her other hobbies, including playing competitive USTA league tennis, gardening, needlepointing, painting, jarring her produce and hooking rugs. Her standard poodle, Rocket, is her pride and joy and keeps her on the path of sanity.

You can learn more about Devon at www.devonpdelaney.com.

Made in United States
Troutdale, OR
11/15/2023

14602571R00125